Being an ethicist was all about c
of a...habit. Anyone could do
and listen, and watch. That's all.

She would be watchful. She would be patient as her father taught her to be when they went looking for elephants thirty years ago. She was only a little girl then, but he taught her to pay attention to the world around her. That was what this moment called for.

She settled back to wait, sure that the reason for Khun Wiriya's nervousness would emerge just as the shape of an elephant would materialize from the overgrowth, if you were patient enough. After all, Khun Wiriya was an important detective. His was a very prestigious position, held by a very important man. This was a man who had no time for social visits, and therefore a man who could be counted on to get to the point quickly. So Ladarat looked expectantly across her desk at the detective, her pencil poised above a clean yellow notepad that she had labeled with today's date.

She hoped she wouldn't have to wait long, though. She, too, was busy. She was the nurse ethicist for the entire hospital, and she had a full docket already. And the Royal Hospital Inspection Committee would be coming to visit next Monday, exactly one short week from now. And not only did she need to impress the committee, she also needed to impress Tippawan Taksin, her supervisor. Khun Tippawan was a thin, pinched woman with a near-constant squint who held the exalted title of "Director of Excellence."

She had so much to prepare. So hopefully the trouble—whatever it was—would emerge soon. And it did.

"I mean to say..." the detective said, "we may be looking for a murderer."

ALSO BY DAVID CASARETT, M.D.

ETHICAL CHIANG MAI DETECTIVE AGENCY

Murder at the House of Rooster Happiness

Mercy at the Peaceful Inn of Last Resort

Last Acts:
Discovering Possibility and Opportunity at the End of Life

Shocked:
Adventures in Bringing Back the Recently Dead

Stoned:
A Doctor's Case for Medical Marijuana

AN ETHICAL CHIANG MAI DETECTIVE AGENCY NOVEL

MURDER AT THE HOUSE OF ROOSTER HAPPINESS

DAVID CASARETT, M.D.

REDHOOK

www.redhookbooks.com

Redhook Books/Orbit
Hachette Book Group
1290 Avenue of the Americas
New York, NY 10104
hachettebookgroup.com

First Edition: September 2016

Redhook is an imprint of Orbit, a division of Hachette Book Group.
The Redhook name and logo are trademarks of Hachette Book Group, Inc.

The publisher is not responsible for websites (or their content) that are not owned by the publisher.

The Hachette Speakers Bureau provides a wide range of authors for speaking events. To find out more, go to www.hachettespeakersbureau.com or call (866) 376-6591.

Library of Congress Cataloging-in-Publication Data

Names: Casarett, David J., author.
Title: Murder at the house of rooster happiness / David Casarett.
Description: First edition. | New York, NY : Redhook, 2016. | Series: An ethical Chiang Mai Detective Agency novel ; 1
Identifiers: LCCN 2016003304 (print) | LCCN 2016015284 (ebook) | ISBN 9780316270632 (paperback) | ISBN 9780316270649 (ebook)
Subjects: LCSH: Nurses—Fiction. | Ethicists—Fiction. | Women detectives—Ficiton. | Husbands—Death—Fiction. | Murder—Investigation—Fiction. | Hospitals—Fiction. | Thailand—Fiction. | BISAC: FICTION / Mystery & Detective / Women Sleuths. | FICTION / Mystery & Detective / Police Procedural. | FICTION / Mystery & Detective / Traditional British. | FICTION / Urban Life. | GSAFD: Mystery fiction.
Classification: LCC PS3603.A833 M87 2016 (print) | LCC PS3603.A833 (ebook) | DDC 813/.6—dc23
LC record available at https://lccn.loc.gov/2016003304

ISBNs: 978-0-316-27063-2 (trade paperback), 978-0-316-27064-9 (ebook)

Printed in the United States of America

RRD-C

10 9 8 7 6 5 4 3 2 1

Ladarat Patalung is a product of my imagination. But I'm fortunate to be able to work at the University of Pennsylvania with a wonderful team of palliative care clinicians who are very real. They make the world a better place every day, and they're just as thoughtful, kind, and compassionate as Ladarat is.
This book is dedicated to them.

Wan jan

MONDAY

CHAPTER 1

IT IS KNOWN THAT POISON IS OFTEN A WOMAN'S METHOD

I have come to see you, Khun Ladarat, about a matter of the utmost urgency."

The comfortably built man sitting on the other side of the desk paused, and shifted his bulk in a way that prompted the little wooden chair underneath him to register a subdued groan of protest.

"A matter of the utmost urgency," he repeated, "and more than a little delicacy."

Ladarat Patalung began to suspect that this Monday morning was going to be more interesting than most. Her conclusion was based in part, of course, on the formal designation of the matter at hand as one of the "utmost urgency." In her experience, that didn't happen often on a Monday morning. Despite the fact that she was the official nurse ethicist for Sriphat Hospital, the largest—and best—hospital in northern Thailand, it was unusual to be confronted by a matter that could be reasonably described in this way.

But Ladarat's conclusion was also based on her observation that her visitor was nervous. Very nervous. And nervousness was no doubt an unusual sensation for this broad-faced and broad-shouldered visitor. Solid and comforting, with close-cropped graying hair, a slow smile, and gentle manners that would not have been out of place in a Buddhist monk, Detective Wiriya Mookjai had been an almost silent presence in her life for the past three years. Ever since her cousin Siriwan Pookusuwan had introduced them.

Ladarat herself didn't have much cause to meet members of the Chiang Mai Royal Police Force. But Siriwan most certainly did. She ran a girlie bar—a brothel, of sorts—in the old city. So she had more contact of that nature, perhaps, than she would like. Not all of it good.

Khun Wiriya was that rarest of beings—an honest policeman. They did exist in Thailand, all reports to the contrary. But they were rare enough to be worth celebrating when one was discovered. In fact, Wiriya was something of a hero. He never talked about it, but Ladarat had heard that he'd been injured in a shoot-out several years ago. In fact, he was a hero to many younger officers who aspired to be injured in a similar way, though of course without unnecessary pain and with no residual disability.

She'd met him before at the tea shop her cousin also owned, although he'd never before come to see her at work. Yet now he had. And now he was sitting across from her in her little basement office in Sriphat Hospital, with just her little desk between them. And he seemed to be nervous.

How did she know that the detective was nervous? The most significant clue was his tie. Khun Wiriya was wearing a green tie. He was wearing a green tie, that is, on a particular Monday, the day of the king's birth. Today almost everyone in Thailand of a mature age—a category that included both the detective and herself—would honor the occasion by wearing something yellow. For men, it would be a tie.

Ladarat herself was honoring the day with a yellow silk blouse, along with a blue skirt that was her constant uniform. They were not particularly flattering to her thin figure, she knew. Her late husband, Somboon, had often joked—gently—that sometimes it was difficult to tell whether a suit of clothes concealed his wife, or whether perhaps they hid a coat hanger. It was true she lacked obvious feminine...landmarks. That, plus oversize glasses and hair pinned tightly in a bun, admittedly did not contribute to a figure of surpassing beauty.

But Ladarat Patalung was not the sort of person to dwell on herself. Either her strong points or any points at all. Those people existed, she knew. Particularly in Sriphat Hospital. They were very much aware of their finer points, in particular, and eagerly sought out confirmation of those points. These were people who waited hungrily for compliments, much as a hunting crocodile lurks in the reeds by the edge of a lake.

If she were that sort of person—the sort of person who dwells on her talents and wants to add yet another to her list—it might have occurred to her to think that her deduction regarding Khun Wiriya's nervousness revealed the hidden talents of a detective. She might have reached this conclusion because she noticed things like the doctor's behavior. And not everyone did.

But she was most emphatically not the sort of person to dwell on her talents. Besides, her perceptiveness wasn't even a talent, really. Not any more than being a nurse ethicist was a talent. Anyone could do it, given the right training. Ladarat herself was certainly nothing special.

Being an ethicist was all about observing. And that was more of a...habit. Anyone could do it. You just had to be quiet, and listen, and watch. That's all.

It was a habit that was a little like finding forest elephants in her home village near Mae Jo, in the far northwestern corner of Thailand. Anybody could see an elephant in front of her nose, of course. But to sense where they *might* be, back in the undergrowth, you had to be very still. And watchful.

In that moment, as the detective fidgeted and his eyes skittered across her bookshelves, Ladarat resolved that she would be very quiet. She would be watchful. She would be patient as her father taught her to be when they went looking for elephants thirty years ago. She was only a little girl then, but he taught her to pay attention to the world around her. That was what this moment called for.

She settled back to wait, sure that the reason for Khun Wiriya's nervousness would emerge just as the shape of an elephant would materialize from the overgrowth, if you were patient enough. After all, Khun Wiriya was an important detective. His was a very prestigious position, held by a very important man. This was a man who had no time for social visits, and therefore a man who could be counted on to get to the point quickly. So Ladarat looked expectantly across her desk at the detective, her pencil poised above a clean yellow notepad that she had labeled with today's date.

She hoped she wouldn't have to wait long, though. She, too, was busy. She was the nurse ethicist for the entire hospital, and she had a full docket already. And the Royal Hospital Inspection Committee would be coming to visit next Monday, exactly one short week from now. And not only did she need to impress the committee, she also needed to impress Tippawan Taksin, her supervisor. Khun Tippawan was a thin, pinched woman with a near-constant squint who held the exalted title of "Director of Excellence." A title that was due in no small part to the fact that she was a distant relation of the Thai noble family. And what did that title mean exactly?

Anyway, impressing the inspector was one thing, but impressing the tough Khun Tippawan would be something else altogether.

She had so much to prepare. Even if she worked twenty-four hours every day for the next week, she would never please Khun Tippawan. So hopefully the trouble—whatever it was—would emerge soon. And it did.

"I mean to say..." the detective said, "we may be looking for a murderer."

Ladarat nodded but suspected that she did not entirely succeed in maintaining a calm, unruffled demeanor. It wasn't every day that she had such a conversation about murder. In fact, she had never had such a conversation.

At least the case of the detective's nervousness had been solved. This was Chiang Mai, after all. A small city. A safe city. Where the old Thai values of respect and courtesy still flourished. A murder here would be...well, not unthinkable. But very, very unusual. Of course Khun Wiriya would be nervous—and excited—thinking that he might have discovered a murderer.

At a loss for words, she wrote: "Murder?" She looked down with new respect at her humble yellow pad, which had suddenly become very, very interesting.

"We received a call last night from a young police officer—a corporal—working at the emergency room of this hospital," Wiriya said slowly. "He called about a patient whose wife had brought him there. When they arrived, the man was quite dead apparently."

Ladarat wrote: "Woman. Man. Emergency. Quite dead."

"It seems that he had been dead for a little while—long enough, in fact, that there was nothing at all they could do for him. So they called the emergency room doctor to fill out the death certificate."

Ladarat underlined "Quite."

"But this corporal thought perhaps he recognized the man's wife," Wiriya continued. "He thought . . . he'd met her before at another hospital. But he wasn't certain, you understand?"

Ladarat wasn't at all sure she understood. She nodded anyway.

The detective paused, choosing his words carefully. Ladarat waited. Thus far she wasn't seeing the need for an ethicist. But she would be patient. You must never approach an elephant in the forest, her father told her. You must always allow it to approach you.

"So the corporal asked the doctor in charge, you see. To share his concerns." He flipped open a small spiral notebook and checked. "A Dr. . . . Aroon?"

He looked inquisitively at her, but Ladarat shook her head. It was no one she knew. But then, doctors were always coming and going. They'd work for a year at this government hospital, then they'd move to one of the private hospitals that paid much more. It was a shame.

"But here it is," Wiriya said. "This woman? Who he thought he'd met before? You see, the last time they met was in the same exact circumstances. She'd brought her husband into the emergency room after he died. In both circumstances, the men had been brought in too late to help them."

She wrote: "Two deaths. More?"

He paused, and they both thought about what this coincidence might mean. Nothing good.

"Some women are . . . unlucky in this way," Ladarat suggested.

"It was a tragedy, to be sure, but this man, was he...an older man?"

Wiriya shrugged. "He was not a young man, it is safe to say. Neither was the other man. About forty-five, perhaps. That is not too old, is it, Khun?"

She supposed it was not.

"And what was the cause of death?"

"For the first, the corporal didn't know." He shrugged. "But for this one, the woman, she said it was his heart."

"His heart? Of course it was his heart. Your heart stops and you die. That's not an explanation, any more than saying a plane crash happened...because the plane, it hit the ground."

Wiriya looked suitably chastened. "Well, that's why I came to you, you see? You have this special medical knowledge. And, of course, you think like a detective."

A detective? Her? Most certainly not. That required skills. And penetrating intelligence, and cunning. She herself had none of those attributes. She would leave detecting to others who were better suited for the job.

"But," she said, thinking out loud, "if he did have heart fail-ure, for instance, there might have been signs that the doctor noticed. Those would be documented in the medical record."

"The corporal said that the doctor didn't write anything. He didn't want to admit the patient because that would mean more paperwork. So he just signed the death certificate."

"I see. Well, then for two marriages to end in death, it is unlucky, to be sure. Still, it doesn't sound suspicious, does it?"

Wiriya was silent. Obviously he thought this situation *was* suspicious, or a busy man like him would not have wasted his time visiting her. Unless...perhaps this was just an excuse for a social call? Highly doubtful. He was a careful, methodical man, to be sure. Most important, a good man. And not unattractive.

But what was she thinking? He was here to ask for her help in a murder investigation. Her, Ladarat Patalung, nurse ethicist. And here she was thinking crazy thoughts.

Still the detective said nothing. He leaned back slightly in his chair and studied the ceiling above his head very carefully. He seemed to be thinking.

About what?

What do detectives think about? Real detectives. They look for patterns, don't they? They look for facts that fit together.

So perhaps there was a pattern here that Wiriya thought he saw. And maybe he wanted to see whether she saw it, too. Perhaps this was a test.

She wrote: "Pattern?"

Well, then. What sorts of patterns might there be?

"From what the young policeman said," she asked, "was there anything that these two unfortunate men had in common?"

"Ahhh." Wiriya shook his head, dragging his attention back down from the ceiling as if he had come to some important decision. "Yes, but I can't make anything of it. You see, they were both Chinese."

Ah, Chinese. Ladarat glanced at the detective. His face was a blank wall, and his gaze was again fixed with intense interest on the area of ceiling just above her head.

The Chinese. Some said that the culture of Thailand could be both gentle and intensely proud because the country had never been invaded. Never colonized. But Ladarat wasn't so sure about that. There were so many Chinese here now, one could be forgiven for assuming that the Chinese had, in fact, invaded.

It would be one thing if they were polite, but they were not.

So quick to be angry. So harsh. So rude. Worse, even, than the Germans.

So it was with mixed emotions that she contemplated the nationality of these men and wrote "CHINESE" in big block letters.

Ladarat would be the first to admit that it was bad to stereotype. One should never judge a book by its cover. Although, truth be told, that was often the way she purchased a book— by looking closely at the cover. Like the new biography of that remarkable woman Aung San Suun Kyi. She had purchased a copy last weekend at the night market down by the Ping River largely because of the photograph of the beautiful woman on the cover, who seemed to be looking right at her, about to offer advice. So there was something to be said for the usefulness of a book's cover. But for people, no, that was wrong.

Perhaps detectives of the private sort could pick and choose their cases. But she was not a detective. She was a nurse. And an ethicist.

Where would we be if nurses and ethicists could pick and choose whom they would help? Nowhere good.

In fact, the slim volume that was sitting in the very center of her little desk had one page that was more thoroughly read than any other, and that was page 18. There was a passage on that otherwise unremarkable page that she knew by heart: "A nurse must always leave her prejudices at the door when she walks into a patient's room."

The book modestly called itself *The Fundamentals of Ethics*, by Julia Dalrymple, R.N., Ph.D., Professor of Nursing at the Yale University of the U.S.A. Ladarat regretted extremely the dullness of the title. It didn't really do justice to the wisdom of this little volume, which she'd discovered in a used bookstore in the city of Chicago in the United States when she was there for a year of ethics education. Not a day went by that she didn't seek Professor Dalrymple's wisdom to answer a question, to solve a problem, or sometimes just to be reminded of a nurse's obligations.

So she would follow the good professor's advice. She would leave her prejudices at the door.

"And the man's name?" she asked.

The detective hesitated. "It was . . . Zhang Wei."

"Oh no."

"Exactly. Oh no."

As she jotted this name down on her increasingly crowded—but increasingly interesting—yellow pad, Ladarat reflected that Zhang Wei was a very common Chinese name. A little like John Smith in the United States. And when a name was common in China, there weren't just thousands of them—there were millions.

"And the previous man's name?"

"We don't know. The corporal can't even remember which hospital it was—apparently he's worked at many. So it's unlikely we'll ever be able to find out."

That sparked another thought that it seemed like a detective might ask.

"And this other death, when was it?"

"Ah. Well, the corporal thinks it was in July."

That was only three months ago. Two months to find another man, get married, and have him die.

"You are sure that the woman was truly married to the man who died last night?"

Wiriya smiled. "So now you're definitely thinking like a detective. No, we don't know for sure. She claimed to be, at least."

She dutifully wrote: "Married???"

"So you think this might be...murder?"

Her first thought was for that unfortunate man, of course. But her next thought, almost immediately, was for the good name of her hospital. What would it look like if they had just let a murderer walk in and walk out? That would be very, very bad.

Especially with the Royal Hospital Inspection Committee arriving next Monday. What would the inspectors think of a hospital that aids and abets a murderer?

And think how they would look to the public. Ehhhh, this was very, very bad. Something must be done.

"Serial murder, yes," Wiriya said. "If there are two cases we know about, there may be others."

They both thought for a moment about what that might mean. A woman out there, somewhere, who was murdering her husbands. But why? Why would she do such a thing?

Then she saw. "Insurance money? She's pretending to be married and then killing them for their insurance money?"

Wiriya nodded. "At least that's a possibility. It's all I can think of," he admitted.

"But then why bring them to the emergency room?"

Neither of them could answer that question, but one piece of the corporal's story struck her. "The death certificates," she said. "It's the death certificates. She's taking them to the emergency room so she can get a death certificate."

He nodded. "She'd need one to collect the life insurance, of course." He was smiling, now. "You're quite good at this."

For a moment she suspected that the detective had reached this conclusion ahead of her. He was, after all, a detective. Perhaps this was a test? Or maybe he was giving her a chance to figure it out for herself? In any case, she was proud of herself for reaching the correct conclusion on her own.

Ladarat Patalung, ethical nurse detective. She liked the way that sounded.

"But...why do you come to me? What can I do to help?"

The detective didn't answer immediately. When he did, she thought for a moment that he hadn't heard her question.

"In your work here, you must have to review...cases?"

Ladarat agreed that she did. There would be questions about a patient's care and she would investigate. Although she wouldn't use that word exactly. She would look and listen and ask questions. She would try to determine whether her colleagues behaved in the proper way. And if they didn't, she would look for opportunities to help the doctors and nurses involved see what they could have done differently. So yes, she was used to looking and searching.

Wiriya thought about her answer for a moment.

"You see," he said finally, "I don't know if there have been other cases at this hospital. And I can't find out without a search warrant. And...well...there isn't nearly enough evidence for one. The chief would just laugh at me." He paused, thinking.

"And so you see, I thought that because of your position, you would have a justification to look through medical records... quietly."

"But what would I be looking for so...quietly?"

"Well, if this woman were a murderer, then we'd need to think about poison. That would be the logical method."

Ladarat nodded, then stopped to think about that. "It would?"

The detective nodded. "Poison is often a woman's method. It is a known fact."

Ladarat wasn't so sure about that. That was a rather sexist thing to say, wasn't it? But presumably Khun Wiriya knew what he was talking about. Still, shouldn't she question everything? That's what a real detective would do. So she wrote very carefully: "Woman = Poison?" And underlined the question mark.

"So," Wiriya continued, "we need to look for evidence of poison. Blood tests, and...so forth."

Ladarat was intensely curious about what the "and so forth" consisted of. Yet she began to see what the detective had in mind. "So you want me to see if there were any lab tests that were ordered."

Wiriya nodded, relieved.

Then Ladarat had another thought. "But if this was only last night, it might still be possible to run new tests on a blood sample." She'd heard of the coroner's office doing such things for suspicious deaths.

"Well, it's not so simple, unfortunately. The body has been taken for cremation already."

"Already? But he only died last night. And wouldn't she need a marriage certificate to be able to obtain the body?"

Ladarat knew that the marriage certificate would be essential in order for this woman to claim the body and receive a death certificate. She'd been involved in a terrible situation last year when a woman wanted to bring her husband's body back to Vietnam to be buried at their home near My Tho. But the poor woman didn't have a marriage certificate, so she couldn't prove that they were married. Eventually the hospital monks had to intervene.

Now Wiriya looked grim. He smacked his solid hand down on the desk in front of him and looked at her with a new respect.

"I knew I was missing something. I knew something was wrong. She had the marriage certificate with her last night." He paused. "You see?"

She didn't. But then she did. Very clearly.

If your husband died suddenly, would you have the presence of mind to find your marriage certificate and take it with you? You would not. You would panic. You would call your family. You would do any one of a number of logical and illogical things. But you would not think to take your marriage certificate to the hospital with your newly deceased husband.

"So that means that the hospital has a copy," she pointed out. "We'd need to keep a copy of the marriage certificate for our records."

Wiriya was nodding enthusiastically now. "So at least we'll be able to get her name. That's good. That's very good." He smacked his palm on the desk again, for emphasis, but more gently this time. And he was smiling.

"Well," he said finally. "This is progress. Perhaps it will be nothing, but maybe..."

He left the sentence unfinished, but Ladarat knew what he was thinking. Maybe, just maybe, they were on the trail of a murderer. They knew that she was out there somewhere, but she didn't know that she was being pursued. That thought gave Ladarat energy and a sense of excitement she hadn't felt in a long, long time.

Being an ethicist was important work, of course. And satisfying. But it wasn't... exciting.

"So you'll do it?"

Ladarat started to say that of course she'd do it. But she hesitated. She was the ethicist, after all. And here she was offering to look through a patient's records. Was that... ethical? She thought so, but...

"Yes, I'll do it."

"Good. And in the meantime, I will ask around... quietly. Perhaps there have been other suspicious deaths..."

They stood up to say their good-byes, and she thought

Wiriya might have lingered just a little longer in her door than was absolutely necessary. But if she had to be completely honest with herself, she didn't mind. She wasn't sure whether that was because he was such good company, or whether it was simply the excitement of the investigation. Whatever the reason, she found that she was a little sad to see the door of her little office close behind him.

CHAPTER 2

THE TRAGEDY OF THE AMERICANS

Ladarat Patalung did not have such conversations about murder every day. It was safe to say that such a conversation was an event and should be treated as such. It should be... marked somehow.

And what better way to mark such an event than with a snack? Just a small something. It was only midmorning. A sweet, perhaps.

No sooner had she reached this gratifying conclusion than her mind began to wander—entirely of its own accord—out the front door of Sriphat Hospital. Down the wide, grand stone steps, it went around the meandering driveway, and to the main entrance on Suthep Road. There, her mind explored the options for a snack that would be appropriate to the occasion.

In giddy anticipation, her hopeful mind wandered along the row of stalls that were reliably arrayed along the west side of Suthep Road. At the first cart there was *khao neow ma muang*—perhaps the simplest Thai dessert (*Khanom*)—slices of sweet, overripe mango on top of a small mound of sticky rice and drenched with rich coconut syrup. Or perhaps *khanom jark*—coconut meat and palm sugar wrapped in a palm leaf and grilled until the coconut and sugar were fused into an intensely sweet toasted candy. Or *khao neow dam*—black sweet sticky rice smothered in finely shredded coconut. Or...

18

She had just decided on *khao neow dam* as being a little more virtuous, when her mind's wandering was pulled up short by a knock on her office door. Deeply disappointed, her mind hurried back up the hospital driveway, through the grand entry hall, and down to the basement, dragging its heels the whole way.

"Khun Ladarat?"

Oh dear. That was a voice she knew well. A moment later, the door opened and the face to which the voice belonged emerged in the gap, framed against the dark hallway beyond. Ladarat suppressed an instant of annoyance as she realized that her mind's culinary wanderings had been so abruptly curtailed by her assistant nurse ethicist. She of all people should know that very few things are more urgent than *khao neow dam*.

Ladarat had just received permission this year to hire an assistant ethicist, and she'd selected Sisithorn Wichasak from more than a hundred applicants. Sisithorn was a new nurse who had just graduated from school two months ago. Young and gangly, she had no discernable social skills whatsoever. She favored big, round glasses; oversize clothes; and wide, open-toed sandals that emphasized her big feet and inelegant toes. Not that Ladarat was qualified to critique anyone's sense of fashion, but she could think of a few pointers one might offer, if one could find the right moment.

In fairness, though, Sisithorn was exceptionally smart. She graduated at the top of her class at Kuakarun College of Nursing in Bangkok, and then she came here to Chiang Mai because she wanted to learn about ethics.

"Khun Ladarat—Khun Jainukul is here." Her assistant was breathless with excitement over such an important visitor. "Will you see him now?"

Of course she would see Dr. Suphit Jainukul. The director of the Sriphat ICU was certainly more urgent than *khao neo dam*, and was not a man to be kept waiting. Nor was he a man who would generally come to visit her in this little basement office. So his appearance was strange indeed.

They greeted each other formally with *wais*—the traditional Thai greeting. A sort of half bow, with palms pressed together at chest level and brought up to the nose as the head was bent. Much more sanitary, by the way, than the Western tradition of a handshake. More sanitary, and more respectful.

Then the director straightened and took the seat that Khun Wiriya had just vacated.

As he did, Ladarat had an unobstructed view of the door, which was still open, framing the face of her assistant ethicist. Sisithorn looked at her expectantly.

"Khun Ladarat...is this a meeting for which I would be needed?"

"Needed?"

"To take minutes. To record." She paused hopefully. "To... document important facts?"

Ladarat sighed. She knew she should be pleased to have such an energetic and ambitious assistant. And for the most part she was. But there were times when such motivation should be curbed. Indeed, in Thailand the word "ambition," *tayur tayaan*, was often used to mean "overly ambitious." And it was not generally used as a compliment.

But to be fair, would this be a meeting for which her assistant would be helpful? She glanced at the director, but his eyes were downcast, paying attention only to the iPhone that rested on a broad palm. He was clearly very worried about something. The director's forehead, she noticed, was wrinkled with concern and lined like a page of sheet music. And his forefinger stabbed at his phone's screen with an irritable energy that was most unusual for him.

"Perhaps..." Sisithorn persisted, "Khun Jainukul would like tea?"

The director glanced up and turned toward the door. He shook his head distractedly. "No, thank you, Khun."

"Or a sweet? I can run to get *khao tom mud*. It will only take a minute..."

Again the director shook his head. "No, Khun. Perhaps another time."

Oh dear. Whatever the director's purpose here, it was certainly serious.

Dr. Jainukul always took tea. And anything else—sweet or savory—you'd put in front of him. He was a large man whose ruddy cheeks, shaved head, and plump fingers belied an indomitable strength of purpose and a deep commitment to his patients. In the ten years she'd known him, she'd seen many bureaucrats make the error of underestimating him.

Yet he did love his food, and especially sweets. And simple *khao tom mud* was his favorite. The national dessert of Thailand, it consisted of small packets of sticky rice and coconut milk and syrup, neatly wrapped in a triangular banana leaf. Ladarat had witnessed the director consume a half dozen with an expansive enjoyment that was contagious, and which reminded her just a little of her late husband, Somboon.

Not today, though. As this large, exuberant man refused Sisithorn's offer without any interest, Ladarat knew something was very, very wrong.

She shook her head at Sisithorn, who also looked suitably concerned. To her credit, she, too, was alarmed by the director's refusal of *khao tom mud* and accorded it the significance it deserved. Without another word, she backed out through the door, closing it gently behind her.

In the moment of silence after the director glanced up again, Ladarat drew her conclusions quickly: *The director is here to ask for my help.*

And: *This request for help is making the director very, very uncomfortable.*

"You have heard," the director asked hesitantly, "about the tragedy of the Americans?"

He offered a weak smile and the rattling skeleton of a laugh that would have been inappropriate anywhere else. But in Thailand, a laugh is provoked almost as often by embarrassment or sadness or anger as it is by humor. Over the years Ladarat had had many opportunities to wonder at her strange culture that could produce such an anomaly.

Ladarat positioned her yellow pad in front of her, turning to a fresh page and hoping fervently that this page would not be as interesting as the last. She wrote today's date. Then: "Americans. ICU."

Then, the most important word she would write today: "Elephant."

She nodded. Of course she had heard about the sad story of the Americans. A young man and his wife. They'd just been married down in the Gulf of Thailand, at a fancy resort on the island of Koh Samui. Then they'd taken their honeymoon by going trekking with elephants in the Golden Triangle, northwest of Chiang Mai.

On their first day in the forest, the elephant on which they'd both been riding just a few minutes earlier turned violent. It trampled the man, damaging his spine and badly damaging his brain. His new wife had been hurt, too, with a fractured pelvis and other serious injuries. Hoping to avoid a tourism debacle, the Thai Air Force had intervened, sending a helicopter into the deep forest to airlift them both back to the best hospital in northern Thailand—hers.

They'd arrived here two days ago, on Saturday. Since then, the wife had woken up, but the man had not. Ladarat had heard, in fact, that there was too much brain damage, and that he was brain-dead. Or close to it. So sad.

She wrote: "Husband? Wife?"

"The man," Khun Suphit said. "He will not be waking up." He shook he head sadly.

"Ever?"

"Ever."

They both thought about this for a moment. It was Ladarat who broke the silence.

"How is the wife?" she asked.

Khun Suphit brightened, just a little. "She is doing better, I'm happy to report." Although truth be told, he didn't look at all happy.

"But emotionally, how is she doing? The knowledge of her husband's condition must be a terrible shock, no?"

Ladarat had always believed that how you feel determines, in large part, how well you do medically. And she was convinced that doctors and nurses needed to attend to a patient's emotional health at least as much as they attend to his physical health. The good Professor Dalrymple offered wise counsel on this topic, which she credited to an American physician named Dr. F. W. Peabody: "In order to care *for* a patient," she admonished, "you must care *about* the patient."

Ladarat looked up from her notes at the director, who, she

noticed, had become strangely silent. He gave a short laugh that reminded her of the sound that a very old and faithful bicycle tire makes when it is deflated for the last time.

It was then that she knew why Khun Suphit was sitting in her office now. She knew why this important man had honored her by coming to her little office in the hospital's basement. And why he looked so uncomfortable.

"You see," he said slowly, "I'm not sure she knows about her husband."

"You're not sure? Ah, Khun Suphit, so you mean you're not sure she understands what you've told her?" Ladarat was almost certain this was *not* what the director meant.

"Well..." Again the sad laugh.

"Yes?"

"You see, we have not told her yet."

"Indeed?"

"Indeed."

So the director did not want to tell the woman. He did not want to be the bearer of bad news, and above all, he did not want to cause distress. So very Thai. And yet so very wrong. Did he not have an obligation to share this news honestly? He most certainly did.

"Ah, I see," she said. "And so...when you do tell her, you are worried that she will be upset. Of course I understand. When you tell her, we should invite one of the monks from Wat Sai Moon." That was the monastery across the road from the hospital. "Would that be helpful?"

He shook his head. "No...I mean, yes, it would be helpful. But it's just that we...I...thought that it might be better if you tell her."

Oh dear.

"I see," she said. "But why would that be?"

Ladarat knew exactly why that would be, but she pressed on. "You know his condition better than I ever could. After all, you're his doctor, and the director of the ICU. Such information should come with authority. Who better to explain his condition and prognosis?"

"Ah," he said. "But you...you've spent time in America. In Chicago." He pronounced that city with singsongy Thai vowels that oddly seemed to fit her memories of the city better than the prosaic pronunciation to which she'd become accustomed.

"I thought that since you know Americans, and how they think," he continued, hurrying, "you'd be better able to explain his condition."

"And what is his condition?"

Relieved to be back on firmer ground, the director stopped fidgeting and assumed the calm, patient demeanor to which Ladarat was accustomed. He smiled sadly and explained that the man's condition was very grave indeed. "He has no evidence of brain function. His pupils are not contracting, and he cannot breathe on his own." He paused. "It is, truly, very bad."

Ladarat nodded, beginning to see why the director wanted her to convey this information. In the United States, she knew, this man would be brain-dead. His life support would be stopped. That would be very sad for the man's family, of course. But at least they would be able to close that door behind them.

But here in Thailand there was no such door for them to close. There were no such hard-and-fast rules about what to do. So it would be difficult indeed to explain the man's situation to his wife. And if his situation were not explained correctly—and perhaps even if it were—she might insist on keeping him "alive" and supported artificially, for weeks or even months.

Their hospital could not afford that. Their ICU was always full, she knew, and there was always a waiting list. As long as the American was there, there would be patients who would not get the ICU care they needed.

Of course she would help. There was no question of that. Wasn't this why she'd been sent to receive ethics training at the University of Chicago? Wasn't this why she had braved a year of extreme cold, and rude people, and bland, salty food? Food, in fact, that was so tasteless that eating a meal was no more satisfying than reading a menu. She suffered all of that for a year so she could bring the principle of ethics back to the best hospital in northern Thailand.

So she would have to help. No question. But this was the director's responsibility as well.

"Then we should meet with her together," she suggested. "I will need to ask you for the medical details and prognosis, and of course, the importance of your position and status will make the conversation easier."

A little flattery, Ladarat had always found, worked wonders with doctors. With everyone, actually. But with doctors more than most.

Yet the director did not seem to be overly enthusiastic about this plan. He looked down at his hands. Then up at the tiny mail slot window set high into the wall behind her.

"You are the expert in injuries of this type," she explained gently. "Everyone knows this. It would seem strange, would it not, if you were absent for such an important discussion?"

This direct appeal to his vanity was her last hope. The director considered for a moment. At last, Khun Suphit seemed to agree that his absence would be strange indeed. He nodded.

"But you will do the talking?"

What could she say? She nodded. "I will do the talking."

The director stood up, at least partly relieved. This meeting had not gone quite as well as he'd hoped, but it had gone better than he'd feared.

And that, Ladarat had always thought, was the way things usually worked out. One's hopes are never fully realized. Or almost never. But on the other hand, one's fears are not usually justified. If she were wise enough to write a book like Professor Dalrymple's, that would be the sort of advice she would offer.

"Then we should go now," the director announced.

"Now?" Ladarat's stomach gave a modest lurch of protest as she realized that there would be no *khao neo dam* in her immediate future. Nor would she be able to begin her work as a detective. Nor would she be able to prepare for the upcoming inspection.

"Right now," the director said. "You see, she has been transferred out of the ICU and is in a private ward. And the man's parents are here. They flew here last night from Alb... Alb..."

"Albuquerque?"

"Yes, that's it. Al-bu-quer-que. And they want to know what is happening."

"I'm certain that they do."

And she was certain, too, that the man's parents wanted their son to get the best possible care. No doubt they were deeply suspicious that anyone could get the best possible care in Thailand, of all places. If he'd had the good fortune to be in a Bangkok hospital, which everyone knew rivaled the best in the United States. Instead, they were here in Chiang Mai. Little more than a point of departure for tourists and trekkers venturing into the wild forests of the Golden Triangle. At least that was what they thought.

So she would need to reassure them that Sriphat Hospital was the equal of any hospital in Bangkok. Or Albuquerque. Or even Chicago, for that matter. But that, she knew, wasn't going to be easy.

As Ladarat rose to follow Khun Suphit out of her little office, her gaze rested for a moment on Professor Dalrymple's wise book. She thought of another wise passage from that very wise book: "One must never tell a patient that there is no hope. There is always hope. It's just a matter of helping our patients hope for what is reasonable."

That was good advice indeed. But what could this poor man's family hope for? And certainly there was no simple aphorism that could offer comfort to his wife. Still, perhaps Ladarat could offer something.

CHAPTER 3

THE ETHICAL RIGHTS OF A BAREFOOT VISITOR

Khun Suphit led the way, swinging his thick arms around a broad middle section as he strode down the low-ceilinged hallway. It was not difficult to remain a few deferential steps behind him as they walked to the north elevators. The director moved very quickly for a man of such . . . roundness.

She caught up with him at the elevator, just as the doors slid open. It seemed to have been waiting for him. Odd how some people inspire the world to give them what they need. Somboon had been like that. Relentlessly upbeat, he always expected the best, and usually received it. Up until the very end, he'd been irrepressibly cheerful. And even hopeful.

But she, Ladarat, was not one of those people. Doors seemed to open for her grudgingly, as if they had better things to do with their time. And people, too, did not step out of their way to help her as they did for Somboon. They didn't hinder her, exactly. It was more that she wasn't . . . noticeable. Ah well.

She and the director discussed their strategy as the elevator took them from the basement up to the ICU on the sixth floor. They would see the man first, they agreed, and review his case. Then they would go to see the wife.

"Together, yes?" she clarified.

"Yes . . . of course, Khun. Together."

A moment later, the elevator doors opened onto a different world. Where Ladarat's basement office was dark, with just a small window close to the ceiling, the hallway that led to the ICU was broad and light-filled, as was the waiting room at the far end. Tall windows offered spectacular views of the mountains that began just a few kilometers to the west, and Ladarat knew that if you looked up and to the left, from some of the waiting-room seats you could see the Doi Suthep temple perched on the mountainside. That must be such a comfort to many visitors, in this Buddhist country.

There were hardly any visitors today, though. It was still early, and many friends and family members needed to travel from the countryside. Chiang Mai was really just a small city in the midst of rich farmland and—to the north and west—endless forests. Visitors might take an overnight bus, arriving midmorning, if they could come at all. They'd pay their respects, and then return home in time to work the next day.

Many patients came from small villages, where people earned money only if they worked. The fields wouldn't tend themselves, and if people didn't work, they didn't eat. So the waiting rooms were often empty, except if a patient came from very close to Chiang Mai, or was in the city itself.

This morning there was only one man in the waiting room, in the far corner, with his back to the wall that separated the waiting room from the ICU. Despite the fact that there was a wide field of empty chairs in front of him, the man was squatting on the floor, his arms cantilevered out over his knees. He was rocking back and forth very slowly, in time to some rhythm in his head.

The man's posture reminded her of the people from the

hill tribes where she'd grown up, near Mae Jo. Coming into town for the day to buy or sell or trade, they'd avoid chairs and benches, preferring to squat as this man was doing. As if there was safety and security in being as close to the ground as possible.

Ladarat looked more closely at the man but was careful not to stare, which would be rude and inhospitable. He was a guest, after all. Moreover, he could be here only because of a serious tragedy, so he deserved her compassion.

She followed Khun Suphit across the waiting room, turning to admire the view. As she did, she glanced over just long enough to see that, in fact, the man did have the long face of one of the Karen hill tribe people. Their light skin was distinctive, too. He was probably from a small village along the border of Thailand and Myanmar, perhaps even on the other side of the border. Most of the hill tribes didn't care about borders—they'd lived here long before anybody thought to divide the Golden Triangle into the territories of Myanmar, Laos, and Thailand.

The man noticed Ladarat looking at him, so she stopped, of course, and greeted him formally as one should greet a guest. Startled by her attention, he got to his feet, revealing very thin arms and legs, with prominent veins and corded muscles. He appeared to be in his forties or fifties but was probably much younger. His body and face had been weathered and molded by a difficult life of hard outdoor labor and just enough food—mostly fruit and fish and sticky rice—to survive.

He stooped, keeping his head at a respectful level below hers. And that was difficult for the poor man, since she herself was only one and a half meters tall. Then he returned her greeting with a mumble that was barely audible and offered a deep *wai*. Joining his hands, palms together, in front of his chest, he brought his nose down to touch his fingertips, bending almost double at the waist. It was as deep a *wai* as Ladarat would offer the dean of the school of nursing, or a high government official.

Yet despite that demonstration of profound respect, the man did not linger. Instead, after a pause that was just long enough to avoid an appearance of disrespect, he scooped up an old gray burlap bag that had been behind him, slung it crosswise over his shoulder, and scurried toward the hallway. It was only as he padded away that Ladarat noticed that he wasn't wearing shoes.

But she didn't have time to think about that, because Khun Suphit was waiting for her at the large double doors to the ICU. He'd been watching her interaction with the Karen man, and now he was nodding.

"Yes, it's strange," he said. "The man arrived here last night. I don't know who he's here to see. He just sits and waits. And he'll run away if you try to talk to him. Last night the charge nurse told him he couldn't stay there all night, so he left, but I don't know where he went. Then first thing this morning he was back."

"If he's from a village, it's likely he doesn't have a place to stay here, or anything to eat," she said. And that is no way to treat a guest, she thought.

He nodded. "I'll make sure the volunteers know to send him to Wat Sai Moon." Many staff prayed at that temple and gave their donations there to make merit. In return, the monks would visit patients and would take in visitors who needed a place to stay.

The man might not want to accept their hospitality. Indeed, he had seemed almost painfully shy and was almost certainly overwhelmed by the big city. It was, in all likelihood, the first time he'd been to Chiang Mai, and almost certainly the first time he'd been in a hospital. So it was all the more important that they make him welcome.

As Professor Dalrymple said: "You must always treat a patient's family as an extension of your patient."

"But..." the director said.

"But?"

He sighed. "I'm only thinking of the Royal Inspectors. They will be here next Monday, you recall?"

She certainly did recall. Indeed, hardly a waking moment in the past month had gone by that Ladarat hadn't paused to recall that impending event. And if she did forget, there were the frequent reminders from Khun Tippawan, the Director of Excellence.

"And it won't do to have this man in his bare feet in our waiting room." He paused, and then, perhaps sensing her impending objection, he asked a question that she hadn't thought of. "Would you see a man like this outside the ICU of the University of Chicago?"

"No, Khun," she agreed. "You would not."

"It's not that it is bad that he is here necessarily. But it is not the sort of scientific and academic image we want to present to the inspectors, is it?"

Ladarat agreed that was probably true. But she also thought that if one of the inspectors were in the ICU, they would want their visiting family members treated with respect and courtesy, no matter what those family members looked like. And whether those family members wore shoes.

But there would be time later to consider the ethical rights of a barefoot visitor. For now, there was work to be done.

As Khun Suphit led her through the glossy steel double doors that swung open automatically, it was as if she'd stepped back in time to her days at the University of Chicago five years ago. Indeed, what she saw was an ICU to make the director proud. The Sriphat Hospital ICU was new and modern, with glassed-in cubicles arrayed around a central nursing station. The place was busy with mechanical conversation. There was the rhythmic whoosh of breathing machines, layered over the background babble of beeps and buzzes and chimes coming from various monitors that were all trying to have their say. It could easily have been the ICU in Chicago where she learned about ethics. Or any other ICU in a major city.

She knew that people in the United States and elsewhere had a tendency to look down on medical care in countries like Thailand. She certainly heard dismissive questions from people in Chicago. Do you have antibiotics? they asked. Or chemotherapy? Or surgery? A brisk walk through this unit would convince them quickly enough that we have all of those things. But, she liked to think, we haven't forgotten about the caring part of medicine the way the West has.

Now they were standing in front of cubicle 8, where the American named Andrew Fuller was lying on a hospital bed. In his throat he had a breathing tube that was connected to a ventilator, which was breathing for him. His head was bandaged, and his eyes were taped shut to prevent them from drying out, but she could see fresh bruises across his right cheek and jaw. There was bruising around both eyes, too. Raccoon eyes, she remembered from nursing school, were a sign of fractures of the bones that surround the eyes. The heart monitor over the bed was blipping along, but that was the only sign of life.

"He looks…peaceful," she said hesitantly.

Khun Suphit winced.

"Do you really think so?"

Ladarat nodded.

"Ahh, yes. Of course you are right, Khun. I suppose he does."

Ladarat nodded again. That was part of the problem. The American appeared to be resting. It was a comforting appearance of peacefulness, but a misleading appearance, too. He looked like he could wake up any second. And once those bruises healed…well…it would be hard for his parents or his wife to believe that anything was wrong. And that would make it much more difficult for them to make a difficult decision. Oh dear.

She had to ask the obvious question. How could the director be sure that the man didn't have any brain function? How was it possible to know that, after such a short period of time? But she couldn't ask in that way.

No. She didn't want to question Khun Suphit's medical expertise. It was, she knew, a delicate situation that she'd faced many times as a nurse. Fortunately, it was a problem for which she had developed…strategies.

"When I tell the family that his brain is no longer working," she said slowly, "they will have questions."

Khun Suphit nodded unhappily. He knew that they would. That was why she was here.

"What shall we tell them?" she asked. "How do we talk to them in a way that will help them to understand his condition?"

"You can tell them three things," the director said. And he didn't hesitate. "First, that his pupils don't respond to light. Second, that the vestibular canals in his ears don't respond to hot or cold water the way that they should. That means that the part of the brain that controls balance and coordination isn't functioning. Finally, you can say that we've done EEGs two times since he's been here, and we've seen no response. So you see, his brain—it is not sending any of the signals that even a sleeping brain makes."

"Eehhh. That is bad."

And it was. Those are the tests that she'd learned about in Chicago. But she also knew that there were other tests, like a brain scan, that Western countries sometimes did. She hoped the family wouldn't ask about those tests, because they didn't do them here. Still, she knew that they might ask.

"And if they ask about a PET scan, what should I say?"

He nodded. "Oh, no doubt they will ask. Or they will have a U.S. doctor call me to ask. We can tell them that although that test is used sometimes in the U.S., it is not used in Europe or most other countries."

"And why is that?" Although she knew perfectly well why not, it would help to give Khun Suphit a chance to practice his explanation.

"Because, you see, it doesn't add useful information. It is no better than the tests doctors can do at the bedside. Ask any expert, they will tell you the same thing."

She knew, then, why the director was so eager to have her translate. This would be a conversation that would be full of conflict. There would be angry words and tears. And, probably, accusations of poor care. Accusations that real "experts" would do things differently. In short, the kind of conversation that would cause all of those involved to lose face.

Ladarat and the director stood there watching as Andrew Fuller's chest rose and fell, knowing that movement didn't mean anything. And knowing, too, that this was not going to be easy to explain to Andrew Fuller's family on the other end of that long hallway.

CHAPTER 4

THE *YIM SOO* SMILE OF THE FEMALE SEX

And indeed it was not.

The first hint of trouble came in the hallway outside the room of Andrew Fuller's wife. His soon-to-be widow. Kate, she was called.

As Ladarat and Khun Suphit approached the door, a new nurse, just out of nursing school at Chiang Mai University, one of the best nursing schools in the country, came hurrying out of the American's room, smiling furiously.

To a *farang*—a foreigner—she might look happy. But one glance revealed her smile to be what Thais call *yim soo*, or "I'm smiling because I don't know what else to do."

If it seems like Thais smile too much, it's not because we have so much to smile about, but because we use a smile for so many occasions. It was a little like what the undergraduates said at the University of Chicago: Drinking is only for after 5 P.M., but it's always after 5 P.M. somewhere.

In Thailand we smile because even if there is nothing to smile about, there may be something worth smiling about someday. Or there used to be. She was sure that those college students were addicted to their drinking and she often wondered whether perhaps Thais suffered from a similar addiction to smiling.

The young nurse rushed between them, slowing only for a

hurried *wai*. Normally she was ambitious and almost obse-
quious, particularly to a powerful doctor like Khun Suphit.
Her hurry was bad sign. A very bad sign.

Khun Suphit paused. Then he sighed. Then—of course—
he smiled. Then he led the way into the room.

It was one of the best rooms in the hospital. Khun Suphit
had made sure of that. Normally used for government officials
and very important *farang*, it had wide windows that afforded
a panoramic view of the deep green mountains to the west. It
also boasted a wide expanse of marble floor and a large sitting
area with comfortable teak and rattan furniture.

Ladarat was in general not in favor of special, private rooms
that gave some patients better treatment than others. The pro-
ponents of such luxurious accommodations said that those
patients do not receive better care, only more comfort, as if
that made injustice more acceptable. In her view, it did not.

And wasn't the distinction between care and comfort a
false one? Don't people who are more comfortable heal faster?
So aren't we giving some people better care than we're giving
others? That is unfair.

Yet she could not fault the hospital for giving special treatment to the Americans. They had been through so much,
compassion dictated that they should offer additional comfort. One could only hope that the Americans would appreciate this gesture, but she suspected that they would not.

Americans—and indeed all tourists—never seemed to
appreciate the hospitality for which Thailand was justly
famous. No matter how hard a hotel clerk or a waitress might
try to anticipate a guest's needs, the guest seemed to take
those efforts as their due. Just what was expected. And they
never smiled.

Khun Suphit's broad back paused in the doorway, obscuring

for a moment the scene that awaited them. Then he stepped backward and to his right, revealing a solid middle-aged American man who was standing with his hand on his hips, blocking their entrance. He had sandy hair and high cheek-bones like a woodcarving, and probably would have been very handsome once. Behind him was the woman Kate, sitting in a wheelchair next to her bed, with a hopeful smile and bright green eyes. Despite the bandages that encircled her head and partially hid her blond hair, you could tell that she was beautiful. This Andrew Fuller had been—for a short time at least—a very lucky man.

Then Ladarat's attention was jostled by a flicker of movement off to her right, and she glanced beyond the man who was blocking their way. Thin and pale, with red hair and a tentative smile, a woman rose from her place on the sofa to greet them with a deep *wai*, in the correct order, first to the director and then to her. Khun Suphit was nonplussed for a second—a first for him, no doubt. But he returned the American's *wai*, then turned to the man, and finally to the girl on the bed. The girl smiled uncomfortably, and the man simply nodded.

Well.

The three Americans looked expectantly at the director, and it wasn't until he took another step backward and to the side, looking directly at Ladarat, that she remembered that she was to do the talking. That recollection didn't feel very good.

"This," she announced an uncertain voice, "is Dr. Suphit Jainukul. He is the director of the ICU. He is responsible for the oversight of Mr. Fuller's care."

"Are you a doctor?" This from the man.

The director turned to her, with a tentative smile, pretending that he didn't speak English. Oh, so very clever. She smiled, too, contemplating revenge.

"Yes, Dr. Jainukul is a doctor. He is a pulmonary physician. And my name is Ladarat Patalung; I am a nurse." Mentioning that she was the ethicist for the hospital would only confuse things.

"You speak English very well," the woman said, peering around her husband's shoulder.

"Thank you. I had the good fortune to spend a year at the University of Chicago studying. And this is why," she continued, "Dr. Jainukul asked me to join you for this conversation as a translator. That," she said somewhat unnecessarily, "is my role."

If the director followed this, he gave no sign. Instead he had assumed a pleasant yet vacant expression of superficial interest. This was his defense mechanism, she knew. Whatever happened, and whatever the Americans said, he would smile his distracted smile, trying very hard to think of the gardening he would do this weekend.

No wonder Thailand has never been in a serious war. We are allergic to conflict, whereas Americans seemed hardwired to seek it out. The man, for instance, was staring at them with a strange intensity. And—what was truly odd—he still hadn't moved aside to let them pass. It would be awkward indeed to get into the room unless he gave way. But the women were nodding and smiling hopefully, waiting for some good news.

Then the man surprised them all. "I'm going out for a smoke. You all just talk about...whatever you need to talk about."

And before Ladarat could explain that he needed to be

here—that they needed him to be here—he slipped between her and the director with a grace that was surprising for a man of his size.

There was an uneasy moment as the four of them who remained looked at one another. Then his wife broke the silence with an awkward shrug and a smile. She sheepishly held up a pack of Marlboro Lights, whose red was anemic and washed out. Knockoffs from China or Cambodia probably. "He left these here. I think . . . I think maybe he's just not ready to talk."

She smiled again, weakly. If she were Thai, this would be the same *yim soo* smile that the young nurse had displayed just a few minutes ago. The smile of helplessness. It's also a way of saying: "I don't find this funny, and in fact it's very painful, but I'm smiling so at least you can smile, too."

That the *yim soo* smile seemed to be exclusive to women was part of its tragedy, and its effectiveness. One felt compelled to smile in sympathy. Especially if one was a woman, too.

But she couldn't explain that to Mrs. Fuller, any more than she could tell her, honestly and directly, that her son was going to die. Instead, Ladarat simply nodded, wondering that it was the man who left, and the women who stayed behind, willing to hear whatever news needed to be heard. Of course, it stands to reason that the women are stronger in these matters than the men. She saw this in Chicago, too. Perhaps it was true everywhere.

Mrs. Fuller gestured to the little circle of chairs just inside the door and pushed Kate's wheelchair over to join the circle.

They all sat and everyone looked at Ladarat.

"How much," she began, "do you know about what has happened to Mr. Fuller?"

That was how one started a conversation of this sort. Professor

Dalrymple was clear on this point. "First you must always find out what the patient and family know. You cannot guess what is in their heads, or in their hearts. You must ask."

"Please," Kate said, "call him Andrew."

Ladarat nodded.

"How much do you know about what has happened to Andrew?" she asked. "About his condition?"

"We know," Kate said slowly, "that he was badly injured. In his head, I mean. And...a spine fracture."

"And...that he hasn't shown any sign of brain function," Mrs. Fuller added. "Yet."

It was uncanny how they finished each other's sentences. Indeed, looking at them side by side, they shared a fresh, wide-eyed openness that made them seem like they could be mother and daughter.

"But there's still hope, isn't there?" Kate asked.

Ladarat translated that for the director, certain he'd understood, but at least she could give him some time to think.

He seemed ready to reply directly to Kate but then thought better of it. Instead, he turned to Ladarat.

"It has been forty-eight hours," he said in Thai. "It's very unlikely that he'll show any improvement if he hasn't already."

"But not impossible?"

Kate and Mrs. Fuller were watching this dialogue with increasing concern.

"No," he admitted slowly. "Not impossible. The chances of recovery decrease the longer he remains unconscious. So every day like this his chances are worse."

"So you wouldn't say that right now, today, he has no chance of recovery?"

He shrugged, then shook his head. "No, it's too soon to say that absolutely."

"Then how long, do you think? It would help if we could give them some time, so they can prepare."

The two women turned to the director. No doubt they were becoming increasingly confused. It was a simple question, they were thinking. Kate had simply asked whether there was hope.

It would certainly be a simple question in America. Any American doctor would have said of course. Of course there's hope. There's always hope. We'll just wait and see. We'll take one thing at a time. And one day at a time. Yet this Thai doctor and nurse were taking what felt like hours to answer a question that shouldn't take more than a few seconds. What is wrong with them?

And poor Khun Suphit was probably equally confused by the twists and turns their brief conversation was taking. Normally, with a Thai family, he would simply say that there was nothing more that he could do. But not with this family. No. They wanted information. They wanted...possibilities. And of course they wanted hope.

Instead, he offered them a smile that meant, among other things, "Things are very grim, and Andrew will never wake up. I'm so sorry for your loss." At least, that's what Ladarat saw. Who knew what the Americans perceived?

Then he said, in broken English: "Things are not good. Not good at all. But to be sure, we wait three more days. No improvement...then no hope." And he smiled.

It was odd how, in that second, the two women seemed to respond so differently. Kate nodded and smiled, as if her beloved Andrew had just gotten a reprieve. But Mrs. Fuller seemed already to be thinking ahead to the next conversation they'd be having in three days' time, and fearing the worst. She looked down and reached for the pack of cigarettes that her husband had left, then withdrew her hand as if she'd thought better of it. But for a moment, her arm outstretched and caught between two impulses, she had a confused look on her face. It was almost as if she'd forgotten who she was, and where she was.

But she came to her senses quickly enough. Putting on a brave face for the both of them, she said that she'd share what they'd discussed with her husband. And she picked up the pack of counterfeit cigarettes and shook it gently, as if it were somehow his representative in this little meeting.

Ladarat stood to leave and the director followed her. But Mrs. Fuller had one more question for them as she walked them to the door. It was plainly something she was reluctant to bring up, judging from her glances at Kate, who stayed behind in her wheelchair.

"You know we have the utmost respect for the medical system in Thailand," she began. She waved her arm at the hospital room and the view out of the oversize windows, as if that were an eloquent statement about the quality of a country's health care. "We know that Kate and Andrew have only gotten the best of care, and we mean no disrespect to...to the doctor." Here she smiled and nodded toward the director. "But my husband...well...he will want to be sure that everything possible is being done, and..."

"And you want a second opinion? A doctor from the U.S.?" Ladarat suggested.

Mrs. Fuller nodded sheepishly. "I think that would help him. Especially if...well...if Andrew doesn't improve. Roger will want to know that we did everything we could."

Ladarat nodded and translated, nervous about how that request would be received. In Thai culture, it would be difficult indeed to ask for such a thing without it being perceived as a slight. And indeed, the director frowned for a second, but just a second. Likely Mrs. Fuller didn't even notice.

Then he nodded and smiled at Kate and Mrs. Fuller. "Of course, I understand," he said in English. "If you give the name of the doctor, and e-mail, we can send all records. And translation."

He offered them both a *wai*, which Mrs. Fuller and then Kate returned. A moment later they were in the hallway.

"That went better than I expected," the director said thoughtfully.

"It was because the man, Mr. Fuller, was not there. That made it easier," Ladarat said.

The director nodded. "You think he didn't want to hear bad news?"

Ladarat agreed that was part of it. But more likely he didn't trust himself to be tough in the face of bad news. And, too, she wondered whether maybe he knew somehow that the conversation would be more productive if he wasn't there. That more questions would get asked and answered if he was absent.

The director stopped next to the elevators, waiting as Ladarat pressed the button to take her back to her basement office. Unlike the director, she couldn't count on the world around her being inspired to come to her aid when she needed it. She would probably have to wait for this elevator for a long, long time.

"There is one other thing I would appreciate your help with," he said slowly. "I hesitate to ask, because it has nothing to do with ethics. But..."

"Yes, Khun?"

"Do you remember that man who was here as we passed through earlier? The one who needs a place to stay?"

Ladarat nodded.

"You are very good at talking to people," he said. "They...
trust you."

"You are most kind." Oh dear. There was nothing more
dangerous than Thai flattery. Because surely that was flattery.
She was not "very good" at anything related to people. And no
one trusted her, with the possible exception of her cat. What
was the director up to?

"So I wondered if perhaps you could try to talk with him.
Maybe you could try to find out why he's here?"

Oh dear.

"But surely he has a good reason to be here? He would not
come to a hospital unless he were visiting a family member or
a close friend."

"Well, you see, there's the fact that he has no shoes..."

Ladarat waited.

"And with the inspection coming, you know...What
would it look like to have him here?"

What would the good Professor Dalrymple do? Sometimes Ladarat thought that everything she herself had accomplished, and indeed most of the decisions she made, could be
credited directly to the good professor's book. But just this
once, Ladarat didn't need to think about that for more than
a moment. The good Professor Dalrymple would try to help.
That was a nurse's duty, whatever the problem.

"Of course," she said finally. "I will try to speak with him."

The director smiled, relieved. "Thank you, Khun." He gave
her a *wai*, a little lower and more formal than he would usually have. She returned it, and they went their separate ways.
He no doubt thinking about his patients and she thinking
about how she was going to solve the mystery of the waiting
farmer.

CHAPTER 5

THE SADNESS OF HALF A HOUSE

It was past seven o'clock that evening when Ladarat finally arrived home, and she guided her pale yellow VW Beetle into the driveway of her little townhouse. She was exhausted, and barely had the energy to drive, but she was willing to believe that the Beetle knew its way back and forth to work by now. She'd had it for sixteen years, ever since she and Somboon had bought it as a second car shortly after they were married. When he died, she'd sold their main car, preferring to keep the Beetle. He'd loved to take long trips in their BMW, driving into the hills or east through the plains and farms of Isaan, but on her own, Ladarat never went far. And for going back and forth to work, the little Beetle was perfectly adequate.

She pulled herself out of the car, closing the door gently behind her. As usual, she didn't bother to lock the doors. This was Chiang Mai, after all, not Bangkok. They didn't really have crime here.

That thought, barely formed, made her pause on the little walkway that led up to her solid wooden door. No crime? But wasn't she in the process of investigating a murder? Well, a possible murder. Just possible.

And that was still all it was, wasn't it? She hadn't even made any progress that afternoon. She just plodded from one meeting to another throughout the morning and spent most of the afternoon wading through piles of guidelines, making certain that they were up to date in preparation for the Royal Inspection on Monday. The hospital inspectors always looked for those dates, she knew. One guideline that was past its expiration date, and they took one point off. One whole point! And if one was behind, then others might be, too.

So she'd spent the afternoon in the company of guidelines that covered every aspect of the hospital's daily life. Guidelines for when the signs should be updated, when employees should wash their hands, and where patients were allowed to smoke. Ladarat even discovered a guideline for the creation and modification of guidelines. That, at least, made her laugh out loud. Simply get rid of that one, and all of the others would be impossible to find fault with.

True, she didn't find any problems. That, at least, made her feel a bit better. But still, it had been exhausting and she was glad to be home.

As Ladarat turned the key in the look, she heard her alarm system, her watchcat, who protected the house during the day.

That's how she thought of him. Literally, in Thai: *maewfawbaahn*. (*Maew* is "cat"; *faw* is "watch over"; *baahn* is "house.") *Maewfawbaahn* means "catwatchhouse," or watchcat. Actually his name was Whiskey, because of his golden fur. But he seemed to appreciate the title and the prestige it conferred. He was a very honorable cat.

Her little home wasn't much to brag about, but she loved it nonetheless. It was a townhouse built in the old Lanna style, with wide-board teak floors, exposed beams, and white plaster walls. There was a small living room and kitchen on the first floor, and a small bedroom, study, and bathroom on the second. That was all. It was to be a starter house for her and Somboon, but they never…started. So sixteen years later, twelve years since he died, here she was, still.

For some time, in the back of her mind, there had lurked the vague notion that she might perhaps…remarry someday. Nothing more than a general idea. Certainly nothing that had taken shape.

Nor would it ever take shape. Statistically speaking, Ladarat knew that she would never remarry. Most people marry once, do they not? And they call themselves fortunate to do so. Perhaps a select few are fortunate enough—and attractive enough—to find love twice. But surely they were in the minority.

And did she have attributes that would justify her place in that fortunate minority? She most certainly did not. She was neither pretty nor intelligent, nor was she a good cook. In short, she possessed none of those qualities that might lead her to think she could find love a second time.

So here she was, with her house and its garden out back. Ladarat was most proud of that garden. Ladarat had no aptitude for growing things, but somehow plants here seemed to thrive spontaneously. Some were native to Thailand, like the Siam tulips around the edges of the patio. Their pretty fluted stalks were just as nice this time of year, in the fall, when they weren't crowned with a flower. There was silver-leafed ginger, too, with stripes down the middle of its leaves that seemed to her as if they were little ladders. There were impatiens by the score, flowering now in a pure white and a fluorescent yellow. And even though they never seemed to flower, the gordonia bushes with tough dark green waxy leaves hid the ugly concrete block wall at the back of the garden. And gold-leafed philodendron with delicate riffled edges popped up here and there according to a whim of their own.

Whenever she came out here—which was almost every day that it wasn't raining—she thanked her good fortune that she was not in Bangkok. Indeed, she had been to that enormous city only twice, and that was more than enough. The first time was with Somboon, on their honeymoon. They'd taken a plane that landed in the enormous Suvarnabhumi Airport outside of the city. The flight was only forty-five minutes, but it took them at least that long again to make their way through the gleaming corridors of the airport, surrounded on every side by marble and stainless steel and glass. She felt as though she were walking through a very wealthy person's endless bathroom. The second time was for a conference about palliative care, and she took the train—a much more pleasant and relaxed experience of travel altogether.

But when she was there . . . oh dear. So big, and so dirty. The air pollution alone was surely the same as smoking a pack of cigarettes every day. And not the major brand imported ones, or even the counterfeits like the gullible Mr. Fuller bought, but the rough filterless cigarettes that were imported illegally from Cambodia. After an hour outside, she felt as though she had a bronchial infection. How could people live in such a place? And why would they want to?

Perhaps it was just as well that there were people with such predispositions. What if every person in Bangkok decided he or she would much prefer the clear skies and cool nights of Chiang Mai? What if all eleven million inhabitants of that big, dirty city took the train north and descended on her little garden? That would not do. Much better that they like the crowded streets and the dirty air, so she could have her town just the way it had always been.

Here in Chiang Mai, she had her garden, and she could sit and hear nothing at all. Or perhaps only *Maewfawbaahn* mewing for attention, and the little red-breasted swallows creating a chorus of chirping from back among the dense gordonia leaves. And that's what she was going to do right now.

Too tired to cook, she'd picked up some *tom nam khon*—spicy prawn soup with coconut milk—and *glooai tawt*—banana fritters—from Khun Duanphen, the Isaan lady who ran the stall at the corner. At least, tirednesss was her excuse. But honestly, Ladarat couldn't cook. She never had been able to. Besides, Duanphen's *tom nam khon* was about the best in Chiang Mai. And she didn't make it very spicy like some of the other stalls did. Too much spice is as bad for you as not enough. So Ladarat put *Maewfawbaahn*'s canned food under the table and settled her slight frame onto one of the two delicate iron chairs that sat before the matching table.

Ladarat was always careful to alternate between the two chairs. There is nothing sadder, she always thought, for a person who lives alone, as when half a home becomes worn out while the other half stays fresh. It's as if a person's incomplete life were imprinted on the world. So everyone would know that she is just half a person.

She would not let that happen. Anyone looking at her small home would note that the chairs are evenly worn and the silverware is evenly tarnished, and even her bed is worn on both sides. That evenness was a comfort to her, although if pressed, she wouldn't be able to explain why it should be so.

Right now, though, she didn't have to explain anything to anyone. She was sitting on the patio in back of the house that she owned, watching the sky above her turn from a bright white to a deep blue with the rapidity and surety of a scene change in a play. There were things she needed to think about, and many things she needed to worry over. Such was life. But she put them all out of her mind for the moment.

It was at this time of day, though, that she missed Somboon most acutely. During the day there were distractions and work; now was the time that people should sit quietly with family and talk over their day. They should tell each other what had happened. And, she imagined, they should ask each other for advice. Sitting here with *Maewfawbaahn* was pleasant enough, and restful. Still, it was now more than ever that she felt as though she was missing something.

But perhaps that was one more thing to worry about. And so she put it out of her mind, setting it on a shelf for later. There would be plenty of time to think about her future. And, of course, to worry about the upcoming inspection. And, of course, the mystery man and the murderer and her own future as a detective. For now, she would sit here savoring the last bites of her *glooai tawt*, with *Maewfawbaahn* happily on her lap, listening to the swallows argue about whatever it is swallows argue about.

Wan ang kaan

TUESDAY

CHAPTER 6

THE HEALTH BENEFITS OF BUTTERFLY PEAFLOWER TEA

Are you well, Khun?"

Ladarat asked out of politeness, as one must. But truth be told, the man facing her across the medical records counter did not look well at all. In fact, he looked harried. His face was pale—even paler than is normal for a man who works in the windowless basement of a large hospital. And his short hair was mussed in odd, swept-back whorls as if he'd been running his hands over his head in frustration, as he did reflexively when he greeted her.

Of course Panit Booniliang was harried. He knew, as she did, that the hospital inspectors were likely to focus very intently on their medical records. The inspectors usually asked for many charts, and when they did, they wanted them immediately. It was almost as if, despite the fact that they were supposed to be interested in how well a hospital cared for patients, they forgot that, all around them, conscientious staff were trying to do just that. When they wanted a chart, they had to have it. So Panit Booniliang was a very nervous man.

He smiled the *yim yae yae* smile, which could be loosely translated as: "Well, it's awful, but really, what can you do?"

This smile, she knew, told the story of why Khun Panit was in charge of medical records. He would do whatever he could to prepare. And still he would be nervous. That was most un-Thai. His worrying was almost American. But in the event, he would realize that he'd done everything he could do and would retreat into the Thai state of *choie*, or imperturbable calm.

Alas, he was not quite there yet, as his roving glances across the wide, neat countertop revealed. He was still looking around for files out of place, as if he might see something that would remind him of a task he had forgotten. She hated to bother him now, but it couldn't be helped.

Ladarat offered her own version of the *yim yae yae* smile and said she needed his help.

"It is about a matter to do with the care that we gave to an unfortunate man in the emergency room last week."

"Yes, Khun?" She had gained at least a sliver of his attention. That was good, but she needed his full concentration for the matter at hand.

"He died," she said. "It seems he died before he came to our hospital, but his death was pronounced officially here."

"I see. And how old was this unfortunate man?"

"I believe he was about fifty."

"And what time did he die?"

That was when Ladarat knew these questions weren't prompted by idle curiosity or by concern. Not that Khun Panit was a heartless man, but his questions were typical of Thais faced with news about the death of someone they didn't know. In a culture that was wrapped in superstition and beliefs about numbers, the story of a man's death—his age, birthday, time of death—provide the raw ingredients for speculation that led, all too often, to a selection of numbers for that day's lottery.

Once she'd even witnessed, much to her dismay, a gaggle

of nursing students speculating about the death of a young woman—a *katoey*. A woman's spirit trapped in a man's body. Unable to cope with that cruel joke of fortune, she'd thrown herself off the roof of the Empress Hotel, one of the highest buildings in Chiang Mai. Ladarat was deeply ashamed of her profession to hear these nurses discussing how many floors the poor creature fell, so they could play those numbers in the lottery.

Panit Booniliang wasn't like that. No, this was just the force of habit. These were the questions one asked. It was a reflex. That was all.

Still, better to cut off further questions to which she wouldn't know the answer—birthdate, occupation...So she was perhaps a little more direct than she would have been in other circumstances,

"We have a problem."

This got Khun Panit's attention.

"I see, Khun. That is bad. What sort of problem?"

He was too polite to ask the question that was no doubt on his mind: What sort of problem could one have with a patient who is dead? Surely this couldn't be a very important problem. Surely it couldn't be more important than, say, preparing for next week's inspection?

She would need to choose her words carefully. She mustn't cause alarm, of course. Yet she must convey the gravity of the situation to a man who was understandably preoccupied.

There was a saying in Thai to which she'd had recourse many times in her career: *Kling wai korn, pho sorn wai*. Roughly: Do whatever needs to be done, to get through the moment.

Odd that in the United States such an aphorism would denote a strong-willed determination and a fundamental belief that defeat is impossible. But the Thai version was an illustration of creative pragmatism. Especially the importance of maintaining grace and smoothness, and a willingness to bend the truth if that's what was required. And in this case, it most certainly was.

"We have received word that the inspectors are very interested in the care of patients who have died," she announced, with what she hoped was a perfectly neutral face.

"Ahhh. This is from...an inside source?"

"It is."

"Indeed?"

"Indeed. That is, they are interested in the care of patients who have died suddenly. They will want to see records of patients in particular like this man, Zhang Wei, who died suddenly two nights ago."

"But why?" Khun Panit could not hide his confusion. "Why would they be so interested in such a patient, when there are hundreds of other patients in this hospital right now?"

Why indeed? That was an excellent question.

"Besides, which," he added, "from what you've told me, it seems that this man died outside our hospital. What could we have done that was good or bad?"

"Ah, but you see, that is perhaps the most important part of the practice of medicine."

"It is?"

Ladarat was as surprised as Khun Panit had been to hear this. But she needed to invent an explanation. Quickly.

"Yes, indeed. When a patient dies, our responsibilities don't end."

"They don't?"

"No, of course not." Ladarat shook her head, warming to

her topic. And wondering what words were going to come out of her mouth next.

Words were like that, she thought. Sometimes they surprised you by appearing. Or by failing to appear. Hopefully that wouldn't happen in this case.

And indeed it did not.

"No," she heard herself saying. "We still have an obligation—a duty—to help support the family. That means offering emotional support, for instance, and the chance to pray with one of our monks. It also means making sure the family has enough information about the cause of the patient's death."

The medical records clerk was nodding now, listening attentively.

"Because if families leave with unanswered questions, and if they are worried that perhaps not everything was done that could have been done..."

"Then there are ghosts. *Phi tai hong.*" He shuddered.

Ghosts? Ah, indeed. Ghosts (*phi*) were commonplace in Thai culture, and *phi tai hong* were particularly feared. They were vengeful ghosts of people who died suddenly, without the necessary preparation or Buddhist rituals.

Were such ghosts real? That was not a question that Ladarat had ever felt comfortable with. It was a wrong question. Unanswerable and unproductive.

A better question, perhaps, was what these ghosts meant to Thai people. That *meaning* was certainly real. And Ladarat had always thought that these beliefs—and beliefs about *tai hong* ghosts in particular—were a way of putting a face to guilty feelings. Guilty feelings for the bad things you may have said or done to a person during life. Or things you should have said but did not. A ghost was a way of doing penance for those things—expunging them through the fear that one felt.

Ah, but she was not a psychologist. Already a nurse, and an ethicist. And now perhaps a detective. That was enough professions for one diminutive Thai woman to take on in her lifetime. She would leave those sorts of theories to those who were better prepared.

The medical records clerk was watching her expectantly, as if waiting for her to confirm or deny the existence of *phi tai hong*. Instead, she simply nodded. "That is one concern, to be sure," she said.

"Then they bring a lawsuit."

"Well, yes, that is another concern," Ladarat admitted. And one that, presumably, Khun Panit knew more about than ghosts, because whenever there was a lawsuit, it was he who was responsible for gathering all of a patient's records. "But there is also the distress and anger and guilt that the family may feel. This is also our responsibility, is it not?"

Faced with such unassailable logic, Panit Booniliang had to agree that this was, in fact, their responsibility.

"But you see," she concluded, "we don't always support families as we should."

"We don't?"

"No." She shook her head sadly. "We do not. It is easy to simply walk away from a patient who has died. And easier, usually, to walk away from his family. They are distressed and sad, and sometimes angry."

"Ah, I see, so these inspectors, they want to see that our staff comforted the family. And that we—"

"Determined the cause of death, and shared that with his wife. Yes. They will want to see this. So," she concluded, "I need to review this man's records, and his laboratory tests, to see whether the inspectors are likely to be satisfied with what they see."

Ladarat was quite proud of herself. And even prouder when Khun Panit nodded once—a quick bob of his head— and disappeared through the double swinging doors behind him. During the short time he was gone, she had the opportunity to think about what she'd said. It was, she decided, as neat an example of *kling wai korn, pho sorn wai* as she'd ever accomplished.

And even better, it was true. That is, as health-care providers they should continue to care for families just as they did the patient. And it was true, too, what she said about walking away. Doctors and nurses today, they didn't want the stress of those conversations. It was easier, they realized, to simply hand the death certificate to the ward clerk and disappear into another patient's room where they couldn't be disturbed.

She was still thinking about that, and how Thai culture was uniquely ill suited for these sorts of difficult conversations, when the medical records clerk reappeared. His smile suggested that he was not bringing good news.

Without saying anything, he held the chart by one corner, letting it flap open. There were no lab results inside, she could see. Nor were there any notes. Nor, honestly, was there anything else. The folder was entirely empty.

"Is it possible," she asked hopefully, "that notes or tests haven't been added to the chart?"

Khun Panit shook his head with a finality that she found disheartening, "No, Khun. A chart cannot be filed if there are pending tests, or if there are notes that need to be written." He paused. "I suppose this is bad for us?"

Ladarat nodded. "Yes, it is bad." Although perhaps not for the reasons she had divulged. No, what it meant was nothing that would give them any clues about whether this poor man's death really was suspicious.

But...there. Stapled to the back of the chart. There were two sheets of paper. She reached for the chart and Khun Panit released it reluctantly.

One was a death certificate. As she'd expected, it had little information. Doctors hardly ever took the time to fill them in correctly. Just the patient's name, and his age, and his diagnosis: cardiac arrest. That's all.

The second page was the other thing that she'd hoped to find: a marriage certificate. Someone had known that they needed a copy to release the body and—better—had made sure to keep it in the chart. You couldn't trust doctors, but the clerks, at least, were reliable.

This was interesting. It was a marriage certificate dated... January 24, 2009. Several years ago. So what did that mean for the man that the corporal saw with the woman just three months ago? If this couple had been married for almost a decade, had she married two men?

She shook her head in confusion. But there wasn't time to figure this out now. The medical records clerk was watching her curiously, and she'd be hard-pressed to explain her interest in this marriage certificate if he were to ask. Hopefully he wouldn't.

There was just one more piece of information she needed. One more...clue. There it was. Anchan Pibul. That was the wife's name.

And an odd name it was, too. *Anchan* meant "peaflower," a local plant that was used to make tea. Ladarat had even enjoyed iced butterfly peaflower tea at her cousin's tea shop. It was a bright, iridescent blue color that didn't seem natural at all, but which supposedly had health properties of anti-aging. It also turned your lips blue in a way that Ladarat had to assume had nothing whatsoever to do with long life. And this particular Peaflower did not seem to be offering her husbands any sort of health benefits whatsoever.

Ladarat thanked the patient medical records clerk and made her way back to her office. Down the long, dim hallway, she found herself thinking about this woman. What was motivating her? Why would someone do what she'd done? Or what she might have done?

There was one person she knew who could help her answer these essential questions. One person who, Ladarat had always thought, knew more about the way that people think than anyone she'd ever met. Her cousin was a successful businesswoman not simply because she had a good head for business but because she had finely tuned sense of people. Particularly for the sorts of motivations that many people kept hidden.

She would go to see her cousin that morning and ask for her advice. That was the logical thing to do, was it not? If you had a difficult case involving ethics, you would call on a nurse ethicist. And if you had a difficult case involving people's more . . . nefarious impulses, who better to ask than someone who runs a highly successful business that exploits those impulses?

But what of the policies that needed to be reviewed? There were still many—most—that she hadn't yet examined. How could she take a morning off work when there was so much to do?

Perhaps she could take them home? She would bring a stack with her, and she could sit in her garden to do them. After a dinner of *tom yum gung*—spicy prawn soup without the coconut milk. A little like hot and sour soup. Such a meal would prepare her for a late session of policy reviews. It would help her to concentrate, would it not?

Ladarat was pondering the intellectual focusing powers of *tom yum gung* as she reached her plain wooden door. That door identified her as "Ladarat Patalung, Nurse Ethicist." She was very proud of that door. It was better than a diploma, in a way. Because it reminded her every day of what she'd accomplished.

And she needed those reminders, she knew. Somboon always said she lacked confidence, and she supposed that was true. So it was good to have a reminder that she had accomplished something. That she was...someone. Ladarat knew that when she stood in front of her door. But unfortunately she did not spend all of her time in front of that door. Although sometimes she wished she could.

Today was not one of those days. Her nameplate was there, as it always was. But today there was a white envelope peeking out from under the door. Ladarat picked it up gingerly with her thumb and forefinger, with much the same sense of queasiness that one might pick a slug off one's Siam tulips.

Opening the single folded piece of paper, Ladarat realized that it was a note from Khun Tippawan. As she knew it would be, the note was written in a careful hand on stationery "From the desk of Tippawan Taksin." Oh dear.

This was the way that Khun Tippawan operated. She had a unique...gift for being invisible. When was the last time Ladarat had seen her? She couldn't remember. She would just leave notes and send texts. Like some...poltergeist? Was that the word?

Ladarat smiled. Her boss was a *phi tai hong*. A vengeful ghost. But her smile faded as she read the brief note.

66

"I came to check on your progress in reviewing policies but was disappointed to find that you were not yet here. Perhaps you have finished all your reviews? Or perhaps you are not taking your work as an ethicist seriously?"

Oh dear. Ladarat knew that she had read through at most 10 percent of the policies she needed to review. The rest would take the better part of the coming week.

And what did Khun Tippawan mean about her not taking her ethicist responsibilities seriously? Ladarat's stomach gave a lurch as she read that. How could Khun Tippawan think such a thing?

Of course she took her responsibilities seriously. Did anyone doubt her commitment? Anyone, that is, except Khun Tippawan? They did not. Ladarat was certain of that. The ICU director himself came to her office to ask for her advice. Certainly that was a vote of confidence.

And yet, her primary obligation was to the hospital. That was certainly true. To Sriphat Hospital, and of course to their patients. So perhaps it was wrong to use her time in any other way?

So as she stood outside her door, staring at the reminder that she was a "nurse ethicist," Ladarat was forced to admit that Khun Tippawan was correct. Her door told her exactly what she was. That door did not announce her identity as a detective. Or as a doctor. Or—most certainly—as a cook. No, it proclaimed to all the world that she was a nurse ethicist.

So that's what she would be this morning. She would walk into her office—the office of Sriphat Hospital's one and only nurse ethicist—and she would review as many hospital policies as a dedicated nurse ethicist possibly could.

CHAPTER 7

THE AMERICANS' STRANGE DESIRE FOR CONTROL

That firm resolve lasted until eleven thirty, when her assistant, Sisithorn Wichasak, came to get her for lunch. Ladarat looked up to find the girl peering through the door, her head protruding from the right-hand edge. Perched there, with only her head visible, she looked a little like a puppet.

She really was pretty, but in an awkward way. Admittedly, her oversize glasses and oversize feet didn't help. The glasses, in particular, gave the impression that she hadn't quite grown up yet.

And in some ways, perhaps, she hadn't. She was so serious, for instance. Like a child memorizing her lines for a school play in which she would impress everyone. She reminded Ladarat of herself, twenty years ago. Hoping that if she worked hard enough, and attended to every detail, success would come to her naturally.

And like Ladarat herself had always been, Sisithorn was a good listener. And a good watcher. She often noticed things that others didn't. She would have been very good at finding hidden elephants.

"You work too much, Khun," Sisithorn said suddenly. "You need to take a break and clear your head. So you can be more...effective." She knew, somehow, that would be the argument that would be most likely to have an impact. The

68

promise that a rest now would make her more effective this afternoon. Very wise for someone so young.

But no. She had too much to do. "I don't have the time," she said. "For me to go down to the dining room, and to take the time for lunch..." The hospital was counting on her. She knew that. To spare even a half hour wasn't right.

But Sisithorn was nodding. "I knew you would say that. That's why I brought your lunch to you."

And she piled through the door, bearing plastic bags that she unceremoniously set down on Ladarat's little desk. Without waiting for permission, Sisithorn began to unwrap and open Styrofoam containers. There was *tom yum gung*—the spicy prawn soup that was to have helped her be productive tonight. And *gang keow wan*, classic Thai green curry that would probably be a little too spicy for Ladarat.

Ladarat sighed, pushing the pile of guidelines away from her. These would wait.

"So tell me," Sisithorn said, "about the American man. Will he survive?" She helped herself to the curry.

"It is bad luck to speculate about such things," Ladarat told her, a little more severely than she'd intended.

She tried a couple of spoonfuls of the soup. Ahh, very good. Just spicy enough, and sour enough to make your mouth water.

"Besides," she said more softly, "it is impossible to know such a thing so soon. Instead, the real question we should be asking right now is..."

"How to help the family," Sisithorn said promptly.

"Exactly so. We cannot do anything more to help the man, Mr. Fuller. But we can certainly help his family."

"But what sort of help do they need?" the girl asked. "Of course we should make them comfortable, as guests. But they are waiting, the same as us. Surely we can't help prepare them for his death, because we don't know if he will live or not. So what can we do?"

Sisithorn wasn't being argumentative, Ladarat knew. She was genuinely confused. She sighed. So clever, but she couldn't put herself in the position of other people. She couldn't experience true compassion.

"Ah, but that is where you are wrong. They are in a strange place, with no one they know," she explained patiently.

Sisithorn nodded uncertainly.

"Imagine...Imagine you are in...Chicago. And you are with a loved one who is very sick and in the hospital. You don't know anybody else. And you don't speak the language. You have no idea what is happening. What would you want? What would help you?"

"*Gang keow wan?*" She smiled.

Thinking back on her year in Chicago, and the sterile hospital cafeteria with its casseroles and meatloaf and mashed potatoes, Ladarat had to smile, too. A little *gang keow wan* would have made her year much more bearable.

"But what else?"

"Ah, I would want...someone to talk to."

"But not just anyone, yes? You would want..."

"A friend."

Ladarat nodded. "Exactly so. You would want a friend."

Sisithorn thought about that for a full minute as she progressed from the curry to the soup.

"But how do we find them a friend?" she asked finally. "Much less a friend who is an American like them?"

"We don't find them a friend, exactly. No one can do that. But we can visit often. We can help them get their questions answered. Americans, remember, want to be in control. They want information. They want people to be telling them what is going on."

"Even if there is nothing they can do?"

"Especially then."

"That is . . . strange."

Ladarat shrugged. "Perhaps. But it is normal for them, just as it is normal for us to defer to the physician. Anyway," she concluded, "we do what they expect. What they need. We help them get information. And slowly they will come to appreciate having us there. We still won't be friends, but we will be helpful in that way."

"I see," Sisithorn said, smiling as if to say she most certainly didn't see. But that was all right. She would take her assistant with her to see the Fullers after lunch.

They talked about other things—the other patients and issues and, of course, the inspections, until finally, triumphantly, Sisithorn unpacked the last item from the plastic bag at her elbow. Proudly, but nervously, she unwrapped her offering. She held out a small package, wrapped in a banana leaf.

Ladarat's favorite: *kanom maprao*. A soft, fantastically rich coconut cake made with coconut milk and shaved coconut. More like custard, it was creamy and sweet with clumps of coconut that would surprise you.

"I know you like this," Sisithorn said simply.

"Thank you, you are most kind." She took one of the three pieces and Sisithorn took the second. That was very thoughtful. And perceptive. How had Sisithorn known that the cake was her favorite sweet? Ladarat couldn't remember ever discussing such a thing. Yet Sisithorn must have paid attention. She must have noticed. She was indeed very good at noticing things.

Ladarat had observed that talent in the past. Like when that Frenchman last month was confused and disoriented, it was Sisithorn, and not Ladarat or even the doctors, who noticed that he got worse whenever his girlfriend came to visit. (It turned out that she'd been bringing him heroin that he'd inject into his legs.)

"I'm so glad you like them. Please, have the last one," the girl said.

"No, thank you. You should have it."

"No, I insist." She wrapped it up and pushed it across the desk, smiling shyly. "Or then you should save it. It will keep."

Ladarat agreed that it would. And she thought that it would be exactly what she'd need later in the afternoon, as she was struggling to finish reviewing all of the hospital guidelines.

"So now we'll go see the American family. We will do our best to make sure their questions are answered."

"And Kate and I will be . . . like friends," Sisithorn added.

CHAPTER 8

TOMORROW IS NOT USUALLY ANOTHER DAY

That was perhaps easier said than done. Mrs. Kate Fuller was not in her room, and so they went looking for her in the ICU, where they found her with her husband's parents in the waiting room. As it had been yesterday, the waiting room was almost empty. And the mysterious man, she noted, was nowhere to be seen.

Truth be told, Ladarat was relieved that the man had not made an appearance. She had too much on her mind, and too much to be nervous about already. Like this meeting with the Fullers. She would address the problem of the mysterious man tomorrow. Now, she needed to focus all of her attention on what was likely to be a very difficult conversation.

The Fullers had colonized the corner of the waiting room that was nearest to the double sliding doors that led to the ICU, and they had completely rearranged it. They'd brought two rows of six connected seats together in a "V" that provided them with a little private seating area, but which effectively reduced the seating available for others. It was not a crisis, as Sisithorn would say, since there were still seats available. And few people. But it was not polite. And Sisithorn looked genuinely surprised. She seemed to be on the verge of saying something as they approached the group, but Ladarat reminded her that the Americans had different customs.

"In America," she said preemptively, "such behavior is not unusual. Americans will often rearrange the world to suit themselves."

Sisithorn nodded uncertainly.

As they drew closer, she could see that the elder Mr. Fuller was reviewing a pile of papers that he held on his lap. He seemed to be trying to sort them, imposing some sort of order. His organizational efforts puzzled her, though. As she got close enough, she saw that they were all in Thai. Could he read Thai? She doubted it. And yet he was shuffling the papers into an order that must have made sense to him.

Sisithorn was hanging back, perhaps drawing some of the same conclusions. And presumably, she was also confused by those conclusions. But no matter. This, at least, was something they could help with.

The two women looked up as they approached and offered passable *wais*—Kate seated in her wheelchair, and Mrs. Fuller standing to greet them. Mr. Fuller barely looked up and offered them something that—charitably—might be counted as a nod.

It was Kate who explained that her father-in-law was trying to make sense of Andrew's medical charts. She didn't need to explain that those notes were entirely in Thai. The elder Mr. Fuller's frustrated expression and the vigor with which he was shuffling papers made that abundantly clear.

After introductions, it was her assistant, much to Ladarat's surprise, who broke the silence.

"Has there been any change?" Sisithorn was looking at the elder Mr. Fuller, as if she was trying to engage him as the most important person there. That was clever. Very clever. Although Ladarat would have preferred it if her assistant had allowed her to speak first. That would have been more proper.

The elder Mr. Fuller shook his head and continued shuffling

74

papers. But then he paused, looking up and seeing them, it seemed, for the first time. That was when he turned to Sisithorn, handing her the top paper in the stack.

"Can you read this?"

Sisithorn paused for a moment, her mouth open in an "O" of surprise. Then she smiled a thin, brittle smile that was perhaps best translated as: *Yim mee lessanai*, the sort of smile that hides wicked thoughts.

Or more specifically: "I'm an assistant nurse ethicist at one of the best hospitals in Thailand and you're asking me if I can read?"

So Ladarat interjected, before they could get off on the wrong foot. She was the one in charge, after all, and she shot Sisithorn a reproving glance.

"We're not doctors," she said. "So we may not be able to explain what everything means. But we could translate, if that would help?"

Mr. Fuller nodded. "They're giving us an official summary translation later today, but I thought...well...I thought that there might be more detail here."

So Sisithorn and Ladarat joined the three in the little "V" that the Americans had created. Mr. and Mrs. Fuller sat on one side, and Sisithorn and Ladarat on the other, with Kate in her wheelchair in the opening between them, closing the triangle. Sisithorn and Ladarat took the pile of papers between them and shuffled the pages into some semblance of chronological order. As they did, Mr. Fuller took out a yellow legal pad, and turned to a fresh page.

Oh dear. What if she said something that Khun Suphit, the director, would object to? What if she made a mistake?

"We can translate," Ladarat offered, "but we can't tell you what some of these things mean. Their...significance."

Mr. Fuller nodded. "Anything would be helpful, I guess."

She and Sisithorn put the stack of papers between them and took turns pulling sheets from the file. First one, then the other, they walked the Americans through what had happened to Andrew in the past three days.

"This," Ladarat said carefully, "is the admission note from Sunday." The three Americans were watching her intently, and Mr. Fuller's hand began to write. She hoped she didn't say anything that was wrong. She hoped even more that Sisithorn would be careful.

"This describes some of his injuries. His pelvis was broken in three places, it says. And his right femur. The CT scan says he has a hematoma—a collection of blood—in the capsule around his liver. That sometimes happens with trauma." She scanned the rest of the report.

"There are other small things," she concluded, "but those seem to be the main problems."

"But what about his brain?" Mr. Fuller asked.

Ladarat looked to Sisithorn, who was holding the neurologist's report. She looked at Ladarat nervously and Ladarat nodded. She could trust Sisithorn not to say anything that was insensitive.

"This is the neurologist's report from yesterday," Sisithorn said. "The neurologist is Dr. Ratana. It talks about the CT scan that they did, and his own exam. It is a summary, you understand?" The three Americans nodded.

"Dr. Ratana describes...what happened to Mr. Fuller, from the reports available." She looked up cautiously at the ladies and especially at the elder Mr. Fuller. She seemed to decide that a review of those details would be too painful.

"He describes those events," she repeated lamely. "And

then he describes Mr. Fuller's neurological status when he arrived here."

"Keep in mind," Ladarat interjected, "that these findings are a day old. They don't include...changes"—she almost said "improvements"—"that might have happened since then."

The Americans nodded. No doubt they'd heard some version of that before. That was yesterday, but tomorrow is another day, as they are fond of saying in the United States.

Of course, tomorrow is not really another day. Usually tomorrow is just another version of yesterday, with slightly different weather and new lottery numbers. But if you're an American, she knew, then sunrise was a promise that any- thing could happen.

Sisithorn looked at her, then at the Americans. Then she began to read again, picking through the information as one might pick through *som tam*—green papaya salad—looking for the crunchiest bits of fruit while avoiding the fiery chilies.

She described the CT scan results: Skull fractured along the parietal bones, at the top of the head. Also a fracture of the orbit, around the right eye. The jaw was broken and needed to be wired in place.

And the brain. This is what the Americans would want to know about. Always so worried about brain function. Although, if you asked her, it seemed that many Americans didn't use their brains for much of anything that was impor- tant. Still, it would be important to these three people sitting in front of her. Sisithorn seemed to know that, so her descrip- tion was particularly careful.

"With respect to the brain," she began slowly after read- ing the entire next paragraph to herself, "there is little visible trauma. There is some clotted blood in the anterior sulcus of the parietal lobe, consistent with a subdural hematoma. That means the blood is inside the lining that protects the brain," she explained. "But it says that there is no other sign of injury."

"So his brain is basically normal." This was from the elder Mr. Fuller, and Ladarat was concerned to hear that it wasn't a question. He didn't ask whether his son's brain was normal, but instead seemed to be telling them that it must be.

Sisithorn looked to Ladarat for help.

"Dr. Jainukul can explain this better than we can," she said. "But the CT scan results only provide a picture of what the brain looks like. It can't tell how the brain is functioning." She searched back in her mind for an example that she'd heard in Chicago.

"When you see a car that's run out of gas," she said, "it looks like a normal car, yes?" The Americans nodded. "But it will not run. Yet it looks like it should. CT scans of the brain can be much the same. They may make the brain look normal—as if it should run—but it does not."

The elder Mr. Fuller, at least, was nodding. Proving once again that to explain medical things to patients and families, you must choose your terms carefully. A metaphor that works for a man will not work for his wife, and vice versa. That insight didn't rise to the philosophical heights for which the wise Professor Dalrymple was so well-known. And perhaps if Ladarat were wiser herself, she'd be able create a saying that would merit inclusion in the professor's little book. But it was true nonetheless. And now, if Mr. Fuller understood, then he could help to explain things to the ladies.

Sisithorn turned back to her, relieved, and Ladarat turned to the next page. This was the neurologist's examination. She read quickly, and summarized.

"Here Dr. Ratana tells about Mr. Fuller's brain function.

Remember, though, that these results are from yesterday. So, he says that Mr. Fuller was not awake. He had no response to touch. That is, he did not move when touched." In practice, she knew, Dr. Ratana would have used painful stimuli, like a pin. But she didn't think the Fullers would want to hear that some foreign doctor was poking their loved one with pins.

"He goes on to describe other tests. These are the tests that your doctors in America will want to see." She summarized the tests that Dr. Jainukul had described in her office the previous morning, omitting the interpretation, which was beyond her. As the director said, those tests included movement of the pupils of the eyes, and response to cold water introduced into the ear canals. Also reflexes. Normally that would be enough, Ladarat knew. But perhaps because Dr. Ratana sensed that doctors in America would be looking over his shoulder, he had arranged an electroencephalogram on that first day as well. She wasn't sure how to explain the results, but it seemed as though there was some brain activity, so that's what she said.

And of course, the elder Mr. Fuller grasped tightly to that little bit of information. Almost immediately, she wished she hadn't said anything about the EEG.

"So there *is* some brain function," he said, slapping both hands on his thighs. "So...he's not out of gas, is he?" He smiled. "Okay, now that's something to go on."

Sisithorn looked at her in confusion, but Ladarat had grown used to this strange and obdurate optimism during her year in the United States. Any good news became the focus of families' attention. You could say that a patient's kidneys were not working, and that he wasn't waking up, and that his liver was failing. But if his blood sugar was normal, that was viewed as a good sign.

It was a little like those fortune-tellers in Isaan who would read your future in tea leaves. If they wanted to find good news—or if they sensed that their client was willing to pay more for good news—they would be sure to find it somewhere. If a farmer came to town on a Saturday, he might be poor and childless, and his wife may have left him. But he could depend on a fortune-teller to say, with perfect sincerity, that perhaps his tiny house would get a new roof in the spring.

Once again, Ladarat found herself thinking about *kling wai korn, pho sorn wai*. To do whatever needs to be done. Anything to get past a crisis.

Not for the first time, she wondered if that rule of thumb was invented to help Thais deal with foreigners. It certainly seemed to be necessary particularly often when dealing with *farang* in general, and Chinese in particular. They were so demanding, and so hopeful. Often there was no choice but to tell a little white lie that would spare them discomfort and spare the hospital embarrassment. So that is what she did.

"Ah, so there is some brain function. You are right. My reference to the car that runs out of gas was not a good one. I apologize. How much function, you should discuss with Dr. Jainukul."

Mr. Fuller had other questions, and Kate did as well. But the older Mrs. Fuller was strangely silent. Perhaps that was just her personality. Ladarat had known women of her generation in the United States who seemed content to let others do the talking. They were paying attention, and listening carefully, but didn't feel the need to be in the middle of things. Those women were often very patient. Those women, she thought, were also very Thai.

She and Sisithorn answered Kate's and the elder Mr. Fuller's questions as best they could, about what tests had been done (many) and what the lab results had shown (surprisingly normal).

They talked, too, about what had been done so far. The ventilator, for instance, and antibiotics to prevent infections. Dr. Jainukul had also used drugs to reduce the swelling in Mr. Fuller's brain. Ladarat described many of these treatments in excessive detail, for no other reason than to make sure the Americans knew how much they were doing, and how hard everyone was working to save Mr. Fuller.

Eventually, though, the Americans ran out of questions. It was clear that all of Andrew Fuller's troubles were fixable, except for his brain. That would be the problem they could do nothing about. They would simply need to wait and see, and that was something that Americans were not good at.

As Ladarat and Sisithorn stood to leave, the elder Fullers stood, too. Whether that was a mark of respect was difficult to tell, but Ladarat wanted to believe that it was. And why not?

Sisithorn promised to come back later that afternoon. She spoke to all of them but looked in particular at Kate, who smiled shyly and nodded. That unfortunate girl could definitely be helped by talking with someone her own age. And someone who was not related to her husband.

But where was *her* family? Surely her parents would have come to provide support? She was not as seriously ill as her husband, but still...Ladarat made a note to herself to have Sisithorn find out.

As they rode the elevator back down to Ladarat's office, she asked Sisithorn what she thought. They were alone in the elevator, and Sisithorn took her time to think.

"Mr. Fuller seems angry," she said finally. "But I don't

think he's angry at us." She shook her head, perplexed. "He is acting as though he's angry at us, but I think he's just angry at what has happened."

Ladarat nodded. "Anger for Americans is like the way that we smile. Just as our smiles can mean many things, their anger can mean many things."

The doors open and they stepped out into the basement hallway.

"But the older Mrs. Fuller," Sisithorn continued thoughtfully, "she is not angry. She wants everyone to get along. She wants harmony."

Ladarat smiled. "Yes, I thought many times during that meeting that she is as Thai as we are." She thought for a moment as they stepped off the elevator. "But the young woman—she is scared. And, I think, she is lonely. Why doesn't she have her family here?"

They both thought about that for a moment. To be alone in a strange land, with a husband who is likely going to die, with no one for comfort besides his parents? That would be very frightening.

Sisithorn nodded her agreement. "I had the same thought," she admitted. "She is the one who needs our help the most. But she won't ask me to talk with her, will she?"

Ladarat shook her head. "No . . . I think she will not want to be . . . a burden."

"A burden? But she is our guest."

Ladarat thought about how to explain this concept of "burden." A minute later, they'd reached her office, and she was still thinking. She shrugged.

"Americans are very . . . independent. Remember how the older Mr. Fuller was reading his son's medical records? In

Thai? Yet he didn't ask someone to explain. He was going to do it himself. Or try to. Well, that is how Americans are."

"Then," Sisithorn said with decision, "I will go back to visit her on my own. I will go in, and I will sit in front of her, and I will listen."

More than a minute after Sisithorn had left her, Ladarat found that she was still standing outside her door. She was staring absently at the sign that proclaimed her to be a nurse ethicist, her key dangling, forgotten, from her hand.

Nurse ethicist. That sign meant that she had skills of ethics and decision making, did it not? And shouldn't she use those skills where they were needed? In supporting the Fuller family certainly. And in the case of the farmer in the ICU waiting room.

Well, why shouldn't she use those skills to protect men like the unfortunate Zhang Wei from being harmed? Was that not ethical work? And wasn't that work as significant as reviewing policies?

That simple insight was what had caused her to pause outside her door. And that was the question that had led her to search her mental index of Professor Dalrymple's wise advice. And that was why she was still standing outside her door, looking perhaps like one of those crew-cutted, heavily perspiring, white-shirted missionaries who tried to find converts.

Khun Tippawan would say, she supposed, that such work was unrelated to the tasks of Sriphat Hospital. That was true, perhaps. But...wasn't one of these deaths declared in their emergency room? So wasn't this the hospital's problem? And wasn't it, therefore, a problem for Sriphat Hospital's nurse ethicist?

Ladarat was strangely elated to find that she could answer

her own question without hesitation. Of course this was her responsibility. And she was hardly shirking her duties as a nurse ethicist by investigating a murder—a possible murder—in which their very own hospital might have been complicit.

So it was with a light heart that she entered her office, exchanged her white coat for her bag, and then exited, closing the door behind her. It was only three o'clock as she passed through the grand hall outside the outpatient clinics. The wide tiled space was often home to musicians and sometimes dancers, who entertained patients and staff alike.

But today there was just a single musician. And she heard his music before she saw him. From the center of the crowded hall, she heard the strange, sad notes of a *lueng* bouncing like raindrops off the tiles beneath her feet. Ladarat altered her course to pass by the small dais where musicians performed and found an older man—perhaps in his seventies—with his small instrument that looked something like a lute. A traditional part of *Lanna* culture, it was one of three instruments in the *salo-so-sueng* ensemble, along with a small fiddle (*salo*) and a reed pipe (*pi so*). Through some sort of strange magic, even its fastest rhythms somehow sounded sad.

So intent was she on the notes that floated and danced around her that Ladarat didn't notice the intrusion of a harsh chirping that couldn't have been more out of place. It wasn't until an older woman and her daughter standing nearby glared at her that she recognized the intrusive signal of a mobile phone. Her mobile phone.

She ducked her head and silenced the phone until she could step away. But as soon as she answered, she wished she hadn't.

"You have not forgotten the meeting of the operating room procedures, have you, Khun? It begins promptly at three o'clock."

"No, Khun Tippawan. Of course not."

But...how did she know?

"Ah, that is good, Khun Ladarat. You see, I saw you enjoying today's entertainment, and I was just a bit jealous."

"Jealous, Khun?"

"Yes, just a bit, you understand. Because I wish that I had time to enjoy music on my way home in the middle of the afternoon. But of course, I have work to do, so I cannot afford such luxury."

"Khun, I..." But the Director of Excellence had disconnected. So Ladarat hitched her bag to her shoulder and turned back to the elevator, preparing herself to spend the rest of the afternoon in yet another meeting.

CHAPTER 9

THE CONSIDERABLE BENEFITS OF A
MATCHMAKER FOR THE SHY PERSON

The rest of the afternoon had been interminable. "Interminable," incidentally, was Ladarat's favorite English word. Odd that there was nothing that meant quite the same thing in Thai, yet the pace of Thai life often called for such a word. Maybe that made sense. Only a people who hoped that everything would have been done yesterday could create such a wonderful word to sum up the futility of that hope.

The director of the operating room wanted to review their policies regarding sterile technique, and they did so, in paralyzing detail. Still, Ladarat supposed that was one area that no one wanted the inspectors to have trouble with, and yet the operating room staff were sometimes so lazy. No wonder some of the private hospitals hired nurses from Singapore and the Philippines—those ladies were much more conscientious sometimes. Sometimes the live-and-let-live Thai attitude was not what you wanted. Like when you were undergoing open-heart surgery.

Then, back in her little cubby of an office, she'd reviewed a dozen more policies, which made her feel a little more confident that she could actually review them all by next week.

So the afternoon had been interminable, but now, at last, she could leave. And she should. Before anything else happened.

She was just rising from her chair and reaching for her bag when the telephone rang. It was Detective Mookjai, asking for an update.

Ladarat was hesitant at first. After all, she had found nothing. And that's what she explained. No note. No lab results. And no record of any blood sample having been taken. In short, a failure. Except...

"Except?"

"A name. That is to say, I have the woman's name. On her marriage certificate. She is called Anchan Pibul." Ladarat paused to let that information register.

"Ah, Khun Ladarat. That is very good. Very good. More progress than I've made."

She smiled at that. She was perhaps doing better at detecting than a real detective?

"And there is a little more," Ladarat admitted. "Although I don't know what it means. The marriage certificate..."

"Yes?"

"It was dated more than five years ago."

There was a protracted silence as the detective considered this revelation.

"Khun Wiriya?"

"Yes, I'm sorry. I was just thinking about what this new information means." He sighed. "I'm not sure. I suspect it means... something."

But what? An old marriage certificate, by itself, meant nothing. She married this man several years ago and then he died. But there was the corporal's story of seeing the same woman with a different man. So either she was married to multiple men at the same time—which seemed as though it would be a lot of work for a murderess—or...

"Is it possible," she said slowly, "that this woman is...recycling a marriage certificate?"

"Recycling?"

"Imagine that she...connects with multiple men, and kills them. Then she uses the marriage certificate to prove that she deserves a share of their life insurance?"

"But that would only work if the men all had the same name."

"Like Zhang Wei?"

"Ahh, yes. A most common name. Perhaps that could be her strategy. Assuming the man isn't really married," Wiriya pointed out, "because surely his real wife would object?"

"So perhaps she preyed on men who were not married?"

"Ah, I see. That is very clever. You are either a very good detective or..." He paused. "You have a bright future as a murderer."

Ladarat wasn't sure how to respond to that assessment, so she said nothing. But Wiriya didn't seem to notice. Instead, he posed a question in return.

"But, you see, there is a very large problem with that... strategy. To be successful, our friend Anchan would need to find men—single men—with the same name. Granted, it is a common name. A common Chinese name. But how would she do that?"

"I don't know," Ladarat admitted. "She seems to be very quick, too, if your corporal is to be believed. Only three months from one death to the next? At that pace, she can't rely on chance meetings, and she couldn't rely on friends, who would become suspicious."

"Perhaps she is placing advertisements somewhere," Wiriya suggested.

"Ah, it would be difficult indeed to use such advertisements to find a man with the right name. But perhaps she is using a dating service, which has a database she could search," Ladarat suggested. "And that would point to a younger woman."

There was a moment of silence on the line, and then Wiriya asked why she should say that.

"Ah, well, younger people are more likely to use services such as online dating." She paused, smiling. "It is a known fact." Like the known fact that women use poison. So there.

And indeed, when she thought back about conversations she'd had, she could only remember hearing about such services from the younger nurses.

"Maybe," Wiriya said tentatively, "older people who use such services are more...traditional. And thus they're embarrassed to talk about them." He paused.

"Ah."

"Ah," she said again.

Then he rescued her. "So you see, it is possible that an older man or woman uses one of these services. But it is also possible that they might use a more...discreet service."

"To avoid embarrassment?"

"Exactly so."

"But there must be dozens of such services," she said.

"Hundreds, actually," he said. "I looked."

She resisted the temptation to ask whether he had looked for personal or professional reasons.

"But can't we simply...question her?"

"Ah, we could, if we could find her."

"But surely her name is unusual. Anchan Pibul? I don't

think I've ever met an Anchan before. You must have data-bases to search..."

"I do, and in fact, I've been looking as we've been talking these last few minutes. There is no record of a phone number or address of such a person in Chiang Mai."

"Perhaps that is a...pseudonym?"

"Perhaps," Wiriya admitted. "But that name was on the marriage certificate. She was listed as his wife, using that name."

Ladarat didn't see how that could mean anything. What would stop her from giving any name she liked. Unless...

"She needed the death certificate to obtain the life insur-ance money. So...that must be her real name." Because cer-tainly she would need to provide some proof that she was actually the man's wife in order to receive the life insurance payment. So unless she had many forged documents that would be good enough to fool a tight-fisted insurance com-pany, then there was an excellent chance that her name really was Anchan Pibul.

"So if that really is her name, and I can't find her," Wiriya said, "then she is making an effort to be hidden."

Which would, of course, make a great deal of sense if your hobby was murdering middle-aged men. It was not the sort of activity that cried out for a high profile.

"Then how can we find her?" Ladarat asked. "She wouldn't use her real name in a dating service profile, I suppose?"

"No, people don't use their real names in what's available to the public. In order to find a person's true name, they must agree to share it with you." Again, she wondered how the detective knew such information. But perhaps it's the sort of thing that police know.

"Then how can we find this woman?" she asked again. They sat in a companionable silence for a moment, thinking.

Was this what detectives did? They made some progress, and then they ran into a dense thicket that prevented any movement. And then, she guessed, there would be a breakthrough. The silence on the phone lengthened.

Now would be an excellent time for a breakthrough to occur.

And then, just like that, it did.

"A matchmaker," Ladarat said. "There might be benefits of using a matchmaker when one is searching for a spouse."

"Perhaps," Wiriya agreed. "Some people will use a matchmaker. They might, for instance, if they were shy, or were anxious about meeting new people." He paused. "But if there are hundreds of dating services, there must be just as many matchmakers."

"Ah, but what if matchmakers—or dating services, for that matter—specialize?"

"Specialize?"

"What if," she asked excitedly, "our woman Anchan is looking for a particular type of man. A...Chinese man?"

"I see...then she might go to a service that specialized in just such matches."

"And such services do exist," she said. "I read about them. Because of the one-child policy in China, there is a shortage of wives. So Chinese men, and particularly middle-aged Chinese men, search for wives in Myanmar and Laos and Vietnam and Thailand."

"Exactly so," Wiriya said. "But...how would we find this person?"

But Ladarat had a ready answer.

"I have..." What was the word the police used? "I have... a source," she said.

"Ah, indeed?" Although he knew perfectly well who her source was. "Well then, you are becoming a true detective."

And in that moment, Ladarat could think of no higher praise.

92

CHAPTER 10

THE LIMITED PATIENCE OF MANGOES

The day wasn't yet over, and Ladarat was a little cautious as she left by one of the hospital's back doors. More than a little cautious, truth be told. It wasn't yet five o'clock and she was hurrying to her car in the parking lot next to the nursing school.

Hopefully Khun Tippawan was not watching her right now. Ladarat looked over her shoulder but saw no one. Only an empty parking lot. Still, there were the windows of the nursing school to her left. Five floors, each with a row of windows as long as a city block. Any one of them could be the lookout post of one of Khun Tippawan's spies.

Did that seem paranoid? Perhaps. But some paranoia was justified, was it not? The Director of Excellence seemed to have an uncanny ability to know when Ladarat was not at her post.

Although surely people realized how hard she'd been working to prepare for the inspection? Still, it would be her luck to meet Khun Tippawan. Or...worse...the hospital director himself. He would joke about how some staff had such an easy life...

She played that scene out in her head several times, making it more uncomfortable with each iteration, until finally she reached her car and heaved a sigh of relief as she slid into the driver's seat.

93

Eeeeeyyy. Fortunately she'd come in early that morning and had been able to get one of the best spots under an immense banyan tree close to the hospital building. Still, it was hot. Whoever it was in Germany who designed these vinyl seats didn't think about weather in Thailand. Her next car would have air-conditioning. And perhaps a radio. A radio wasn't truly necessary, of course. One always had one's thoughts for company. But it would be nice to hear another voice, for a change.

Then she patted the Beetle's dashboard gently, feeling disloyal. Not that she'd be getting a new car anytime soon...

Ladarat threaded her way out of the university hospital complex and onto Suthep Road, and then cut over to Arak—the westernmost side of the perfect square that encircles Chiang Mai's old city. She followed the road around the square—south, then east, then farther east on Sridonchai Road toward the Ping River.

Farang thought Chiang Mai was old and quaint because they mostly saw the old city. But out here, and on the Ring Road in particular, you could be in a suburb of Chicago. There was a wide divided highway with big stores and supermarkets and gas stations. She didn't like this part of Chiang Mai, because it was ugly. But she was proud of it, too, in a way. Proud not that her town could boast strip malls, but that those strip malls could coexist with traditional Thai values. At least for the time being.

She turned left at Charoen Prathet Road, which led north to Tha Phae, the tourist avenue that led from old city down to the night market and the river. Anything *farang* wanted—from girls to elephant hair bracelets—they could find along this half-mile stretch of road. But this wasn't her destination.

There was an unnamed *soi*, or small street, about halfway

down Tha Phae, where she could usually find a parking spot. It was little wider than an alley; nevertheless this *soi* was filled with *farang*, many of whom would nod appreciatively at her yellow Beetle. Some of the older ones were perhaps remembering fondly their own motoring history. If she ever sold the Beetle, she decided, patting the dashboard again for luck, she would park it here with a big "For Sale" sign in English. She'd find it a good home with a car collector in . . . California.

She found a parking space even more easily than she'd hoped and greeted the owner of the fruit stand across the street, whom she knew by sight.

The mangoes looked particularly good. Still partly green, they'd mostly turned a promising warm yellow. She gave one a gentle squeeze. Ahh, almost ripe.

"I'll be back, Khun. Save one for me."

The man smiled and shrugged. "You cannot expect a ripe mango to wait for you. Mangoes—they are not a patient fruit."

Ladarat nodded agreement. Fruit stand philosophy was oddly comforting right now. But not helpful.

She didn't need a sackful of ripe mangoes where she was going. But a bunch of bananas would be perfect. She bought them and paid 30 *baht*, or about a dollar. She waved her thanks and crossed the small *soi*, entering an even narrower alley. It was shadowy here, and a few degrees cooler. Still, she hurried. This wasn't a neighborhood she liked to be seen in.

Even if you had never been to this part of Chiang Mai before, just the names of the businesses around her would tell you in no uncertain terms what this street was all about. There was the Cowboy Bar, and the Paradise. And the Shangri-La.

This was a street that catered to the worst appetites of *farang*. Big greasy meals and T-shirts and women. And women. And more women.

Every other business, it seemed, had the same stylized figure of a naked woman with long hair. It was as if someone, somewhere, had decided that this was the universal symbol of a girlie bar, in much the same way that traffic signs had become international.

Halfway down the street, though, the businesses lining the *soi* seem to lose their focus. There was an electronic repair shop, and a small crockery store, and a kitchen supply warehouse. Beyond that was another plain storefront that announced itself simply as "The Tea House." That business had the same stylized woman's figure in the lower-right-hand corner of the door, but the little sign was the only indication of what went on inside. And that, Ladarat knew, was exactly the way that her cousin Siriwan Pookusuwan wanted it.

Ladarat slipped through the oversize wooden doors, a little surprised that they were unlocked. Usually they weren't open until after six o'clock, to discourage the odd traveler who wandered in looking for tea. They served tea, of course. But anyone looking for tea was probably in the wrong place. The place was a brothel, although Ladarat was careful never to call it that.

As her eyes adjusted to the dark, the contours of the large room emerged, stretching back into the dim corners. There were century-old teak floors and walls, with a large sunken table more than five meters long in the center. Wood carvings and silk tapestries lined the walls, and a Buddha to her right watched over the entrance.

That Buddha was the ubiquitous Thai *Hing Phra*. Many places of business had one inside, just as they had a *Saan Jao*, or spirit house, outside. It was a balance that Ladarat found comforting. Outside you'd pray for luck and good fortune or good crops—all materialist things. But inside you'd pray for harmony and enlightenment. She paused and knelt, depositing the bananas as an offering in hopes of her own enlightenment regarding matters of detection.

As she rose, out of the darkness a man materialized in front of her. A blond *farang*, the biggest she had ever seen. Easily two meters tall, with broad shoulders and a crewcut, the man looked like he'd been designed by a Thai casting director who'd been told: "Give me a typical big American surfer."

The man turned toward her, holding up a hubcap-size hand. "We're not open..." he said in English. He looked nonplussed for a moment, then switched to heavily accented but perfectly serviceable Thai. "Hello, so good to see you, Khun Ladarat." He offered a high *wai*, which she returned. "And how have you been?"

"Well, I thank you, Khun Jonah. And you?"

"Krista's pregnant," he burst out, unable to contain himself. "It's going to be a girl," he said shyly.

"That's wonderful. I'm so happy for both of you." And she was.

Jonah had had a rough life. As a tourist just out of college, he'd gotten involved in a scam to run drugs to Koh Samui to make enough money to travel on to India. But as many unsuspecting *farang* are, he'd been caught and had ended up in prison for five years. He'd gotten hepatitis in his third year and had been transferred to Sriphat Hospital, where she'd met him when his family had come over to try to get him released. She had translated for those meetings, and much to her surprise, their director had gotten involved and had intervened.

Somehow—she wasn't sure how—Jonah had been released. You'd think he would have left Thailand immediately, but he hadn't. His girlfriend, Krista, had come over to live, and he'd taken a series of jobs as a bouncer at some of the bars around the old city, where his size had been enough to quell most *farang* disturbances before they started. One look at him, and even the most inebriated Australian would decide he'd rather make trouble somewhere else. But not always, and sometimes he had to wade in.

It had been after one such brawl that he'd ended up in the hospital and Ladarat had met him again. He had asked her, jokingly, whether she knew of a bar where he would be less likely to get hit over the head with a full bottle of Mekhong whiskey. And much to his surprise, she'd said yes.

"Please, sit," he said now. "I'll get the *mamasan*."

Ladarat took off her pumps at the door and padded over the polished teak floors to the large table. She was met by a smiling, bright-eyed girl with the broad, pretty face of an Isaan farmer, who offered her a *wai*, and a cool glass of ginger tea and an iced towel. Her name was on the tip of Ladarat's tongue.

"It's so good to see you again," the girl said. "It's been so long. You are well?"

"Yes, very well. Thank you. And you..."

Kittiya, that was it. "Ya" was her nickname.

"Khun Ya? And your family?"

The girl smiled proudly. "My parents' house is finished, and my brother has passed his civil service exams with honors. So he will be starting work in the Ministry of Health next month."

What she didn't say, but they both knew, was that Ya had paid for that house, and her brother's education, as well as a herd of twenty water buffalo, out of her earnings at the Tea House. Also unspoken were her plans for the future. Many girls from Isaan came to Chiang Mai or Bangkok and found they liked the flashy, glamorous life. But not Ya. She would probably escape soon. One day, she would simply disappear and go home to begin a new life.

"Well, that is very good. I am so happy for you."

"Thank you." She gave another deep *wai*. "I must sweep upstairs."

Jonah and the girls all cleaned, and mopped, and cooked, and prepared drinks. The Tea House didn't employ people for those jobs. At first Ladarat thought this rule was the tightfisted result of her cousin's efforts to cut costs. But it was really just Siriwan's way of making the Tea House seem more like a home, and their customers more like guests. It was odd for a business of this type, but not too different than what she tried to do in the hospital.

That was just one way that this place was different than many of the other so-called "girlie bars" on the street. So different, in fact, that it was in a category of its own. There were no bar fines, as there were at other places—payments the man had to make before a girl could leave with him. All "business" was transacted here, where the mamasan could keep an eye on things. And where Jonah could intervene forcefully if there were any difficulties.

There were half a dozen spacious rooms upstairs, as clean and as large as hotel rooms. Men often spent the night, staying for breakfast in the morning, and money changed hands surreptitiously. Many men who were repeat customers would simply hand the mamasan a wad of baht when they entered, trusting her to deduct the appropriate amount. And almost all customers were repeat customers. You couldn't find this place unless you had heard about it from a friend. There were no advertisements, and no touts out on the street.

And there was none of the shenanigans of other places. No pickpockets or laced drinks. And no hidden video cameras in the rooms upstairs, which Ladarat had heard about. Some bars, she'd heard, made most of their money from blackmailing wealthy *farang* whose Thai vacation had been captured on digital film.

Ya and four or five other girls, all in sweatshirts and leggings, flitted around the large room dusting and scrubbing and lighting candles in the sconces on the walls. Ladarat sat quietly and sipped her tea, feeling for a moment strangely as if she were part of a family. Which, she supposed, she was.

"Ah, cousin. So good to see you. You have been staying away from me?"

"No, cousin, just very busy." They exchanged *wais* and then hugs.

Her cousin, Siriwan Pookusuwan, was four years older but looked ten years younger. She'd kept a girlish figure, she claimed, because she was surrounded every day by young beauty that rubbed off on her. She had clear pale skin and long flowing black hair that was usually tied up primly in a bun.

"And how is my learned ethicist nurse?" There was a teasing note to Siriwan's banter that some might mistake for jealousy, but that wasn't the case at all. They'd gone their different ways, that was all.

Siriwan had worked for a time as a tour guide, and then had gone into business for herself. She'd done well, but not in a way that Ladarat ever could have emulated. Business wasn't for her, any more than the careful work of a hospital ever would have appealed to Siriwan. Ladarat could barely balance her savings passbook every month. She'd often thought that there were a limited number of genes for various traits in a family, and Siriwan had obviously received all of the money genes.

It was true, though, they didn't see each other often. But perhaps that would change.

"Now I'm not just a nurse," she said with an arch, mocking boast. "I'm...a detective."

That pulled her cousin up short, and she paused, with a glass of iced tea halfway to her lips. Slowly she set it back down on the table.

"I see," she said slowly. No, actually, she didn't. "A what?"

"A detective."

It wasn't often she could surprise Siriwan. Whenever they met, her cousin always had wild stories of *farang* and her girls, and tales of politics and intrigue. Mostly Ladarat just listened. In fact, she'd always felt as though Siriwan's four-year seniority had dogged their relationship all their lives. But now, at last, after forty years, here was something of Ladarat's that piqued Siriwan's interest.

And so Ladarat told her cousin about the mystery of the dying men. And about Wiriya. And about Anchan.

Siriwan's eyes seemed to open just a little wider when Ladarat mentioned the mysterious peaflower lady, but perhaps it was her imagination. She waited until Ladarat had told the whole story, and then sat back in her chair, taking a sip of iced ginger tea, and thinking carefully.

Ladarat knew her cousin well enough to know that she couldn't rush her. Although Siriwan could be a decisive businesswoman, and a ruthless one, she would always take her time when presented with new information. It was as if she had some sense that told her when an idea was ready, much as the fruit seller could sense a mango's ripeness.

Finally she spoke. As usual, she cut straight to the heart of the matter.

"So you think this woman is killing these men for their life insurance, and you want to find her before she finds another victim?"

Ladarat nodded. "Exactly so. But how can we find her? That's the difficulty. We have a name, but it's a name that doesn't appear in the Chiang Mai city directory that Khun Wiriya has access to. She could be anywhere."

"Are you sure it's the insurance she's after?"

"But what else could it be?"

"Ah, cousin. For someone so educated," she said teasingly, "you are not very worldly. Perhaps this is...fun? Perhaps she likes the thrill? Or perhaps," she added thoughtfully, "this is a vendetta of sorts. Perhaps she doesn't like men because of a bad experience in the past and hunts them down."

"Just because she can?"

"Precisely because she can. Perhaps there's no financial motivation at all."

Ladarat couldn't understand that at all. Murder...for a thrill? Even murder for money was very difficult to understand, but at least she could grasp the premise. But for fun?

"But it could be the life insurance, though, couldn't it?"

Siriwan was thoughtful. "Yes," she admitted finally. "I suppose. But life insurance payments are often generous. One such payment would be enough to set many people up for a good life. And certainly two should be adequate. She could buy a house, open a small shop, and hire someone to run it..."

As Siriwan spoke, it sounded as though she were talking about her own fantasy retirement. But that was rubbish. Her cousin would be bored in an instant.

"And besides," Siriwan continued, "there is often a waiting period for life insurance. If they are married today and he dies tomorrow, most insurance companies would look askance at that."

So Ladarat explained about the old marriage certificate, and advanced her theory that perhaps Anchan was reusing it for subsequent men.

Siriwan nodded. "Then she is very clever." She paused, thinking. "And very thoughtful. This is not a vendetta, or if it is, it's a long-term campaign."

"And that," Ladarat insisted, "is why I need to find her."

Siriwan didn't ask why. She'd known Ladarat all her life, and knew that once she'd been given a task, she had to finish it. Whether that was eating a plate of her mother's *gang keow wan*—Thai green curry—that was far too spicy, or finishing a fellowship in the cold and unfriendly city of Chicago, if it was an assignment, she would finish it.

"Let me think about it," Siriwan said finally. "I can... make inquiries."

"But quietly," Ladarat cautioned her. "Quietly. If Peaflower knows that someone is looking for her, she'll go somewhere else and start again, and we'll never find her."

Siriwan nodded, and Ladarat rose to leave. As her cousin walked her to the door, they passed Jonah, and again Ladarat wished him the best of luck. She was truly happy for them both. He had earned some happiness.

As Siriwan opened the door to see Ladarat out, she thought of one last question.

"You said that she did this before? You're sure?"

"I think so," Ladarat answered. "That's what the policeman told Khun Wiriya. Of course, he can't be sure."

And not for the first time, she realized that quite a bit hung on that corporal's recollection. What if he'd confused

Peaflower with someone else? What if that was a different woman entirely? Then there was no case here, and she wasn't a detective. She was just playing a detective, and wasting everybody's time.

She'd almost convinced herself that might be the case, so she was surprised by Siriwan's next question.

"This other man... was he also Chinese?"

Ladarat paused. "I don't know for certain. But it seems likely, doesn't it? If she's doing this for life insurance, then she'd want to find men with the same names. But would that help us find her?"

"It may," Siriwan said. "If she is interested mostly in Chinese men, well, that might mean something very different." But she didn't say what that something was.

Just then the door opened and two older *farang* with neatly trimmed beards pushed through the doors. As their eyes adjusted, they saw Siriwan and Ladarat and offered formal *wais*, then took off their shoes and *wai'd* the Buddha by the door.

"Two of my best clients," Siriwan whispered. "They work for the World Bank. I have to go. But I'll telephone you tomorrow or the next day." They embraced again and Ladarat stepped out into the fading afternoon sun, wondering whether the mangoes had waited for her.

Wan put

WEDNESDAY

CHAPTER 11

A BRIEF BUT ILLUMINATING CONVERSATION

Despite the fruit seller's warning, those mangoes had, in fact, waited patiently for her return. Ladarat had bought three and had eaten them all last night for dinner, with sticky rice from Duanphen on the corner, and mild red chili paste. It was about as simple as a meal could be, the white rice smoothing over the sweetness of the mango and absorbing the heat of the chili. The quintessential Thai meal, it was all about balance.

Maewfawbaahn had sniffed around and had even tried a piece of mango. He seemed bemused but appreciative. Who ever heard of a cat who ate fruit? But it was good that he had an open mind. Everyone should all aspire to be as open to new things as her cat was.

Didn't Professor Dalrymple say that a nurse must grow a little every day? Then *Maewfawbaahn* had certainly grown a little last night. And she, Ladarat Patalung, would need to grow a little more today.

Indeed, now she had no time to think of cats and mangoes. Or of murder investigations. Now, she had to utilize her budding skills as a detective to do her work as a nurse ethicist. That is, she would need to be an *ethical* detective.

Because Ladarat knew she couldn't postpone a meeting with the mysterious man outside the ICU any longer, and she was nervous. So nervous, in fact, that she hadn't even gone to her office first to drop her handbag and put on her white lab coat, fearing that she would lose her nerve for this conversation. If she'd even stopped there, she'd seek refuge in paperwork and would put this meeting off till tomorrow. Then she'd never do what needed to be done. So Ladarat forced herself to go straight to the elevator and pushed the 6 button, with a sense of purpose mixed with foreboding.

She knew, somehow, that this would be her best chance. She would get only one good opportunity to talk with the man. She needed to make it count.

As Professor Dalrymple said, one must always make the most of every encounter with a patient or family. It can take years to recover from one wrong word that undermines trust.

As she stepped onto the empty elevator, Ladarat reflected that the man had seemed . . . skittish on Monday. Like a forest creature. And today he would almost certainly run away if he sensed that she were a threat. Or if she asked too many questions. Or maybe if she asked him any question at all.

Just as the doors began to close, a young man—little more than a teenager—slipped between them and moved politely to the far corner of the elevator. Ladarat thought about what questions might be safest to ask the man outside the ICU, as she rode the elevator up to the sixth floor. She thought, too, about what her strategy should be. A strategy, she knew, is a very good thing to have.

The elevator stopped on the second floor and more passengers joined them. Then again on the third floor, and the fourth. Some passengers left, but Ladarat noticed that the young man remained.

With every stop, the young man would glance at her in a way that could only be called surreptitious. The way you might look at someone whom you think you know. His eyes flicked up to Ladarat's face in quick forays, without seeming to focus, but then would dart away just as fast.

As the elevator passed the fourth floor, she turned to the man and smiled, but he looked straight ahead. That was both odd and rude. He seemed young, though with Thai men it was often difficult to tell. In his early twenties, perhaps. And dressed neatly in trousers and a white short-sleeved shirt that still had the creases of its package. He'd apparently dressed in new clothes, but he wasn't poor, to judge from the large gold watch that seemed to weigh down his left arm. It was of the complex sort that men seem to favor, with dials within dials, and all sorts of buttons on the side. It was truly as large as a clock but was intended—somehow—to appear sporty.

Perhaps he was here to visit a relative? That would explain his neat appearance. Yet he was carrying nothing. Surely a visit to the ICU would require some sort of gift? And he was going to the ICU. Ladarat was certain of that. That was the only elevator button that was illuminated.

Then, at the very last second, the young man lunged forward and pressed the "5" button. The poor elevator seemed confused by this sudden change of plans and lurched up, then slowed. The young man seemed embarrassed that he had discomfited the elevator in such a way, but still he said nothing. Staring at his feet, he waited until the elevators doors began to slide open, then slipped through, and out onto the fifth floor.

Ah, the obstetrics wards. Perhaps that would explain the young man's confusion. He was a new father.

She would have known that, Ladarat realized, if she had engaged him in conversation. She pondered this fact as the doors slid shut. There were limits, perhaps, in what one could discover by observation. Perhaps one must also talk, and listen.

Perhaps she could just...have a conversation with the man outside the ICU?

That was easy to say, but much harder to do. How could she simply have a conversation? How could she walk in and start talking with the man as if they were friends?

Especially if the waiting room was empty, she thought as the doors opened onto the long, deserted hallway. What if he's there but no one else is? She couldn't exactly take a seat next to him, could she?

Ladarat was still mulling that problem over, getting no closer to a solution, while she walked down the hall. So when she reached the waiting room—which was almost empty—she was hardly relieved to see the man resting on his haunches, his back against the wall that separated the waiting room from the ICU. He'd been in the same position the day before, she remembered. And in much the same place.

It was then that she realized that the man had discovered the only place in the whole waiting room that gave an unobstructed view of the mountains to the north. He'd picked the only spot, in fact, from which you could see the Doi Suthep temple.

Without thinking or planning, Ladarat made her way across the empty waiting room toward where the man was sitting. She was careful not to look at him, though, as she navigated around the rows of chairs. Although she sensed that he was watching her closely.

Instead she looked out the window. She was looking so intently, in fact, that she barked her shin on the edge of one of the hard plastic seats. She said something that was not particularly polite, and only then, again without planning it, looked at the man and smiled. He looked down and away.

Not an auspicious beginning, granted. Still, it was a start.

She drew closer, until she was only two meters from him. As she approached, Ladarat was careful to look only out the window, watching the landscape of the mountains shift. Finally she could see what he saw: a view of green forest that stretched up into the low clouds. Unmarred—unless you looked very closely—by roads or buildings or power lines. And far off to the right was the Doi Suthep temple, one of the oldest and most sacred Buddhist temples in all of Thailand. Beyond that stretched Doi Suthep National Park, a vast expanse of forest just outside Chiang Mai.

She made a high *wai* toward the temple and then stood there, admiring the view for a moment. Partly she wanted to put him at ease. But also, it was a spectacular view, and one that she had not really appreciated before. To see such mountains just outside a city was remarkable. And to have that mountain capped by such a temple...well...it was at times like these that she couldn't imagine working anywhere else.

Finally she turned and offered a *wai* to the man. He returned it more deeply than was strictly necessary. Again, it struck her that he had mistaken her for someone of importance.

But as Ladarat looked at him more closely, she had a different impression. He was, very clearly, a farmer. He had broad, calloused, leathery feet flattened from years of hard work without shoes. His loose-fitting T-shirt was soiled and worn, and his thin cotton trousers had been patched many times. And the bag next to him that she'd noticed yesterday was homemade. It had been constructed entirely of old burlap of the sort that was used to make rice sacks, stitched together with rough twine.

He had showed her such respect, she realized, not because he thought that she was important but because he thought of himself as unimportant.

She found herself in an awkward position, standing over him. In other circumstances, to stand over someone would be considered rude. One should always show respect by putting oneself at a level that is no higher than the other person is. And meeting someone in a prominent position, it was customary to duck and bow. And perhaps even to sit, putting yourself beneath them.

But in this situation, she suspected, if she were to crouch on the floor next to him, he would find it disconcerting. Perhaps he would think it was improper. Perhaps it would frighten him away?

So she compromised and sat on a bench nearby. She was still gazing out the window, careful not to make eye contact. But out of the corner of her eye, she thought she could see him tense. The bag disappeared from her peripheral vision, as if he was gathering it to make an escape.

She could not let that happen. She had come so far. And here she was, sitting right next to him. All that remained was to begin a conversation. But what should she say?

She looked at the man and smiled in a way that she hoped would be disarming. But he was watching her with a wary look that you might reserve for a large, unpredictable animal that was too close for comfort.

Of course, if he was a farmer, then all of this—the whole hospital, indeed the whole city—must be foreign to him. It would be like putting her in the middle of the forest. At night. Everything would be a potential threat. He must be feeling much the same thing.

"I love this window," she said simply.

The man glanced up but didn't move.

"There are houses and buildings on that mountainside," she said quickly, "but you can hardly see them. Especially during the monsoon season, when we get rains every day, the forest seems to grow and covers everything."

She was talking too fast, she knew. She was nervous. But the man, at least, was still paying attention.

"It's like the village I'm from. All trees, not many buildings." She smiled. "Not like here."

"And . . . where are you from, Khun?" He had a brittle, raspy voice that sounded as if it had seen too many cigarettes over the years.

But at least he'd spoken.

"From near Ban Huai Duea School," she said quickly. "It's on the Pai River near the border with Burma. Near Mae Hong Son."

"I know it," he said quietly. "It is good country."

That was an odd phrase, and she wasn't sure what he meant. "Good" as in good for farming? Or did he mean that the people there were good? Both, she thought, were true. But how did he know?

"And you, Khun? Are you from near there?"

For a split second he looked away from her and out the window. In that moment, she saw his face in profile and he looked . . . sad. Very sad. What she had thought initially was humility was also sadness.

It wasn't just that he doubted his importance; he doubted himself.

Without speaking, he turned back to her and rose in a fluid motion, using only his calloused heels to propel himself off the floor. In a second his tattered bag was draped across his shoulder and he made a high *wai* to her, and to the temple on the mountain. Without a word, he padded across the waiting room, his bare feet flapping on the tile floor. No more than a second later, he was gone.

Ladarat watched him hustle across the waiting room and then began to follow him. She wasn't tracking him exactly. Yet she wanted to see where he went when he wasn't in the waiting room. Would he take the elevator at the end of the hall? Or would he keep going to the cafeteria in the next building?

But she was surprised when she rounded the corner. She stood at the end of the long corridor, not ready to believe what she was seeing, or not seeing. The man had disappeared. There was an elderly couple with a young woman, and a young man on crutches with a nurse at his side, practicing walking. But the man was gone.

Where could he have disappeared to? He couldn't have taken the elevator—there was no way he could have reached the far end of the hallway that quickly. Could he? Most certainly not.

And the rooms along the hallway were all for doctors. Their doors were closed because they were out on rounds. Perhaps he could have slipped into an office, but why? She had not been chasing him, and he had no reason to be frightened.

This was indeed mysterious. Ladarat supposed his disappearance should add to her sense of failure. Not only had she been unable to learn why he was here, but now she didn't even know where he went.

And yet, in a strange way, she felt like she had succeeded. She had determined, for instance, that he was a farmer or a laborer. He was either from around Mae Hong Son or at least had lived there once. And she knew—or thought she knew—that he was very sad.

It was true that she wasn't much closer to solving the mystery of the strange man in the waiting room, but she was more confident now. She had, in fact, had a conversation with the man. They had talked, which was more than anyone else had been able to do, wasn't it? It was.

And perhaps she was being too hard on herself. Perhaps she would have a second chance to speak with him.

She could now see how that conversation might unfold. She would greet him, and he would greet her. She would stare out the window. And then she would say something about her home village.

That would be all. She would simply say how lovely it was at the end of the monsoon, as the weather began to cool. How the forests were still green, and how the Siam tulips would bloom abundantly in the forest clearings. She would say something about that, and then she would be patient. Eventually, she was certain, he would talk with her.

You couldn't rush things like this. You couldn't behave like an American. You had to have patience.

Unaccountably cheerful, she stood up. She should check on Mr. Fuller, since she was here. And then she had some unfinished business in the medical records department.

CHAPTER 12

THE STRANGE EPIDEMIC OF FAIR SKIN

But Ladarat's cheerfulness after the encounter with the mysterious man faded almost immediately as the large automatic doors swung open to admit her to the ICU. The unit was unaccountably quiet. The doctors must be in a conference, and there were only a couple of nurses at the nurses' station, one of whom greeted her with a *wai* as she approached.

It was...Kanchana? Yes, Kanchana. Plain-looking and dependably friendly, she was a graduate of Chiang Mai University. In the lower half of the class. Yet only a few years out of nursing school, she was steady and reliable. Too bad her parents had saddled her with such a name. *Kanchana* meant "golden," and surely that was an impossible name to live up to. Ladarat was grateful that her name was one of those Thai names that didn't mean anything, so there were no lofty expectations of her.

Yet Kanchana tried so hard. Both in her studies and in her appearance. Her skin—eeeeyyy! It was an unhealthy, unnatural white. This whitening fad among young women was mystifying.

You want to put some chemical on your face that makes you look like you're dying of some horrible illness? How is that appealing to a man? Do you think a man will say, "Oh yes, I want that one. The woman who is terminally ill—that is the woman for me."

And this whitening *was* a disease of sorts. It had been infecting her nursing students, more every semester. And now some young nurses like Kanchana. It was truly an epidemic.

"You are here to see the American, Khun?" Kanchana asked.

"Yes, Khun." Ladarat paused. "I suppose there has been no change?"

"No," the girl said. She looked at a chart on the counter just to her left. "His vital signs are stable, but he is still on the ventilator, and..."

"And he hasn't begun to wake up?" Ladarat finished the sentence for her.

"No, he hasn't." She looked around carefully, as if there could be other Americans lurking in the bandage cabinet or behind the rack of intravenous supplies. "And Dr. Jainukul is very worried. He says there is nothing we can do."

Hmm. That was bad. This young nurse needed to be careful about language.

"There is always *something* we can do," she told Kanchana gently. "It's just a question of what is possible. Perhaps we cannot cure him. But we can maintain him on the ventilator for the short term. And of course we can ensure that he is not suffering."

Kanchana nodded uncertainly. But what Ladarat said was true. As Professor Dalrymple points out, one must never say that there was nothing that one can do. One can always do something.

"It's just a bad phrase to use," she explained gently, "because it suggests there's nothing that we can do to help."

"Oh, but there is much that we can do to help, Khun. And we are. We are keeping him comfortable and we have him on a breathing machine, and medicine that is controlling the swelling in his brain..." She paused. "Ah, I see. You mean we need to be sure to tell them what we can do, and what we *are* doing?"

"Exactly so," Ladarat said. "You must be honest, of course. But honesty requires telling patients and families about what you can do as well as what you can't."

She left Kanchana thinking about that bit of advice. And Ladarat found herself thinking about it, too, as she walked back to the elevator. It was wise counsel, she knew, but in the wrong hands it could be a little white lie. It could be misused, for instance, to give the wrong impression of what was possible. A particular risk in Thailand, she thought, where the temptation was great to relieve and assuage and calm. If a white lie could accomplish that, well...

Not for the first time she found herself thinking about how patients and families have hopes for results that are sometimes not realistic. Thais were not immune, of course. Especially government officials, who thought that doctors and nurses should be able to do anything. But Thais, in general, were much less susceptible to this disease of optimism than the Americans. She shook her head. The Fuller family was going to have difficulties.

Passing through the waiting room and into the hallway that led to the elevator, a small sign caught her eye. Funny she'd never noticed it before. Suddenly she knew where the mystery man had disappeared to. And she suspected she knew where he might be hiding when he wasn't in the waiting room.

She'd test her hypothesis later, but for now she heaved a sigh of relief. That was one less thing she had to worry about. At least her mystery man was just a man, and not some disappearing ghost. And even better, now she knew where to find him.

ANOTHER ASPIRING DETECTIVE

Ahh, Khun. You are back so soon."

If Panit Booniliang was delighted by her untimely reappearance in his domain, he was doing an excellent job of concealing his enthusiasm. He was smiling, of course. But he looked worried.

As indeed he should. It was safe to say that the poor man had good reason to be worried whenever Ladarat appeared. With the inspection close at hand, he didn't want to find new instances of poor documentation. Not that it was his fault, of course. He couldn't control what those doctors upstairs did. But still, these requests would come to him and he would be...tainted.

"Don't worry, Khun. I don't need you to find more charts," she hastened to reassure him. "I had...an idea. I wanted to ask you whether it would be possible."

"An idea?" Panit put down the short stack of charts he was holding. Then, thinking better of it, he picked them up again. "What sort of...idea?"

"Well," she said slowly, "you remember the death of the man I asked you about yesterday?"

The medical records clerk nodded warily, and his right hand floated up and raced through his unruly hair like an animal that had escaped its cage.

MURDER AT THE HOUSE OF ROOSTER HAPPINESS

"Well, you see, I'm worried that this man's death might not be as straightforward as it seems."

He looked at her curiously, and then set the charts down very carefully onto another pile. Then he paused to square off the edges with two palms.

How much should she tell him? She would need to pique his interest, certainly. He would not be willing to help otherwise. She needed enough curiosity to entice him. Especially with the inspection coming. He would not tear his attention away from his stacks of charts unless she gave him a reason that was both interesting and compelling. So in a split second, and without planning, she decided to tell him the truth.

"I have some evidence that there may have been...foul play involved." She paused. "In that man's death."

Now Panit was looking at her with slack-jawed amazement. But his next question surprised her.

"So you are like...a detective?"

This is the question you ask someone who tells you that a patient may have been murdered? You quiz them about their career and job responsibilities?

"No, Khun. I'm hardly a detective. I am just a nurse." Khun Tippawan had seen to that.

"But it's as a nurse, and as a nurse ethicist," she clarified, "that I was asked to look into this matter."

"Asked? By whom?"

But she shook her head. Some parts of this story were probably better omitted. She didn't want to mention the good detective, and besides, she didn't want to make this seem as though it were an official police inquiry. But then what should she say?

"When I heard about this man's death, you see, I was not quite honest with you." She glanced at Panit and found, strangely enough, that he did not look particularly surprised by this admission. Emboldened, she pressed on.

"Something struck me as familiar, but I couldn't quite remember what it was. Then it came to me last night: A colleague at another hospital told me of a story of a woman who had dropped her husband off in the emergency room in the same condition a year ago."

"When you say 'the same condition,' Khun Ladarat, you mean to say..."

"I mean to say he was dead. Yes. The woman dropped off a man who was dead. They were very suspicious about this behavior, because she did not seem grief-stricken. She seemed very...matter of fact."

"So did they involve the police?"

"There was no evidence, apparently. My friend looked for this woman but couldn't find her. But when I saw this case, I thought..."

"Our murderer is back." He looked positively excited by the news that there was a killer in their midst. The wrinkles on his forehead danced.

"So you want to know if there have been other instances like this at our hospital or at other hospitals? I see, I see." Now he was rubbing his hands together.

But she was two steps behind him.

"Other hospitals? But how can you—"

"Oh, I have friends. We all know each other. At least at the bigger hospitals. Public, private. Makes no difference. We all have to work together when patients are transferred, so we know each other well. In fact, we have a cricket league we play in together."

Who would have known?

"I'll ask. People don't think that we pay attention to what's in these charts, but I assure you, Khun, that we most certainly do. We mark the stranger cases. We're...alert. If there's a murderer out there, we'll find her."

He seemed positively gleeful. Could it be that everyone wants to be a detective? Perhaps she was not the only aspiring detective in Sriphat Hospital. Perhaps they could form a detectives' club. With a cricket league.

Ladarat smiled and thanked the medical records clerk. This was good. He seemed as though he needed a distraction from the impending inspection. And this task should be enough of a distraction for him.

A few minutes later, she stood waiting by the elevator. And waiting. And waiting.

Not for the first time, Ladarat was struck by Thai dependence on elevators. Then she had a thought. She turned around and made her way back down the hallway, pushing open the door to the stairwell. It led down several more flights to the subbasement, she knew. And all the way up to the sixth floor. But she had only two flights to go up. She could do this.

CHAPTER 14

THE VALUE OF *CHOIE* IN HANDLING SURPRISING NEWS

There was an *incident*," Sisithorn whispered from behind her as Ladarat felt a tug on her left arm. She'd just emerged from yet another meeting to prepare for the inspection. That meeting had gone long and—even worse—now she had extra work to do. And now here was her assistant latched on to her elbow like a barnacle.

"It occurred in the *ICU*," she said breathlessly as she steered Ladarat down the hall. "I've been waiting *forever*."

For how many consecutive sentences could this girl speak in italics? Ladarat was mildly curious. Surely she couldn't maintain these slanted syllables much longer?

And indeed she could not. Now Sisithorn paused as if to create suspense. She looked at Ladarat, wide-eyed, her pupils the diameter of Siam tulips behind her oversize round glasses.

But Ladarat had long ago learned that an imperturbable calm—*choie*—was the best way to meet any news that someone seemed to be holding back. If you express surprise or an intense need to know whatever is being concealed, that simply inflates the value of the information. Then it becomes impossible to say for certain whether that information truly was important. The best way to determine whether news is important is to assume it is not.

"Ah, really?" was all she said.

But Sisithorn's enthusiasm wasn't dampened. Still clutching Ladarat's elbow, she steered them down the west hallway and Ladarat realized they were heading toward Kate's room. The story would emerge in its own way, she knew, in its own time.

Sisithorn had been coming out of the ICU, she said finally, checking on the American, when she saw a commotion in the waiting room. Kate seemed to be hysterical. She was in a wheelchair, and she was being propelled down the hallway away from the ICU by her mother-in-law.

"She kept saying something about a 'killer.' But she wouldn't explain."

"A killer? In this hospital? Ah, Khun. This poor girl—she's been through a great deal. Perhaps she is...confused."

Sisithorn shook her head. "No, Khun, I don't think so. I followed them, naturally," she said.

"Naturally."

"And I tried to talk with Kate. But it was only her mother-in-law who would tell me anything. And she said that Kate had been fine just a few seconds earlier. Her mother-in-law had been wheeling her down the hall, and Kate was chatting away. Then all of a sudden Kate just became agitated as they were proceeding down the hall about the time they entered the ICU."

"But Kate didn't see anyone to prompt this outburst?"

"The mother-in-law didn't think so. Of course, when Kate began to cry, she said she stepped in front of the wheelchair and she saw the backs of several people they had passed in the hallway, but she couldn't say which of them had make Kate upset."

"So they were about to enter the ICU? Perhaps it was a . . . flashback?"

"I don't think so, Khun. Remember you sent me to speak with her this morning? Well, I did, and we had a very long talk. Mr. and Mrs. Fuller were not there, so we spoke for more than an hour. She seemed very clear in her head. As if she were back to normal, you know?"

Ladarat nodded. Perhaps it wasn't a flashback. But then what was it? Since obviously this outburst wasn't prompted by a real killer, then what was it?

They had stopped outside Kate's hospital room. The door was closed, but Ladarat and her assistant were whispering. Ladarat eyed the door nervously, in case it should open suddenly.

"She also seemed very strong this morning," Sisithorn said. "Not just strong like a woman trying to wear a brave face, but truly strong. Deep down. She told me that both of her parents died when she was very young. And that she was put . . . in a home with other children's parents?"

"Ah, foster care. It is not uncommon in the U.S.A."

Sisithorn shook her head. She started to speak, but it was plain that there was nothing she could think of to say. The idea of placing a child with strangers was almost impossible to understand.

"Anyway, she did well and worked hard in school and went to a good college—Swarthmore—that is a good college? In the state of Philadelphia, yes?"

Ladarat nodded, thinking it would be best to leave the U.S. geography lesson till another time.

"So," Sisithorn concluded. "She seems very strong. She has endured much tragedy in her life. This is very, very bad, certainly. But she is also very hard to . . . damage. I don't think that bad memories of her time in the ICU would cause her to lose her head in such a way. Something must have happened."

So whatever had made her hysterical must have been very bad indeed. But what?

Just then the door to Kate's room opened. And a second later, it was obvious that they were not going to find out. Mr. Fuller was standing in the doorway, with meaty arms crossed over his big American chest. He didn't even feign an attempt at a *wai*, even when Ladarat and Sisithorn offered their politest greetings. Instead he just began talking. Very quickly.

"I don't know what kind of place this is, that you would let people wander the hallways who'd upset my daughter-in-law like that. Don't you have any control over who gets in here? Or who wanders around? Is this a hospital? Or just some slum where anyone wanders in?"

He went on like this for a full minute, his big chest becoming even bigger as he talked, and his red face even redder. He was talking about security and "dangerous people," and said in so many words that his daughter-in-law would be safer out on the street in New York than she was here.

It was impossible to get a word in without being rude. Fortunately, he was talking too fast for Sisithorn to follow, so she'd assumed the fixed, false smile of ignorance: *yim thak thaai*. That means roughly, "I don't know what's going on but I'm smiling anyway, because...well...it can't hurt."

But Ladarat was getting most of the message. It seemed that he thought that someone had done, or said, something to their daughter-in-law. This, despite the assurances of his wife, who, Sisithorn promised, had seen no one.

Could Sisithorn have been wrong? Perhaps, but unlikely. Certainly her English was good enough to understand such a key fact.

And of course they wouldn't be able to talk to the wife, who presumably was back there in Kate's room. They'd never squeeze by those broad American shoulders.

This harangue was not helpful, but what to do? The American was causing a disturbance in the hallway, and a group of passing nurses edged away, smiling woodenly as they surreptitiously watched the American. Now the American was at risk of doing or saying something embarrassing, which she should try to prevent if she could.

So she waited patiently for a break in his tirade and interjected smoothly, "Of course, you are right. We will ask security to watch carefully, and perhaps they could speak with Kate when she is able?"

The American nodded, perhaps uncertain what this ready agreement meant.

"That is good. I'm sure that Kate is too tired to have visitors right now, so we'll come back." She offered a *wai* and Sisithorn followed suit.

She was surprised to see the American assay a clumsy attempt at a *wai* himself. Hands clasped as the Catholics pray, it looked more like an attempt at isometric calisthenics than a formal demonstration of respect. As a *wai*, it as an abject failure. Yet he was to be commended for trying. Wondering at the oddness of Americans, she took Sisithorn firmly by the elbow and led her down the hallway the way they had come.

They'd walked perhaps twenty meters before her assistant spoke up.

"Wouldn't it have been helpful to talk with Kate?" she asked. "Surely we'd need to find out who she saw. What can security do without some sort of description?" She thought for a moment as they waited for the elevator. "We don't even know whether she saw a man or a woman."

"He wouldn't have let us talk with her," Ladarat pointed out.

"But how can you be sure? That doesn't make sense."

"Because he was angry. And he felt as though he should have been there to protect his daughter-in-law, but he wasn't."

"So . . . he is making up for that by protecting her now? From us?"

"Exactly so." Perhaps that didn't make sense, but Ladarat had a strong feeling. And her feelings were often right.

"So what do we do? We have no idea who this person is. Or whether there even is a real person. Maybe it was just a . . . hallucination."

"Perhaps," Ladarat agreed. Perhaps it was. But she didn't think so. She was pretty sure Kate had seen someone, or something. And they wouldn't begin to determine what that was until they talked with her. So there was no point in speculating about it now.

It was only as the elevator doors were opening that she realized what had registered in her mind. Gripped in Mr. Fuller's right hand had been a few pages of white paper, rolled into a cylinder. The relentless pressure of his meaty fist had begun to crumple it in the middle like a soda can. Those pages could have been anything, but Ladarat had a strange feeling that the big American had been reading the translation of his son's medical records.

She was tempted to go back to see if he had questions. That, after all, was their job. She hesitated, thinking, as Sisithorn stepped into the crowded elevator. But even if it was their job, he was too upset right now. Sisithorn looked at her strangely.

"I forgot something," Ladarat said simply. "We'll meet later." And the elevator doors closed.

She turned away from Kate's room and headed toward the other end of the hall. She had declined the elevator because there was something much more simple she needed to do. She needed to take the stairs.

Smiling, Ladarat turned left and pushed through the door that led to the stairwell. She paused on the sixth-floor landing as the door swung shut behind her, enjoying the quiet. Of course the stairwell was empty. Thais never take the stairs.

And yet...this particular stairwell was not quite empty. Just below her, Ladarat could hear the soft padding of rubber soles on the concrete steps. Those soles, and the feet to which they were attached, seemed to be moving quickly. Very quickly.

Ladarat saw a man's left hand on the railing of one flight as it turned the corner, then it disappeared. A moment later, it reappeared, attached to an arm that extended from a freshly creased white short-sleeved shirt. And on that arm was a familiar, oversize gold watch. Ladarat barely had time to consider where she had seen such an arm recently when the face of the young man who was a new father peered up at her quickly. Then his face disappeared and his feet seemed to redouble their efforts to move as quickly as possible.

CHAPTER 15

A REPORT FROM THE CHIANG MAI
MEDICAL RECORDS CRICKET LEAGUE

A few minutes later, down in the basement, Ladarat tapped lightly on the door to Panit Booniliang's office in the rear of the medical records department. She had never been back here before, because she had always met the director of medical records at the front desk, from which he guarded his domain. But this afternoon there had been a pleasant young man stationed in Khun Panit's usual place.

She'd been taken aback at first—his resemblance to Panit Booniliang was so strong. It was as if the good director had lost forty years in a day. But of course, he was Khun Panit's nephew, Chaow (which meant "quickness of mind") Willapenna. Usually he worked in the far back, filing X-rays. But today he'd been promoted to the front desk.

Farang could never appreciate the Thai penchant for nepotism, but it made a world of sense. If you hire someone from your family, you know exactly who you are getting. There are no surprises. And if there was one thing you could say for certain about Khun Panit, it was that he hated surprises. Which was why this conversation was likely to be uncomfortable. At least, it would be if her hunch was correct.

131

Panit Booniliang came to the door and gave her a deep *wai*, which she returned. Surprised at the sudden escalation in formality, she took a seat as he closed the door behind her. This was indeed strange.

The medical records clerk sat behind his desk and pulled a stack of medical charts toward him. As was his habit, he squared them with thin, elegant fingers, so that their edges lined up perfectly. Then he began to flick a corner of the top chart with a fingernail.

Still he said nothing. He looked from her to the charts and back but didn't speak. It wouldn't pay to rush things, she knew. Khun Panit would speak up when he was ready.

But her composure began to dissolve a moment later. As she looked at the stack of charts, she noticed that each one was thin. Very thin. There couldn't be more than a few scant sheets of paper in each one. Just like the chart of the man, Zhang Wei, who had recently died.

She had a sinking feeling as she realized that this would be a difficult conversation indeed. No wonder Khun Panit was so reticent.

And yet…she felt excitement, too. This was a real murder mystery. Or it might be.

She'd just reached that conclusion when Khun Panit began to speak. He was avoiding her eyes now, which confirmed her worst fears about those charts.

And there was the fact that he was smiling. It was the smile known as *yim yae yae*, which meant, "I know things look bad, but getting upset won't make things any better, so why not smile?"

"I must admit, Khun Ladarat," he said slowly, "that I doubted your idea that there might be murders." He paused, flicking the corner of the top chart more frequently now. "I mean, murders involving this very hospital? Unknown to us? It was inconceivable."

He paused, thinking, as he squared the slim stack of files one more time.

"And yet I did as you asked. And I found these." He pushed the pile of charts toward her, as if they were trash he wanted to get rid of. And perhaps they were. They were evidence that the orderly world he'd created was beginning to fray around the edges.

"There are eight charts," he continued. "Eight separate people. All of them were brought into Casualty in the early morning hours. The first about five years ago. And the last—the man you asked me about—only two days ago."

That seemed impossible. Eight men killed?

"But, Khun, how do you know that they were..." What was the word?

"Connected?" He smiled sadly. "That is the term, I believe? You see, I am not a detective, so I do not have all of the right words as you do. But I think that is the word for which you were searching." He smiled again.

There was no malice in his teasing, she knew. He was actually paying her a compliment. She had uncovered these murders, and he was giving her credit.

"I can't be certain, of course. But it is not a coincidence. Look at the name on the top chart."

She did. It was Zhang Wei, the man who had died two nights ago. But...the date was wrong. The date was from two years ago. She looked at Mr. Booniliang, who nodded.

She looked more closely at the stamp on the upper-left corner of the chart. It was for Central Chiang Mai Memorial Hospital, about two kilometers southeast, near the river.

"Exactly so. Look at the next chart," he suggested.

She did. It was from about six months later, but bore the same name, and the stamp of yet another hospital.

The real shock came with the third chart. She checked the stamp first—it was her own hospital. Three years ago. But with the same patient name.

Quickly, she flipped through all eight charts and found three from her hospital.

Mr. Booniliang looked grave. And he was no longer smiling. "I don't know which is worse," he said. "The fact that there were three deaths in our hospital, or the fact that there were five in other hospitals."

She thought about that for a moment. There was something about this that was nagging at her. Then she realized what was wrong.

"There are three hospitals in this pile," she said.

Panit nodded.

"Three deaths at our hospital, three at Memorial, and two at Changpuek."

Panit nodded again, looking worried.

"Khun?"

"Yes?"

"How big is your cricket league?"

"We have four hospitals," he said sadly.

"So at least there is one hospital where these deaths are not happening," she said. "That is cause for some relief." Ladarat was duly relieved.

But then she noticed that Panit did not look relieved.

"Well, you see, my friend at that fourth hospital just had gall bladder surgery, so he was not able to help me."

They both sat there quietly, pondering that information. But she wanted to be certain.

"So you mean to say that you inquired at three hospitals and there were suspicious deaths at all three?"

The medical records clerk nodded. "That is what I mean to say."

"Ah." It was the only reply she could think of.

There were half a dozen hospitals in or near Chiang Mai. There was Lanna Hospital and Siamriad to the north along Route 11. And McCormick Hospital, to the east of the river. And those were just the ones that were very close.

She looked at the medical records clerk, who was still nodding. "So you see? This is a problem, Khun. A big problem." He paused. "If you doubt me still, look at the names of these men's wives." She did, flipping through the stack as she had before, but looking this time at the line on the first page that listed the patient's next of kin.

She looked up again at Panit, who was once again wearing the *yim yae yae* smile.

"Eight men with the same name . . ." she said.

"Married to the same woman," he finished her thought.

"Peaflower," they said in unison.

Suddenly very serious, Panit Booniliang leaned across the desk. "You must find her," he said. "You must find this woman. She kills a man regularly. So she will kill another very soon."

Ladarat nodded uneasily. Khun Panit's hard work had confirmed her worst fears, but it hadn't done much to help her solve the case. The stakes were higher, certainly. But her job wouldn't be any easier.

She thanked the medical records clerk and made her way out past his smiling nephew. Out in the hallway, though, her thoughts turned back to the conversation she'd just had. She thought, too, about her observation that her job hadn't gotten any easier. She thought about that very hard, in fact, as she made her way down the hallway to her office.

But this wasn't her job, was it? It was not. She was... unqualified.

A simple look into medical records was one thing. But a murder? A serial murder? Eight men? As Khun Tippawan would no doubt tell her, she was a nurse, not a detective.

She should call Khun Wiriya. She should let him know what she'd found. And she should tell him that she could no longer help. She would tell him what she knew, and then she would go back to being a nurse ethicist.

CHAPTER 16

A HIGHLY INEFFICIENT WAY TO CATCH A CRIMINAL

But things did not work out in the way that Ladarat had planned. Not quite. She had tried to call Khun Wiriya, but he hadn't been in his office. His secretary gave Ladarat the detective's mobile phone, but he didn't answer that either. She left a message, and then—what else?—went back to work.

There were seventy-three policies left to review, and not nearly enough time. She couldn't afford to spend precious hours on a murder investigation for which she was so poorly equipped. As she worked her way through policy after policy, checking expiration dates, she moved them from the left side of her desk to the right. Each wave of migration from west to east across her desk gave her a tiny but noticeable breath of satisfaction. And then she'd turn to the next one in line.

Yet she found that she could not keep herself from thinking about this Peaflower murderer. Indeed, in the gap of concentration that opened as each policy passed from one pile to the other, she thought for just a second about her investigation.

During each momentary respite between policies, her thoughts circled around one very simple question. What would make a person kill again and again and again like that? But no answer came to her. So she would move on to the next one.

Eventually, though, her thoughts began to follow one another down a common path, and that path led her back to the question of Peaflower's motives. At some point after the twenty-ninth policy but before the thirty-fifth, she began to wonder if her focus on life insurance was incorrect. Sometimes, she knew, when you see a problem initially in a particular way, it is hard to set that initial impression aside. It becomes part of the way that you see the world.

Is that what she was doing? Had she become nearsighted, looking only for Peaflower's financial gain? Was it a vendetta after all, as Siriwan had suggested? Her cousin was a woman of the world and surely would know about such things.

Or perhaps—just perhaps—this wasn't murder at all. Could there be another explanation? Could there be a simple explanation that didn't involve murder?

As Professor Dalrymple warned her readers, a nurse must always take a step back and look at ethical problems—and patients—with fresh eyes.

That was what she must do now. Reevaluate.

And that was precisely what she was trying to do when the phone on her desk rang, startling her out of her reverie. The official Sriphat Hospital Policy on the Appropriate Care of the Elderly Patient slid out of her right hand and fluttered under her desk. Reaching one hand for the phone and extending the other under the desk, she answered as she scrabbled blindly for Policy No. 04-5829.

But she stopped scrabbling and straightened up as she heard the voice of Khun Wiriya. He sounded tired. Tired and... beaten down.

He must have a very hard life. Always chasing bad people.

That must be debilitating. Always thinking about the worst in everyone. That must be even worse.

And in that moment, she realized that she was being self-ish. How could she think of abandoning the job that she had begun? This was something she had committed to do. So it was her responsibility. She had to finish.

And that is why, as she told Khun Wiriya what she had found, she found herself falling into the role of a detective.

"So what does this mean?" she asked when she'd finished.

"It means we have a problem."

"But . . . you don't sound very worried."

"Oh, I am worried. Very worried indeed. I think we have a woman who has killed many men and is likely trying to murder another one soon. So I'm very worried. But worrying won't help protect the next man she has set her sights on."

"Then what will?"

"Finding him before she does."

"So you have a plan?"

"For a start, I'll look for men with the same name in Chi-ang Mai."

"And warn them?"

"No, I'll investigate them. I'll find out who they know and who they've been in contact with."

"That is your plan?"

"I didn't say it was a good plan."

Indeed, that seemed like a highly inefficient way to catch a criminal. A little like posting policemen outside every bank in case someone tried to rob it. But he was the detective, not her.

After they'd said their good-byes, though, as she was fin-ishing the pile of policies on her desk, his answer contin-ued to nag at her. There were many men out there with this unfortunate name who were at risk. It was, after all, one of the most common of Chinese names. Less common in Chiang Mai, of course, than in mainland China. But still.

As she finished gathering her policies into a neat pile, she squared them just as Khun Panit liked to. Then she remembered the policy that had slid under her desk. She retrieved it, putting it in order. She was glad that she'd insisted that each of their policies have a unique number that denoted the year in which it was created. She'd invented that system herself several years ago to try to keep track of a growing stack of policies. Now each policy had a unique number that could be tracked. One number per policy. It was the sort of order that Mr. Booniliang would appreciate.

She was gathering up her handbag and turning off the light when those numbers gave her an idea. She stopped in the doorway, the office dark behind her except for a streak of light sneaking through the narrow basement window. It was a long shot certainly. And probably not worth exploring. And yet...she was increasingly certain that Khun Wiriya's strategy would not help him find the murderer.

This idea Ladarat was thinking about might not find her either. But at least it was something. And besides, if they both looked in different ways, perhaps they might compare results?

And in the back of her mind, she admitted, there was the tiny hope that perhaps she would succeed where the detective had failed. Not a realistic hope, she knew, since he was a detective and she was only a nurse. Nevertheless...

But she was too tired to think about this right now. She would go home, and she would get something satisfying. Perhaps *gai pad pongali*—yellow curry rice with an egg whipped in. Like a savory curry pudding. Usually more of a winter dish, but perhaps Khun Duanphen would make an exception. And maybe—if she was very lucky—there would be *glooai tawt*. She would sit on her patio and share her dinner with *Maew-fawbaahn*. And she would read the biography of Aung San Suun Kyi, with the compelling cover, because it was important to learn about inspiring people whenever one could.

CHAPTER 17

SABAI SABAI!

Khun Ladarat, you work too hard!" Khun Duanphen was beside herself with indignation. "The hospital, to keep you late like this. It's not right!"

"Ah." Ladarat smiled. She had heard this before. Indeed, when hadn't she heard it? The small woman who plied her griddle and wok like an orchestra conductor managing a chorus of strings and woodwinds always seemed to take Ladarat's tardiness as an affront to all that is sacred about Thai life.

To think that she would take her work seriously! To think that she would work so hard, and forget to enjoy life! She should—

"*Sabai sabai!*" Duanphen said happily.

A ubiquitous Thai phrase. It was like the American sixties, all rolled up into one word. It meant something like "take it easy" or "easy does it" or "take one day at a time" or simply "relax."

"But, Khun, where would we be if everyone said that all of the time? There would be no hospitals, and no government. No streets, and no electricity..."

The food seller just smiled. "Oh, you know that things would work out somehow. We don't need all of this, you know. We could be happier without anything at all."

Was that really true? Perhaps Khun Duanphen was very wise. Or perhaps she was exceptionally simple. Sometimes it was difficult to tell.

Duanphen handed her a Styrofoam container with her *gai pad pongali*, and then handed over a second container that was very warm. Little wisps of steam leaked from the corners. "For you, Khun. A small something. Because you work too hard."

Ladarat sniffed. "Ah...*glooai tawt*?"

Duanphen nodded.

Banana fritters. Made with dwarf-size apple bananas that were extra sweet, and firmer than the larger bananas that Khun Dole mass-produces. She didn't let herself have them very often. They were very fattening. But she did love them. They reminded her of her mother's kitchen years ago. She'd come home from school and in the kitchen would be her mother or her grandmother—sometimes both. They would always make something special for Ladarat, and Siriwan, if they'd walked home from school together as they often did when they were young.

She thanked Duanphen, promising to work less hard in the future. As if that were really possible.

A few minutes later, she was sitting happily in her little garden. She decided to eat the *glooai tawt* first. They were, after all, much better when they were fresh and very hot. It wouldn't do to let them age. Loyal *Maewfawbaahn* slunk closer after finishing his dinner of canned cat food and waited patiently. These fritters were really too good to share, but he was a good cat.

And had anyone burglarized her house today? They had not. So he was doing his job. And a leader has to reward her subordinates.

She picked up the remaining one third of the banana and set it down gently in front of the cat. He sniffed at it gingerly. Then licked it. And a second later it was gone. Amazing.

She'd left the *gai pad pongali* inside, but she was too tired and lazy to get up and bring it out. Besides, the *glooai tawt* had been very filling. Enough for dinner, although not a very healthy one, to be sure.

She sat back in her chair, resting one hand on *Maewfaw-baahn*, who bounded up onto her lap. Ladarat looked up and noted that it had become cloudy. It would probably rain tonight. There were no stars, and yet still plenty to see, as the city lights played against clouds that shaded from light to dark in wide swaths.

Watching the clouds, and thinking about her day, she found herself wondering about this mysterious woman, Peaflower, who was causing such trouble. Ladarat had promised herself that she wouldn't think about this case tonight, but she couldn't help it. Could it be that Peaflower had a vendetta? That she hated these men?

The fact that they had the same name gave her pause. What if someone of that name had harmed her once? Or her family? And this was her revenge?

But no, who would do such a thing? To kill people with the same name who were unrelated? It was crazy.

To do that once, perhaps... That would be a hot-hearted crime. What Thais called *jai ron*.

It had always fascinated her that the Thais said someone was "hot-hearted" while Americans—and everyone else, it seemed—said such a person was "hot-headed." The Thais understood that the heart was the seat of the emotions and assumed that anyone who was acting aggressively or out of character must therefore have an overactive heart. But the

Americans, who saw the head as the seat of reason, saw such behavior and decided that the brain must have switched sides. That the brain must have become hot instead of cool.

It was typical of the Americans to find such a roundabout explanation for things. And typical, too, of the Thais to find the easiest answer.

The easiest answer?

She smiled to herself. That's it. The easiest answer.

It had to be money. It had to be. Insurance or ... something. Perhaps there was revenge, or ... other motives. But there was money involved. Suddenly Ladarat knew that with complete certainty. One must always look for the simplest answer first.

Even Professor Dalrymple said as much. "The most common diagnosis," she counseled, "is always the most likely diagnosis."

It was wisdom such as this that made Professor Dalrymple a useful companion to have in one's head.

And there was no point at this stage of the investigation in looking for crazy theories. The simplest answer was the most common one. And what motivation is more common than greed? Peaflower was looking for money.

She thought about that a little longer as *Maewfawbaahn* fell asleep. She thought she heard the distant rumble of thunder that the clouds overhead had promised, but it was only his purring.

Ladarat moved and stretched as *Maewfawbaahn* slid, complaining, onto the flagstones at her feet. There would be time enough to be a detective tomorrow. For now it was enough that she knew—or thought she knew—that money was the issue. Now at least she had a motive. That was enough for a detective, at least for tonight.

Wan pareuhatsabordee

THURSDAY

CHAPTER 18

WHAT WILL HAPPEN WILL HAPPEN

Perhaps the lazy portion of her mind that covertly subscribed to the philosophy of *sabai sabai* had listened to what Duan-phen had said the night before. That she worked too hard. That she worked hours that were far too long.

Because Ladarat forgot to set her alarm and didn't wake until past eight o'clock. She might not have woken even then if it weren't for *Maewfawbaahn*, who wanted breakfast. Now. He could be very insistent, that cat.

So it was much later than usual when she arrived at the hospital. All of the shady spots in the parking lot had been taken an hour ago, so she had to leave the Beetle in a far corner, right next to the fence. There was no shade nearby, and even though she left the windows partly open, she knew that the insides of her little car would be like an oven by the end of the day. Ah well. This was the price she paid for being lazy.

Ladarat thought about that proper form of justice as she made her way slowly across the gravel parking lot and through the back door of the hospital. Most Thais wouldn't have that reaction, she knew. Most Thais wouldn't think that they deserved something bad to happen to them because they were lazy.

Waiting for the elevator to take her to the sixth floor, she wondered why she had these ideas. She thought...like an American.

She had the work conscience of an American. Why would that be? One year in Chicago was hardly enough to explain it. And besides, she'd always had these feelings. She was still pondering this anomaly as she walked down the hallway and came to the ICU waiting room.

It was late in the morning, so Ladarat wasn't surprised to find there were perhaps half a dozen family groups scattered among the chairs. The men were dressed in a mix of clean but worn work clothes, but many of the women wore traditional Lanna-style long skirts. They'd brought children and games and, of course, food, making the little waiting room look like it was hosting a small village that decided to take a trip to the big city.

But she was surprised to see the mysterious man here. Tucked into the same corner in which she'd found him yesterday, he was keeping a watchful eye on the crowded waiting room. Hunkered down on his haunches as he'd been the day before, he had the quiet patience of a man who could remain in one place forever, out of the flow of time.

She'd gone straight to the waiting room, so she didn't have her white coat or badge. And she had her handbag over her shoulder. She looked as though she were visiting someone. At least, she hoped she did. That was her plan, if you could call it a plan.

Ladarat made her way slowly across the crowded waiting room, greeting family members and stepping around children playing on the floor, who *wai'd* respectfully. Careful not to step over anyone, which would have been a mark of disrespect, she was having a difficult time maintaining her balance, and her dignity.

From their dress and the respectful *wais*, she guessed that most, if not all, of these families were from the countryside. Up in the Northwest perhaps. Or over toward the Laos border in the north. This was perhaps the first time that some had been in a hospital. She hoped that things would end well for them, but she was afraid that, for many, they would not.

The most common cause of an ICU admission, after all, was an accident. Especially young adults who rode scooters without helmets. That didn't usually end well. Still, the good doctors and nurses here did what they could.

Now she was in front of the window, where she looked out at Doi Suthep temple, as she'd done before. As nonchalantly as she could without being disrespectful, Ladarat turned to offer a *wai* to the man crouched on the floor, who returned it, watching her carefully.

She hadn't prepared a strategy. She told herself that she wanted to be spontaneous. But the truth was that she wasn't sure what she should say. She wasn't at all sure that something would come to her in time.

But then, just as she began to panic, she heard herself asking the man if the person he was visiting was doing well?

"I don't know," the man admitted. "But I'm sure he's getting the best care."

Oh—this was bad. Very bad, from an ethical perspective. He was visiting a family member but could get no information? Presumably the doctors had not talked with him because he seemed simple. But that was no excuse. Even the simplest person from the country could understand the facts, if they were explained properly.

As Professor Dalrymple admonished her readers, "A failure of the patient to understand medical information is really a failure of the doctor or nurse to explain that information."

There would be time for that later, though. Right now, it was good that she'd determined—almost by accident—that this man really was visiting someone. Is that how detectives operated? You make a guess and then discover whether you're right? If so, she would make a very good detective, as she was always guessing. And sometimes, even, she was right.

"But why don't you know how the patient is doing? Surely the doctors have told you something?"

In that moment, the man looked terribly, terribly sad. Of course he was sad. To visit someone with the commitment that he'd shown. Here day after day. But unable to find out how a patient was faring . . . well, that would be awful.

"Ah," the man said. "But I cannot ask. I don't have the words. I am a simple man." He shrugged. "I will wait. I will find out."

"But perhaps . . . perhaps I could ask for you?"

The man seemed to be considering that offer for a moment. His gaze left her face and skipped around the room as if he were looking for an answer along the far wall, or in the food basket a young woman was unpacking over by the window. Perhaps he found it, because a second later he turned to her and got to his feet in a flowing, graceful movement that reminded her once again of a forest animal.

"No, Khun. Please don't trouble. I . . . I don't even know the man's name." He offered her a deep *wai*, which she returned, puzzled. A second later he was hurrying across the waiting room, stepping gingerly around families without losing speed. Again she had this image in her head of a wild animal moving through the forest, sidestepping obstacles with ease that would stop humans in their tracks. It was a strange combination of grace and purpose, she thought, as he disappeared.

Much more slowly, she followed, avoiding the curious looks of the families around her. She doubted that they had over-heard the conversation, but they must have been puzzled by the well-dressed city woman talking with the rough-looking man.

She wasn't disheartened to see that the hall was empty when she reached it. Instead, she smiled to herself. She hadn't really expected to see his retreating back.

Why not? Because she was a detective, of course.

But what now? What would a detective do?

She stood there for a moment at the waiting room entrance, thinking. A detective, she decided, would look for witnesses.

Turning back to the waiting room, she caught sight of a face that looked familiar, on the far side of the waiting room. It took her a second glimpse of his profile as he was staring down at his mobile phone. Then she recognized the man in the elevator. The man in the stairs. The man with the wife in obstetrics.

But...if his wife was in the obstetrics unit, what was he doing up here on the sixth floor? Before she could ponder that out-of-place fact, the man snapped his phone shut and looked up at her. His eyes widened in surprise and he hustled around the corner and disappeared.

Why were people running away from her? This seemed to be a strange epidemic. This running from the ethicist.

Where was she? Yes. Witnesses.

Ladarat caught the eye of the young woman who had been unpacking sticky rice and fried vegetables from a basket. Now she held a small child on her lap. She was alone, which was not good. So perhaps that meant her husband was in the ICU?

She smiled at Ladarat and seemed to want to talk. Whether

she was the best witness wasn't the issue, Ladarat reminded herself. What was important was that she might have something to offer. One never knows.

So she greeted the woman and asked if she was well.

The woman smiled. A *yim soo* smile, which meant "as well as can be expected." But she didn't seem to want to talk about her troubles, and instead asked about the man in the corner.

"Do you know him, Khun?"

Ladarat shook her head. "I met him yesterday—we spoke briefly. I know nothing about him, but he seems... sad."

And in that moment, she thought his sadness seemed out of proportion to his trouble in getting information. Not out of proportion, really. It's just that it was a different sort of sadness. But maybe that was just her imagination.

"Do you know him, Khun?"

The woman shook her head. "No, we've never spoken. But he's been here for several days, I think. I just arrived two days ago and he was there. And he is here at the strangest hours. Often early in the morning and late at night. I heard one of the other women here saying they thought perhaps he lives in the hospital."

"Do you think any of the other families here knows him? Have you seen him talking to anyone?"

"No." She shook her head emphatically. "Never. He never talks to anyone. What's even stranger," she whispered, "is that he's always in that corner. Always the same place. Never on a chair, but always on the floor."

"You don't know anything about who he might be visiting?"

"No, I don't know." Then she was thoughtful for a moment. "But he's been here longer than most of us." She gestured at the other families in the room. "So whoever he's visiting has been here for a long time. Though I've never seen him go in back." She pointed at the doors to the ICU. "All of us go back and forth and visit for at least an hour a day, but I've never seen him go back there."

Ladarat thanked the woman, wishing her the best of luck with her troubles. For a moment the woman looked surprised.

"Ah," she said. "Thank you, but what will happen will happen. It is out of our hands."

CHAPTER 19

THE *JAI DEE* DETECTIVE

It was fortunate indeed that Ladarat came to the ICU bearing good news. Some good news, at least. Because as soon as she walked through the door, she found herself in trouble.

"Khun Ladarat," the head nurse said, scolding. "Where is your white coat? And your name badge? Where is your name badge?" The head nurse was a sharp-featured, rough-tongued bossy woman even in the best of circumstances, and the impending inspection had made her particularly irascible today.

So Ladarat apologized profusely, trying to catch the attention of Dr. Jainukul, who seemed to be finishing a phone call at the nurses' station. As the head nurse calmed down, she deigned at least to tell Ladarat that the American was unchanged. Then, as soon as the director hung up the phone, she stalked off to berate some other hapless employee.

The director, at least, was pleased with the news she shared.

"So at least now we know that he is waiting for one of our patients," he said, sitting down next to Ladarat. The director pulled a stack of charts over to him and began to glance through them, signing the first three without even looking. "Of course we suspected that, but this is good to know for certain."

"But there is one fact I don't understand," Ladarat said.

And she told him what the man had said about not knowing the patient's name.

That caused the director to pause in mid-signature. He even put down his pen. Dr. Jainukul looked surprised at first. Then his eyes widened in confusion.

"How could this man be waiting for a patient whose name he doesn't know?" He thought about that for a moment. "Perhaps...perhaps you misunderstood him?"

She shook her head. "No, Khun. He was very clear about that. He did not know the patient's name."

Dr. Jainukul was still shaking his head, so she was reluctant to give him any more information that would confuse his day. But he had asked her to be a detective, and so she needed to tell him everything she'd learned.

"There is one other thing," she said. "You see, I think he may be sleeping here in the hospital."

"He is sleeping in the hospital? But that is very bad. The inspectors will not like that at all if they find him. How do you know this?"

"I don't, know for certain," she admitted. "But..."

In truth, she wasn't sure how much she should tell him. Now her hypothesis sounded like fiction. And the steps she'd taken to find out seemed ridiculous. Still, it was something the director needed to know, wasn't it?

"Well, yesterday we were talking and he disappeared suddenly. I followed him out to the hallway and he disappeared. I knew he couldn't have reached the elevator at the end of the hallway in time, so I reasoned that he must have taken the stairs."

Dr. Jainukul was starting to smile, just a little. Though she couldn't tell yet whether that smile would be at her expense. But she'd already begun, and it was too late to stop now.

"So later I took the stairs myself. As you know, Khun, we Thais don't like to take the stairs."

The director was nodding agreement. "I never take the stairs, it is true. Although perhaps I would lose a few kilos if I did more often." He smiled and began signing charts again. "But what does this have to do with our mysterious man?"

"Well, I took the stairs all the way down to the basement. I thought that the stairs, and particularly the stairs at the lowest floor, would be unlikely to get much use. It would be a perfect place to hide."

Now the director was grinning. "Of course. What better place to hide in a country of lazy people than in the stairwell?" He paused. "So you found him there?"

"Not exactly. But I did find a space under the last flight of stairs in the basement where the wax was worn. As if someone had been sleeping there," she concluded.

"But why has no one discovered him? And why . . . why was there this place where the wax was worn? Surely the cleaning staff polishes that floor every night."

It had taken Ladarat a little while to work that out, too, and she was impressed that the director had arrived at that question so quickly. But at least she had an answer.

"You see, all of the cleaning staff are preparing for the inspection. They began the least-trafficked areas two weeks ago and there haven't been any cleaning staff down there since then, except to sweep up quickly. So you see, no one would find him. And no one would polish the floor after he'd slept on it."

Dr. Jainukul was nodding, impressed. "So we should send hospital security to find him and remove him?" The director glanced at her stealthily between signatures.

Was he suggesting this course of action? Or was he asking her advice?

He would be tempted to evict the man, certainly. Doing so would solve this problem for him. But she could also tell that the director was a gentle man, with a good heart. He didn't want to lose face with the inspectors. But neither did he want to hurt this man. Especially now that Ladarat had determined that he was here for a patient. She smiled her uncertainty and waited for the director to come to the right decision. Most people, she knew, came to the right ethical decision on their own.

And when it became obvious that Ladarat wasn't going to agree, he shrugged. "So we can't ask security to remove him. No, that would be wrong. But then what can we do? We can't have the inspectors find him, can we? To have them see him in our waiting room would cause us to lose face, but if they were to find him sleeping in a stairwell..." He shuddered.

"I think that is very unlikely, Khun. He is a country man. Someone used to rising very early. I'm guessing that he is awake and gone by four thirty or five at the latest." She smiled. "Even the most aggressive inspector will not be searching the hospital basement at five A.M."

The director smiled, too, and she knew that she had won.

"So what should we do?" he asked. "You are the ethicist. What is the right course of action?"

What indeed? She wasn't sure. But she knew they couldn't remove the man.

"Perhaps if you were to give him information about the patient he's waiting for, that would allow him to spend less time here?"

"Yes, but we don't know which patient."

"Well, he's been here for several days . . ."

The director was nodding. "Yes, I see. So he must be waiting for a patient who has been here for several days." He paused. "But you know there are thirty-two patients in the ICU right now, and more than half have been here for several days."

Then Ladarat thought of something else. The man had said "he," hadn't he? She was sure of it. She offered this information to the director, who scratched his chin thoughtfully.

"Well, that might help. But as you know, Khun, we get many accident victims, and most are male. Men seem to be much more stupid when it comes to traveling fast on motorcycles. There are only"—he thought for a second—"six women here now. But that will help. Even if we can narrow the possibilities down to a dozen patients, I can begin speaking with our nurses to see if anyone has talked with the man."

He put the last chart on the pile and smiled. "Now these are all ready for our inspection."

They said their good-byes, and just as she was leaving, the director stopped her and thanked her for her efforts. "You are truly a *jai dee*." A good-hearted person.

A week ago, Ladarat would have thought that was the highest compliment anyone might pay her, and she thanked the director for his kindness. But then he surprised her by offering a compliment that pleased her even more.

"And . . . you are a very good detective."

The warm glow of Director Jainukul's compliment carried her the rest of her long day. There was the meeting to review the credentials of their credentialing staff, for instance. Because, of course, those responsible for assessing the merits of physicians needed to demonstrate their own merits. And there was a committee meeting to agree on policies for the use of opioids like morphine, which were necessary for pain, but which could be abused. And, of course, there were policies to review. And more policies. So much work, in fact, that Ladarat had not even availed herself of the food sellers in front of the hospital. One of their most loyal customers, she let them down today, snacking instead on a small portion of mango and sticky rice from the hospital cafeteria.

But finally, her day was over. At least, her day as a nurse ethicist was over. And she was still feeling virtuous and valued and...clever, from the director's kind words.

She felt so good, in fact, that she was momentarily nonplussed by the scrap of paper adorning the windshield of her yellow Beetle, tucked under a tired windshield wiper. It was not a parking ticket. Nor was it an advertisement, she realized as she drew closer. Because the page was blank, and that would be a highly ineffective way to advertise anything. It was simply a page of paper.

In the back of her mind, Ladarat recognized that this might be a message from Khun Tippawan. Certainly she seemed to favor such indirect means of communication. And yet there was the fact that this page was blank. Or was it?

Ladarat removed the mysterious page from its resting place, looking at it carefully. Nothing. It was only as she turned to open her car door that she thought to check the other side. And there the message was difficult to miss, and most definitely not the work of Khun Tippawan:

Khun Ladarat: Your car, it is very nice. An antique no doubt. It would be a shame if anything were to happen to damage such a fine machine that has lived so long and in such excellent health. Give up your Peaflower investigation now, and your car will live for many more happy years.

It took Ladarat several long minutes to calm down after finding the message threatening her little car. Her pulse had raced at first, at the very thought that someone might consider harming such a blameless vehicle. Who would consider doing such a thing?

Then, of course, she looked around. Surreptitiously at first, then more boldly. Was this Peaflower woman out there somewhere, watching her? Or did she have an...accomplice? But the parking lot was empty. Yet someone was almost certainly out there somewhere, watching her. Ladarat found that possibility even more disturbing than the threat to her Beetle had been.

A few minutes later, sitting in the front seat of her still-stationary Beetle, Ladarat had a second thought that made her pulse race all over again. Not only was Peaflower watching her now, but that woman had almost certainly been watching her this morning. How else would she have known which car was Ladarat's? So Peaflower had been watching, and waiting for her to arrive at work. Or—much worse— Peaflower had followed her from home.

Eeeyy. That was very disturbing indeed. It was one thing to be chasing a murderer, but another thing entirely to be chased by one. Once again, Ladarat felt her heart bouncing up and down in her chest like a monkey in a cage.

And yet...Ladarat was pleasantly surprised to note that her pulse soon returned to normal. Or nearly normal.

Ladarat thought of calling Khun Wiriya, and indeed she knew that she should. But it was getting late, and she had a stop to make before she returned home. And besides, if she were honest with herself, she would have admitted that this threat didn't seem real. It seemed like something one would see in a film, or read about in a book. People—real people— did not make threats like this. Against an antique car? Really?

Ladarat tucked the offending piece of paper in her glove box and started the Beetle. Her car, fortunately, seemed unimpressed by the threat that had just been leveled at it. In fact, it seemed to spring to life with more vitality than usual, as if to prove to its owner that it, too, was undeterred. So she put her faithful car in gear and pointed it toward the Ping River.

THE VERY LOW PRICE OF GENUINE HAPPINESS

The fruit seller was where he always was. Today, though, he wasn't looking at Ladarat but at the Beetle. He seemed to be eyeing her car appreciatively. The man even stepped out from behind his booth as Ladarat emerged, sneaking a glance over her shoulder at the car's odometer.

"*Sawat dee krup, ajarn.*" He often addressed her with the honorific *ajarn* reserved for teachers, and Ladarat had never bothered to correct him. "I've been waiting for you to return."

Ladarat paused. That was unusual.

"Ah, really?" Even to her, that sounded like a poor rejoinder.

"Yes, Khun. There's a man—an American. He is looking for just such a car as this. Of course, I didn't tell him about yours..."

Of course, that's exactly what you did.

"But I thought of you immediately. You wouldn't be interested in selling it, would you? I could get you a good deal with this man. A very good deal, I'm sure. He seemed very wealthy. And I could find you a new, modern Japanese car. Or Korean? You like Korean? Much better value for the money. I can get you a top-quality Korean car, for just a fraction of what this man would be willing to pay, I'm sure. You'd have money left over..."

"No, thank you, Khun. I don't think so. Not today. But I'd like a bunch of bananas, if it's not too much trouble?"

The man looked downhearted, but not for long. In his line of work, he probably took chances and was rebuffed all the time. Ladarat hefted the bananas in the plastic bag he'd given her. ("Free! No charge! Special for you!") Then she made her way down the small *soi*, toward the Tea House. The whole way, she thought about the man's proposition. Not about what he was offering. She'd never sell the Beetle.

No, she put that out of her mind. But she was still thinking about what the man said. About his being an intermediary.

This woman, Peaflower. Perhaps she has an intermediary of sorts. Someone who can help her find the men, and who can set up a meeting. Perhaps that was a matchmaker, as they had guessed initially, or perhaps it was a friend or acquaintance.

But who?

She pushed through the double doors, offering a deep *wai* and the bananas to the *Hing Phra* Buddha shrine just inside.

One of the girls greeted her, seeming genuinely pleased to see her. She ran to get the mamasan. Then Kittiya—Ya—brought a cool towel and a glass of tea, and Ladarat thanked her.

But Ya didn't leave. She simply knelt on the floor, just out of reach. She didn't say anything but seemed to be waiting expectantly.

In all of her visits, Ladarat had never spent much time with the girls alone. Now she wasn't sure what to say.

It wasn't that she had moral objections to prostitution. It wasn't that the girls were doing anything wrong. And yet Ladarat had always found it difficult to live and let live when it came to the sex industry. Too much bad happens as a result of all the money that it creates. The abductions, the drugs. No, Thailand should do away with it. At least as much as it's possible to do away with something like that.

But that would be harder here than almost anywhere else in the world. Not just because of the *farang* who come here, but because of the way the population accepts prostitutes here. So many work to support family members, and they're honored. A woman like Ya who works for five years in Chiang Mai to put her younger brother through school, and who builds a house for her parents, and buys them a herd of buffalo...

Well, what can you say about someone like that except that she has made much merit? Back in the village they worship her. It would take an ordinary businessman a lifetime to earn that amount of respect and merit for charitable works.

Ya was crouched a few feet away, looking at her expectantly. Ladarat took a sip of the tea and thought about what a detective would do. A detective, she decided in an instant, would ask a routine question to put the person at ease.

"Please, Khun. Keep me company."

Ya rose and sat primly on the edge of a chair, keeping her head respectfully below Ladarat's. Still, she said nothing.

"And where are you from, Khun?" she asked the girl.

"Ah, I'm from Mai Charim District, in Isaan."

"Yes, that is beautiful country. Very peaceful." Ya nodded and smiled. She seemed to be coming to a decision to speak.

"And so..." Ya said hesitantly.

Ladarat nodded encouragement and took a sip of tea.

"The mamasan says that you are not only a nurse, but you are now a detective." She seemed suddenly wide-eyed with admiration. "How does one get to be a detective, can you tell me?"

Ladarat smiled and almost laughed, but caught herself just in time. And besides, it would not do to have people talking about her detection work. It was bad enough that Peaflower was aware. Even worse, what if Khun Tippawan were to find out? No, some activities are best kept quiet.

"No," she said firmly. "I am hardly a detective. I am a nurse, it's true. But as for the detective part...well..."

She wasn't a detective, that was for certain. But she wasn't *not* a detective, if that made any sense. Or she wasn't *not* a detective in the same way that, say, the fruit seller on the corner was not a detective. She was, perhaps, a little closer to the detective end of the spectrum than to the not-detective end. But that wouldn't help her answer the girl's question.

"No," she said finally. "I'm not a detective. I'm just assisting the police in a routine investigation. I won't be arresting anyone." She smiled. "And I certainly won't be sending them to prison."

"But that's all right, I didn't want to become a detective," the girl said.

Well, that was good. But then why was Ya looking at her expectantly? Slowly she began to think through the possible options. She didn't want to become a detective and so...

"So you want to become...a nurse?"

The girl's plain face lit up in a smile. She nodded.

"I've always wanted to become a nurse. My mother wanted to as well, but her family didn't have the money to send her to school. My parents didn't have the money either but, well..." She waved her tiny hand at the room around her.

"I've been here for two years and the mamasan makes me put half of what I earn in the bank. Half! Can you believe it? At first I thought it was a joke. But at the end of the first month, I realized how much I was saving, and now that my brother has passed his exams, I can send myself to nursing school." She paused. "But..."

"Yes, Khun?"

That seemed to give her encouragement.

"But I don't know if I have the right...temperament to be a nurse. I believe I am able to learn—I always did well in school. But would I...fit in, do you think?"

Ladarat smiled and tried to appear very, very serious. In truth, it took the best Thai traits of patience and flexibility and diplomacy to work in both jobs, she thought. She was pleasantly distracted for a moment by how Khun Tippawan, the Director of Excellence, might greet this assessment. And further, by that shrewish woman's reaction if Ladarat were to suggest to her that she might have a future in the sex industry. She couldn't suppress a smile.

"I think..." she said.

"Yes?"

"I think I would need to know more about you from the mamasan, but I think perhaps you could be a very fine nurse. And if she agrees, I would be pleased to write you a letter of reference."

"Oh, Khun, thank you!"

And Ya offered her a deep *wai*, and then another, backing across the room. Then she ran skipping down the hallway to the back stairs.

It was astonishing how little it took to give genuine happiness to someone else. That sort of happiness had a very low price. Especially if that person deserved something good. That seemed to make true happiness even less expensive somehow.

She sat pondering this truism for a few moments when another girl she hadn't met materialized next to her chair.

This girl was hauntingly beautiful, with long black hair and white skin, and a willowy grace that reminded Ladarat of the palm trees that she and Somboon saw on their honeymoon on Koh Samui.

She offered a *wai* and crouched down next to Ladarat, keeping her head well below Ladarat's. For a terrifying moment, Ladarat thought that this girl, too, wanted to go to nursing school. What were the odds of that? And perhaps the entire house wanted to go to nursing school. All dozen or so girls. What would she do then?

But fortunately the girl told her that the mamasan asked her to come back to her office. Then she rose, as fluid and as graceful as a giraffe. Ladarat followed her as she glided down the hallway, feeling clumsy and oafish by comparison.

Her cousin was waiting for her and gave her a hug. Ladarat took a seat across from her cousin's desk as the girl glided out and closed the door. The office was small and cramped but comfortable. There was the small desk, made of smooth, glossy teak. And plain white paneling lined the walls. On those walls were pictures—most in color—of more than a hundred girls. All of them had worked at the Tea House at one time or another. And most, Ladarat was pretty sure, had gone on to better things.

That was one accomplishment that Siriwan prided herself on. She really thought of her Tea House as a sort of finishing school that would give girls a leg up in the world. They'd emerge after a few years with more savings than many Thais amass in a lifetime, a decent command of English and perhaps some French or German, and the ability to carry themselves with poise and elegance. That was her dream, anyway.

And mostly her girls followed that dream. But there were a few pictures that were turned toward the wall. Not many—perhaps half a dozen. But enough to show that Siriwan wasn't always successful. Ladarat had asked her once what had happened with those girls, but her cousin had said only that they broke the rules. That was all. There was no room at the Tea House for girls who were disrespectful or dishonest or who broke the rules. (But neither, she was quick to point out, was there any place at all for men who did the same thing. Jonah would see to that.)

"So," Ladarat said. "Have you learned anything?"

Her cousin was strangely hesitant. She was always the outgoing one, and was hardly shy. And yet she seemed reluctant to speak. And there was her choice to meet back here in her office, with the door closed behind them. Yes, she definitely seemed nervous. But why?

"I may have some information for you." She paused. "Or I know someone who may have some information. But, cousin, you must promise me that you will be very careful."

"Careful?"

"You are working as a detective, but...you know you are *not* a detective, right? I mean to say, you know not to take the sorts of silly risks that a real detective would take?"

Ladarat nodded. She knew. "I'm no detective, I know that. I'm merely helping our friend Khun Wiriya."

Her cousin smiled, relieved. "Good. I was worried that perhaps you might be taking this too seriously. As you take all of your work." She smiled again, but not unkindly. It was a joke between the two of them, that despite the fact that her cousin was the mamasan at a brothel, devoted to pleasure and good times, she had always been Ladarat's equal in terms of seriousness. Serious in terms of her business acumen, for instance. And both serious and ferocious in her protection of her girls.

"Well, in that case, I can tell you about a woman who might be able to help you. She runs a brothel that is not so law-abiding."

"How so?"

"I know there have been . . . complaints. Complaints of girls making videotapes of clients and selling them, for instance." She shook her head. "It is bad for our business. Very bad. It means the police look at us doubly carefully."

"But what might she know about this woman?"

Here her cousin looked worried.

"I don't know. She wouldn't tell me. But I will say that it was she who came to me."

"She did? But how?"

"I was making inquiries of other mamasans who run brothels that cater to Chinese men, and word got out. So she called me this afternoon, asking to meet me. I told her that I was actually asking for a friend, and she seemed reluctant at first. In fact, I thought she was going to hang up. But she agreed to meet with you."

"So this is good, no?"

But Siriwan was thoughtful. "I'm not sure. Yes, it could be helpful. And it is good that she came to me. It suggests . . ."

"That she has something that she wants to get off her chest."

Her cousin smiled. "Exactly so. Something she wants to get off her chest." She looked at Ladarat appreciatively. "Perhaps you are a good detective." She smiled. "But there is another possibility," she continued. "You must also consider that maybe she knows something, and that she wants to prevent you from asking questions. It is possible, cousin, that this is a trap."

"A trap?"

"Exactly so. Remember that there is murder involved. With serious penalties for anyone connected. If this mamasan is connected..."

"She could be scared."

"Indeed."

"So who is this woman?"

"Her name is Wipaporn Chakrabonse. She is ethnic Chinese and owns a bar right next to Dok Mai Market, on the river. She's the co-owner, actually. I heard that she got into business trouble a year ago and she had to bring on a partner who got her out of trouble. That's when things changed and I started hearing complaints."

"So what did she tell you about this woman we're looking for?"

"She wouldn't say over the phone. But she did say she'd meet you tomorrow night."

Her cousin didn't seem overjoyed to be able to convey this news.

"I think you should take Jonah," she said.

"But shouldn't he be here with you?"

"I can spare him for a night."

"No, there's really no need. I'm sure I'll be fine."

Ladarat's answer was a simple reflex. A natural reflex certainly. But when she stopped to consider the note that was now stored in her Beetle's glove box, she was less certain that this reflex was the wisest response.

Up to this point, Ladarat had assumed that the threat to her beloved Beetle came from Peaflower. But what if that threat came from this mamasan, Khun Wipaporn? Or from both of them, working together?

Should she reconsider the offer of a bodyguard?

But her cousin, who knew how stubborn Ladarat could be, did not press her case. Instead, she simply slid a piece of paper across the desk. It was Tea House stationery. Who had stationery made for a brothel? On it was the woman's name, Wipaporn Chakrabonse, and a number: 9283.

THE $30 RAMBUTAN

The fruit seller wasn't at his post. He'd left his cart unattended, which was strange. But presumably he knew that no one would take a mango uninvited. Even a *farang* would know better.

She was going to walk by, but a fresh pomelo salad with dried shrimp and sticky rice would be very good tonight. Pomelo—oversize, mild grapefruit—were almost always in season in Thailand. And with some dried shrimp from the corner 7-Eleven and some dried chilies, it made a foolproof meal. Even she could manage a pomelo salad. Ladarat took a look around for the owner and then stepped behind the cart, pulling out a plastic bag and selecting two of the ripest pomelo. She put two 20 baht notes under an avocado at the bottom of the pile, sticking out far enough to be seen by the fruit seller but not enough to tempt passersby who had sticky fingers.

She looked up to see a young blond man—a *farang*—standing in front of her. He was wearing a tank top and cutoff shorts, a White Sox baseball cap, and a three-day growth of beard. American. He was holding a fruit delicately between thumb and forefinger, head cocked to one side.

"What...is this?" Definitely American.

And probably a recent arrival. He hadn't been in Thailand very long if this was the first time he'd seen a rambutan. The golfball-size fruits with spikes were ubiquitous most of the year. But they took some work to open, and most *farang* didn't bother.

"It's a rambutan," she said.

If he was surprised by her near-perfect English, he didn't show it. Or perhaps he thought that all Thais spoke English as well as he did.

"Do you... eat it?"

For a moment she was confused by the strange American use of pronouns. Did *she* eat it? No. Too much work. Do other people? Most certainly. Otherwise, what on earth would it be doing sitting on a fruit seller's cart?

"You have to cut it open," she explained. "Then you eat the wedges inside and spit out the seeds."

The young man looked dubious. Then he handed over a bill: 1,000 baht.

She shook her head. "No, that's thirty dollars. Too much."

The young man smiled sheepishly. He reached into a pocket and pulled out a wad of maybe 5,000 baht in various denominations. She took the smallest note she could find—20 baht—and held it up. He nodded happily.

"Be careful about carrying that much money around," she warned him. "You have more than many people in this neighborhood earn in a month."

The young man's brows furrowed in concern, and she realized that he was really quite young. Maybe not even eighteen.

"But I thought Chiang Mai was safe?"

He also still didn't think there was anything unusual about having this conversation in fluent English with an apparent fruit seller, which showed just how out of his depth he was.

"It is very safe, compared to Bangkok or... Chicago." She smiled as the boy looked confused. She pointed at his hat. "The White Sox? Wrigley Field?" The kid nodded happily.

It must be nice to be so unfazed by events. If traveling halfway around the world and meeting someone who spoke perfect English, sold him a rambutan from a fruit stall, and talked about the White Sox had not affected this boy's outlook one bit, then what would?

There are people like that who are so trusting that the oddest events don't seem to register. And those people all seemed to come to Thailand as tourists.

The kid nodded uncertainly and ambled off down the street, the corner of a 1,000-baht note peeking from his back pocket. Yes, Chiang Mai was safe, and the chances that he would get mugged were very low. But fingers in these streets were quick and deft. The chances of that 1,000-baht note reaching its destination were slim indeed.

She tucked the boy's 20-baht note alongside hers and thought about leaving the fruit seller a note. Ah, well. Let him wonder.

CHAPTER 22

THE CASE OF THE FROWNING DURIAN

Ladarat was so pleased with that image of the fruit seller's pleasant surprise that at first she didn't notice the change that had overtaken her Beetle. She paused, with her fingers gripping the door handle. Looking down at the driver's seat.

That seat should have been empty, she knew. She was not sitting in that seat, so it should be empty. But it was not.

The seat was occupied by an object that looked vaguely familiar. It was an oblong fruitlike object, about eight inches in diameter, covered with short, sharp spikes. What registered in her mind was not the object so much as its eyes. Its face, actually. Its spikes had been carefully trimmed to create the appearance of a face.

That rudimentary face had small eyes, an even smaller nose, and what might charitably be described as a frown. And each of these facial landmarks seemed to be emphasized by holes that had been carved into the object. That's what she noticed first—that there was a frowning face staring up at her from the driver's seat of her Beetle. Even in light of the oddness-to-date of her week, this struck her as being rather unusual. One did not generally find such things in one's car. Even in the busy, surprising life of a detective, she imagined, such things were unusual.

Her brain did not immediately register the nature of the

fruit that had been artistically enhanced. Actually, it's safe to say that her brain did not register the fruit's identity at all. That detective work was performed by her nose.

Even with the car door closed, and the windows rolled up, her Beetle was surrounded by a thick miasma of smell that was a mixture of putrefying garbage, raw sewage, and rotten eggs. If that scent were visible, it would perhaps look like the ripply emanations that you see blanketing a hot parking lot. Ripples and waves of a smell that could only come from one perpetrator. In that moment, her nose realized that her beloved Beetle had been vandalized by a durian.

Of course, Ladarat was not intimately familiar with the rigors of crime and detection. There were many things she did not know, and indeed would never know. And yet, in this one instance, she was quite certain of one thing: This could only be a threat.

Even with no knowledge of the criminal mind, the combination of the note earlier that afternoon, and the frowning durian, she recognized with total clarity that she was being warned away from the Peaflower case. That was her first thought.

The second thought took longer to form, but she had time. Plenty of time.

Ladarat carefully opened the driver's-side door and picked up the offending fruit, then walked very fast about twenty meters to a trash can. The street was almost deserted and no one gave her a second glance as she deposited the fruit, its frowning face positively glaring at her as it fell backward to its doom.

Ladarat opened both of the Beetle's windows, and also the little triangular windows on either side of the dashboard. There was very little breeze, but there was some. Her Beetle would air out in time. So she waited, leaning against the hood. She waited, and she thought.

She did not need to think much about the meaning of this threatening fruit. Its significance should be clear to even an obtuse observer. Even to someone who knew nothing about detection and the criminal mind. So she didn't think about the fact—and indeed it was truly a fact, if ever there was one—that this was a warning.

Nor, at first, did she think about whether she should heed that warning. That is, she did not think seriously about whether she should give up on the Peaflower case.

No, as she waited for her beloved Beetle to smell a little less like it had been filled with a week's worth of rotting garbage, she thought about who might have done this. She thought very, very hard about this question.

There was, obviously, Peaflower herself. She could have left that note on her windshield, and the durian on the driver's seat. That would be the simplest answer.

And yet, there was a problem with that theory. If Peaflower were the durian perpetrator, then how did she know? How could Peaflower possibly know that she, Ladarat Patalung, was tracking her down? Ladarat pondered that question for several minutes, without appreciable results.

She sighed, stood up, and leaned in through the open passenger-side window. The durian's aftereffects were still quite strong. Overpowering, really. So she had more time to think.

Her thoughts, unfortunately, were not very productive. At least, they were not productive in the sense that they provided her with answers. Yet they were highly productive in the sense that they succeeded in making her very nervous.

Because she realized that this episode of fruit-based intimidation could only have happened in one of two ways. First, and perhaps most likely, Peaflower had learned of her detective activities and was trying to warn her away. That, Ladarat knew, meant that someone had told Peaflower about those detective activities. That is to say, Peaflower had an accomplice. Several accomplices, perhaps.

These would presumably be accomplices who knew about Ladarat's activities. People who knew about them, and conveyed the news of Ladarat's investigation to Peaflower. That was troubling, because there were very few people who knew about Ladarat's activities. Detective Mookjai, of course. And Ladarat's cousin. Both were beyond suspicion. That left Panit Booniliang, the hardworking medical records clerk and cricket aficionado. He should also be beyond suspicion, should he not?

The very impossibility that these three individuals might have warned Peaflower led Ladarat inevitably to a second possibility, which was equally implausible. Perhaps one of these accomplices had actually done the warning. That is, one of these accomplices had placed the note on her windshield and the frowning durian in her Beetle. They might be protecting Peaflower, or if their role in her crimes was substantial, they might be protecting themselves. Yet that seemed inconceivable.

That left a third possibility—that it was the mamasan Wipaporn Chakrabonse who had discovered Ladarat's investigation and was warning her away. And that, Ladarat knew, had to be the case. It was the only logical explanation.

But was Khun Wipaporn acting on her own to protect herself? Or was she working with Peaflower to protect both of them?

That was the most important question. If the mamasan was interested primarily in protecting herself, then perhaps she might be open to persuasion. She might even be willing to give evidence to save herself.

But if the mamasan and Peaflower were working together... well... that was very bad. If that were the case, then Ladarat suspected that her meeting tomorrow night with Khun Wipaporn would be a trap.

Ladarat poked her head through the passenger-side window once again. She noted a slight improvement. But driving, she thought, would still expose her to toxic levels of durian fumes. She resolved to wait a few more minutes.

As she settled back into position on the Beetle's hood, she had two thoughts more or less simultaneously. The first was that she should inform Detective Mookjai of these latest... developments. He would want to know.

But it was as she was reaching for her mobile phone in her bag that she had the second thought. And this was a thought that froze her right hand in mid-reach. If someone had left a note on her car, and had left a frowning piece of fruit in that same car, on the same day, then that someone must be... following her. And in all likelihood, someone was watching her right now.

Ladarat tried to maintain a calm demeanor for the benefit of this unseen watcher. A watcher who, hopefully, could not see her hand trembling. She took out her mobile and dialed the detective's number. As she did, Ladarat scanned her surroundings in a way that she hoped was surreptitious. That is, in the way that a detective might scan her surroundings to identify watchers. Because if ever there was a proper time to behave like a detective—even if one was not—this was such a time.

Perhaps her observations were surreptitious, but they were not productive. Her scan of the darkening street and shuttered shops revealed only two dogs poised at the end of an alley, a group of three schoolgirls heading home, and a young *farang* couple holding hands and looking around at the closed shops in wonder, as if this were the most exciting street they'd ever walked down.

Ladarat pushed aside a twinge of something that could only be called jealousy. She remembered when she and Somboon were like that, many years ago. Wherever they were was the best place they had ever been, because their future was glowing so brightly.

None of these individuals, however, could possibly be Peaflower's accomplice. So if Ladarat was being watched—and she had to assume that she was—then she was being watched rather expertly. By someone, presumably, who was very talented at watching. And that sort of person was not a person to be trifled with.

The detective didn't answer, and so Ladarat left a brief message explaining that someone had placed a note on her Beetle, warning her away. She left out the information about the durian, although she couldn't say why she omitted it. It seemed both silly and frightening at the same time. She wasn't sure whether to make it into a joke, or to grant it the gravity that perhaps the threat deserved. So she said nothing.

As Ladarat put her mobile away, she stuck her head in through the passenger-side window one more time, hoping that perhaps the fumes had dissipated. They were slightly reduced but were by no means gone. At this rate, she would be here all night. So, taking a deep breath, she opened the driver's-side door and got in, hoping that if she drove fast enough, she might encourage the fumes to leave.

By reflex, as she was pulling away from the curb, she turned to wave at the fruit seller. It was only then that she realized that the good man was still not there. The whole time she had been waiting for the durian's effects to wane, he had not been at his post. And it was now well past seven. Normally he'd be packing up about now.

So where was he? And did his extended absence have anything to do with the frowning durian? That was too much to try to figure out. Particularly on an empty stomach.

One should never try to think too hard on an empty stomach. Particularly about matters of ethics and morality.

So she would go home, driving as rapidly as safety permitted. With her head out the window if need be. And she would make herself a pomelo salad. And she would think about recent developments. And she would decide whether to continue with her activities of detection.

CHAPTER 23

ONE SHOULD NOT BLAME FRUIT FOR OUR DISAPPOINTMENTS

The pomelo salad had not been quite as good as Ladarat had imagined it would be. In large part, that failure could be attributed to the aftereffects of driving home, marinating in the stink of durian. It proved to be difficult indeed to work up any appetite under those conditions.

But on further reflection, she had to admit that disappointment was inevitable if you try to imagine how things would be. You get an idea in your head of how nice a fresh pomelo salad would be, and then you start filling in details. Just how crunchy the fruit would be, with a very specific tartness. And you imagine just how spicy the chilies would be. And it's all wonderful until you take that first bite. Then it's not what you imagined and somehow that makes it less good.

If you had no expectations, that bite might have been wonderful. You would be pleasantly surprised. But if you had those expectations, then the event itself was bound to be a disappointment, if for no other reasons than it was different. That failure was not the fault of the pomelo—one should not blame fruit for one's disappointments. So as a general rule, you should be careful what you expect, since that will determine how happy you'll be.

And Ladarat was not happy. There were too many things to worry about. And—what was worse—she was worrying about what she needed to worry about. Like the inspection, of course. And Director Tippawan. And then there was Peaflower. And the durian and a car that smelled as though a large forest animal had died in its front seat.

What should she be doing to better prepare for the inspection? What could she be doing?

And what should she be doing to catch Peaflower? And should she be doing anything at all?

And there was the man in the ICU waiting room. She needed to do something—anything—to solve that problem before the inspectors arrived.

And her smelly Beetle...

Eeeehhh. It was enough to make her want to quit her job and go back to being a regular nurse. She would care for patients during her shifts, and then she would go home. She would do her job, and do it well. And she would go about her life. She would read books and buy strawberries, and drink tea. She would do what normal people did. What Khun Duanphen advised her to do. She would not work so hard, and she would not think so much. *Sabai sabai.*

Yet...that would be boring, would it not? And besides, it was difficult to remain unhappily worried for very long. After all, this was the perfect time of day, with the best possible Chiang Mai weather. *Maewfawbaahn* was asleep, the night was cool enough to need a sweater, a thin gray wool cardigan that was one of her favorites.

As Ladarat let go of her worries, she found, as she often did, that her thoughts meandered along of their own volition. Those thoughts didn't seem to move in straight lines but instead went forward and backward, crisscrossing one another in unpredictable ways. Sometimes they moved slowly and sometimes so fast that she couldn't keep up. But they moved. That was the thing about thoughts. They would work hard for you if you just let them do what they want to do.

Tonight, several thoughts were rambling around in her head. There was the Peaflower investigation, of course. And the question of whether she should give it up. She let those thoughts go where they would. Perhaps she would solve the case. Or perhaps she would decide not to solve it. Either seemed like a good outcome of thinking. So she let those thoughts wander off to wherever it was they wanted to go.

That left her to think about other thoughts that were less freighted by worry. And indeed, it was in moments like these that Ladarat found that she could think about expectations and happiness with the detachment of a philosopher. That was the best definition of luxury she could imagine—to think about things because you wanted to, not because you had to.

There was that young man who bought the rambutan. His expectations, it seemed, were almost nonexistent. He was surprised by nothing. He was, she was certain, a happy sort.

But he also didn't notice things. His expectations were so vague and ill-formed that nothing struck him as odd or unusual. She smiled. An elephant could amble down Praisanee Road along the Ping River, and that young man would probably take it in stride. He might not even notice.

That vision of an elephant wandering past a 7-Eleven on the river road led her to think about the wary country man outside the ICU. He was also a foreigner in a strange land, just as the American was. If he saw an elephant, he wouldn't be surprised. He might even feel relieved. Here was something that was familiar. But everything else was foreign to him. He was nervous. And wary.

But what about these men who were being murdered? She knew that her thoughts would turn back to that case eventually, whether she wanted them to or not. That's the way thoughts worked.

What about those men? What did they expect? For this to happen again and again, without anyone sounding the alarm, they must all be like the young American. They must be wide-eyed and unsurprised by anything.

But where would Peaflower find such men? How could she reliably locate men who would be unfazed by whatever she did to them? Unsurprised by whatever requests she made regarding life insurance?

That was when Ladarat had the insight of a true detective.

She thought about the wide-eyed American and the man in the ICU waiting room and the distance between them. The sort of trust she'd seen in the boy this afternoon was for the young. An older man, particularly one in a strange environment, like that man in the ICU or these Chinese men, would be cautious. He might be stupid. But he would notice things. He would be paying attention.

So it followed that this woman, Peaflower, was very, very clever. She was leading these men down a very carefully tended path. They were seeing what they expected to see. She'd eliminated any unpleasant surprises. If they expected elephants prancing down Praisanee Road, then she gave them elephants.

Ladarat pondered that for a while as *Maewfawbaahn* purred comfortably on the chair next to her.

But what did that mean? How could Peaflower do that? How could she give these men exactly what they expected?

And—a related but more important question: How would she get these men to do what she wanted them to do?

DAVID CASARETT, M.D.

Ladarat tried to put herself in the position of a Chinese man who had met—somehow—a woman. How might that happen in such a way that these men were led along smoothly and effortlessly?

It would have to be like a mahout leading an elephant. Her father had told her once that the mahouts didn't actually tell an elephant where to go or what to do. A 50-kilogram man can't tell a 1,500-kilogram beast what to do. The beast would laugh at the man. If elephants could laugh, that elephant would certainly do so.

But a clever mahout can make an elephant *want* to do something. A clever mahout can guide the elephant's expectations. A clever mahout can induce the elephant to think that kneeling, or raising a leg, or moving to one side is exactly what the elephant wants to do.

That, Ladarat was certain, was what Peaflower was doing. Somehow, she was setting up situations and expectations in such a way that these men thought it was the most natural thing in the world to sign over their money to her.

And that conclusion led Ladarat to an unexpected decision. If these men were making choices of their own volition, they were not victims in the usual sense. They were... volunteers.

And as Professor Dalrymple cautions, we must always respect people, even if we don't agree with the choices they make. That is, we must respect the values that underlie that choice, and the person to which those values are connected, even if we think the choice that person is making is unwise, or even dangerous.

These men were choosing to trust this Peaflower woman. Ladarat was convinced of that. They were walking into this situation with their eyes wide open. They were making a choice to trust her.

188

And the voluntary nature of these choices, she decided, placed them outside her area of responsibility as an ethical detective. She could not pursue an investigation of them any more than she would question the free and informed choice of a patient, no matter how unwise. And no matter what the consequences.

Instead, she would call Khun Wiriya in the morning. She would tell him that she could no longer try to be a detective in this case. The notes would cease, her Beetle would be safe, and perhaps eventually she would forget the smell of a ripe durian. And she would devote herself to the upcoming inspection and to her work as an ethicist. That is, she would be a nurse and an ethicist only. Surely those were enough titles for one person?

Maewfawbaahn rose and stretched his cat muscles. Then, without pausing to look at her, he paced regally toward the back door, knowing that she would follow. As she did. That cat had an excellent sense of when it was time to stop thinking and go to bed.

Just inside the back door on the small kitchen counter, her mobile phone was blinking, signaling that a text had arrived. Ladarat's first thought was that the message was from Khun Wiriya, and her heart gave a little skip of excitement. But then, just as quickly, she thought she might just ignore that message. She was not a detective anymore, was she? She was not. She would devote her time to being an ethicist, as she should.

But maybe this late-night text was related to her ethical duties? What if there were an ethical emergency? They did happen, she knew.

Eventually her sense of duty won. As she was picking up her mobile, Ladarat pondered the strange thought that only a few days ago, she would have assumed that any late-night communication was just such an ethical emergency. A patient who wanted to leave the hospital against medical advice, for instance. Or a family that disagreed about the best course of treatment for a child. But now, strangely, her first thought was of murders and mysteries and detection. Well, that would change.

It was largely thanks to that conversation in her head that Ladarat was almost smiling as she read the brief text from Khun Tippawan, instructing her to be at the hospital promptly at 8 A.M., to do the job for which she was hired.

The text was brief and impolite, as was usual for the director. And for texts in general, Ladarat supposed. And yet she found herself smiling.

Because that was exactly what she would do. She had already come to that decision herself, although perhaps she hadn't entirely realized it. Now she did. Ladarat would arrive at Sriphat Hospital early. And she would work late. And she would be an ethicist only.

Wan suk

FRIDAY

CHAPTER 24

THE LEAPING PEN

Dr. Jainukul was nervous. More nervous, even, than he'd been when he first asked for Ladarat's help with the American. Now he was fiddling with a pen—rolling it over his hand as if he'd trained it to do some strange gymnastic routine. It might look clever to an American, but she recognized it as a rare and entirely unintentional display of nerves that—she guessed—the confident director was convinced he'd successfully concealed from the world.

Of course she would humor him. It would be worse by far to cause him to lose face by asking him if he was nervous. And asking him would be pointless. Because who wouldn't be nervous, sitting here in the ICU conference room, about to discuss what to do with Mr. Fuller?

At least Mr. Fuller's family wasn't here. Ladarat had suggested that the director might want to meet with the other doctors and nurses first, before he spoke with the family. And she'd wanted to have this meeting early. Khun Tippawan would hear of the meeting and she would know that she, Ladarat Patalung, was once more a full-time ethicist.

Besides, it was important to have a meeting, and to have it as soon as possible. You must always know what you think in advance of any formal discussion with the Fullers, she told him, quoting the wise Professor Dalrymple. You must know

193

what you think, and you must be clear about what you know, and what you don't know. A meeting with the Fullers would not be the time to argue among themselves. Much better to discuss the issues thoroughly in private first, which was why they were having this meeting in a fourth-floor conference room, far away from the ICU.

She'd learned that lesson in Chicago, and of course from Professor Dalrymple. But in fact it was a rule that was not terribly useful here in Thailand. Indeed, there was usually little room for discussion. The director would decide, and others would agree. That was the way Thai culture solved problems. It was always better to agree about a bad solution than to disagree about a good one. And it was always better to agree with your director, so they would.

"I've reviewed the results of all of the scans one more time," he was telling the group. "And I see no cause for optimism."

The small assembled group was listening intently, although in truth there was very little the director was saying that was new. The director sat at the head of the table, next to the ICU fellow—an ICU specialist in training. Ukrit Wattana was a tall man, for a Thai. With sharp cheekbones and square black glasses, he looked like an awkward adolescent who hadn't quite grown up. But he was very intense and respectful. And people said he was very smart. That he would take over as the ICU Director one day.

The tough head nurse came next, across from the ICU administrator, who was a nice woman, and pleasantly competent, but who was unlikely to have any opinion whatsoever.

They were all quiet, showing respect by listening. Not like the Americans she met in Chicago. To show respect and agreement, they talked, generally saying the same thing that the most senior person has said, but in a different way. In the

United States, an important person's opinion is like a stone dropped into a small pool—it creates waves that echo back and forth endlessly. Such a noisy waste of time.

In Thai culture, we show respect by listening. By being quiet. That's not better, really. But Thai meetings are generally much more peaceful. And shorter.

Next to Ladarat, Sisithorn was sitting quietly, taking notes. She had taken extra time with her appearance this morning, hadn't she? More than usual perhaps. And today her hair had been brushed out instead of corralled in a bun, the way Ladarat wore hers.

For a moment, Ladarat was just a little offended that her assistant should find her own style. But, of course, that was silly. Especially since Ladarat would be the first to admit that no one with any sense whatsoever should emulate her style. That road to fashion led nowhere.

It took a moment for Ladarat to notice the other difference. Her glasses. Sisithorn wasn't wearing her glasses. Had she gotten contacts? She would find a way to ask carefully. Surreptitiously. As a detective would.

"It has been six days since his accident, and there is no meaningful sign of recovery." The director paused, and his right hand juggling his pen picked up its tempo.

"We've tried to reduce his sedation every day for the last two days in hopes of improving his level of consciousness, but without effect."

Now the pen was flipping over his hand like that migrating fish—a salmon?—leaping out of the water of a river again and again to swim upstream.

"And the brain scan of yesterday shows no significant swelling that could be the cause of his lack of responsiveness," he continued. "So... are there any questions?"

Here the pen escaped gravity entirely, whirring through the air to land in the lap of the ICU administrator, who, smiling and blushing, delicately placed the pen in front of the director without shifting her attention. Everyone around the table laughed.

"Thank you, Khun." He smiled at the table in embarrassment and picked up the pen. But when the administrator edged backward in her chair, the director covered the pen with his hands, making a little tent. He seemed almost relieved that his migrating pen had been trapped.

"So it's my recommendation that we tell his parents and his wife that there is nothing else we can do to prolong his life." Then, to Ladarat's considerable surprise, he turned to her.

"What sort of reaction do you think we can expect, Khun Ladarat? You have lived in America. You have seen these sorts of discussions before. You are more American than we are. What do you think they might say?"

More American? Odd that she'd never thought of herself as American at all. But the director meant it as a compliment. Didn't he?

Ladarat thought for a moment. What indeed? They would not be pleased, she knew that much. And they would be reluctant to agree to stop treatment. But the reason was difficult to put into words that would not cause offense.

"This will be a shock to them, of course," she said hesitantly. "A very great shock."

"But it is obvious that he is dying," Dr. Wattana said. He turned first to the director, and then back to Ladarat. "Isn't it?"

"Yes," she agreed. "It's obvious enough to us. But sometimes...it takes some time for your heart to catch up with what your head knows to be true."

As Professor Dalrymple said, we use our heads to make decisions for ourselves, but we use our hearts to make decisions for our loved ones.

Dr. Wattana seemed as though he was ready to argue, but the director laid a restraining hand on his shoulder.

"I see. So you think they may need more time to . . . come to terms?"

Did they? That was part of it. But not all of it.

"They may need more time, it's true. But . . ."

"But they may not trust our opinion," the director said, finishing her thought for her.

"Exactly so," she said, relieved that it she did not need to say what they all knew.

Dr. Wattana looked as though he was going to argue, but again the director laid a hand on the young man's shoulder.

"Of course they may not trust that he will get the best care here. Why would they? This is a small city in a small country, halfway around the world from the United States. How could he know that he will get the finest care here?"

Everyone around the table thought about that for a moment.

"Well, we cannot convince them that we provide excellent care. They will need to see that for themselves. And then perhaps their experts back in the U.S. will review our records and will agree.

"But," he continued, "perhaps you could meet with the wife this afternoon? Just to see what she is thinking?"

The director was looking at Ladarat with eyes that flicked back and forth in an unbecoming way over a fixed, wooden *yim haeng* smile. It was the dry, slightly apologetic smile that you would offer when you are asking someone to do something that you know is not right. Or, say, when you are asking for a loan of baht that you know you cannot pay back."

She nodded. "Of course I will."

She sighed. Of course. This case was full of all the kinds of discomfort and awkwardness that Thais hated. But if she could act like an American and put those anxieties about conflict behind her for a few minutes, then of course she was the right person to talk to the Americans. Besides, who else would?

The director smiled a genuine smile. A true smile of relief as if a weight had been removed from his shoulders. As indeed it had.

And Ladarat smiled, too. It was good to be an ethicist again. Just an ethicist.

"Then it is agreed that you will talk to the wife." He looked at his watch. "It is two P.M. She is in the ICU and should be leaving soon. Perhaps you could talk to her in the waiting room as she leaves? Perhaps ... perhaps you could help her to trust us, just a little more?"

Ladarat agreed that she would, but she knew that more trust wasn't the only answer. It was true that the Fullers had no reason to trust Thai medicine, but even if they did, they would not give up so easily on a young man. All the trust in the world wouldn't induce people like this American family to make that decision before they had to.

But she couldn't explain this easily to her colleagues around the table. They were being logical and reasonable, she knew. It's just that this wasn't a situation in which logic and reason were likely to be particularly helpful. They were thinking with their heads, as Professor Dalrymple would have said, but the Fullers were thinking with their hearts. So instead she nodded and said that she would do her best.

Trust. Ladarat pondered that as the meeting adjourned. No, the Americans would most certainly not trust Thai doctors, just as she'd said. And that made her think of something else... but no sooner had her brain registered the presence of another thought waiting in the wings than that thought vanished. But she felt that there was something, somewhere, that she was missing.

CHAPTER 25

THE NATIONAL THAI SLOGAN

The meeting had officially ended, but Ladarat knew with the certainty of experience that there would be chatting and gossiping. Especially if there was tea left. She'd seen meetings like this trail off over an hour. Call it traditional Thai laziness, and to a *farang* that's what it would look like.

But it was deeper than that. Thai culture was not well suited to modern medicine, with its rules and requirements. And, above all, its demanding pace. Everything else about the Western world—law, tourism, even business—could be made to fit the relaxed, easygoing Thai view of life. But medicine wouldn't fit.

Especially when people work together for the benefit of others, as in medicine, relationships matter. You cannot be in a hurry. You cannot rush past the formalities of greeting and inquiring after another's health. If you hurry past those niceties, you pass by the structure that allows us to work together.

But after ten minutes of such conversation, Ladarat decided that she needed to leave. She touched Sisithorn's elbow and steered her quietly out of the room and down the hall. They didn't have time for endless discussion today. Sisithorn apparently was thinking the same thing, and she turned to the right as they left the conference room, heading toward the ICU.

"So I talked with the young Mrs. Fuller, as you suggested, Khun." Sisithorn was nodding as she spoke, but she seemed puzzled about where to start.

"And so what did you talk about?" They'd reached the elevator, and this one was usually very slow. So they had some time. But not much.

"Well, she was born in Ann Arbor? Ann Arbor. Yes. It is in..."

"Michigan," Ladarat suggested.

"Yes, Khun. I believe that is correct. Michigan. She grew up there, and her parents had both taught at the university there. That is where she and her husband met. They were both graduate students there."

"And what else did you learn about her family?"

"His studies focused on business. Business administration, I think she said? And she studied international relations. Diplomacy? Yes, diplomacy, I think that was it."

"But what of her family? Surely there is someone?" A good thing the elevator was so slow. It would take hours for Sisithorn to get to the point.

"Ah, but that is difficult."

That was when she knew why Sisithorn had hesitated. It wasn't that she didn't know what was important. It was that she'd stumbled on an awkward topic. But what?

Ladarat had only a moment to wonder about what might be causing her assistant such distress before she was distracted by the sight of a flowering bush that materialized next to them. The bush was not really a bush, of course. It was an enormous bouquet. The biggest Ladarat had ever seen—so tall that the

DAVID CASARETT, M.D.

crowning orchid brushed the ceiling. And so wide that its bulk completely hid the person carrying it. Ladarat glimpsed only a pair of thin, pale forearms grasping the basket, the left one of which was adorned by an enormous gold watch.

The mobile bouquet hovered there, just to Sisithorn's left, as if it, too, were waiting for the elevator. But Ladarat was almost certain that this bouquet was not interested in taking the elevator.

Ladarat wasn't sure why she felt uneasy, but that young man's reappearances were strange. Very strange. This was a large hospital, and to encounter the same person so many times was not consistent with chance. Then she thought of the note on her car, and the durian. She thought of those things and she became very worried.

Was this young man working with Peaflower? Was he here to threaten her?

Her mind entertained other, wilder possibilities, too. Like perhaps this young man was an advance spy sent by the Royal Hospital Inspection Committee. She'd heard of such things. And indeed, that would be a relief. At least that was something that she was familiar with. But Ladarat knew that a far likelier explanation was that this man was an accomplice of Peaflower's.

Ladarat peered around the shrubbery to confirm that this was indeed the young man she'd encountered several times before. She nodded, satisfied, just as Sisithorn opened her mouth to ask what on earth she was doing.

"Come this way," she told Sisithorn.

"But the elevator will come if we wait," Sisithorn said, confused.

Of course she would say that. That could be the national Thai slogan.

202

"The stairs are faster," Ladarat said simply as she marched farther down the hallway.

Sisithorn was lagging behind and Ladarat was pretty sure she'd stopped in her tracks. She couldn't hear the click of Sisithorn's heels on the tile floor behind her, but she smiled and marched on.

"Come along," she said over her shoulder. "We have work to do."

As she'd expected, Sisithorn caught up with her, click-click-clicking in her hurry not to be left behind. The only force in Thailand stronger than a benign laziness was the intense and all-encompassing fear of missing something. So they pushed through the door to the stairwell together.

Sisithorn looked at her for a split second as Ladarat held the door open for her.

"Is this a habit you learned in Chicago, Khun?" she asked.

Ladarat smiled. Perhaps she was more American than she'd thought. Maybe the director had been right. Maybe she was at least a little bit American. And was that such a bad thing? Well, yes. It probably was.

"It's only two flights," Ladarat pointed out. "And we can talk as we go." She waved her hand at the empty space around them. "And we have complete privacy," she pointed out.

Sisithorn seemed to be thinking as they climbed in silence up half a flight of stairs and then they reached the fifth-floor landing. Ladarat was perhaps breathing a little heavily. Not that she was short of breath, of course. But a little faster than usual. Just a little.

Actually, she checked the pulse in her wrist surreptitiously, holding both hands in front of her so Sisithorn could not see. One hundred and ten. Well, maybe that was a little high, but surely some elevation could be attributed to the excitement of going to see a patient, could it not? Of course it could. But they should stop to rest at the second landing. It wouldn't do to walk out into a busy hallway looking as though they'd just run a race across Chiang Mai.

"This is not difficult, is it?" Ladarat asked over her shoulder.

"No, Khun," Sisithorn gasped. "Not at all."

Ladarat smiled. Still, she slowed her pace so they would not embarrass each other by gasping like beached carp when they arrived. Slowly, one step at a time, they ascended the next flight and came to a stop at the landing. Sisithorn was breathing a little rapidly, too, Ladarat was pleased to note. In fact, she'd say they were about even, despite the fact that Ladarat was older by twenty years. So there.

"Now," she said as soon as she was breathing a little easier. "What is it that is difficult about the young American's family?"

"Ah, well you see, Khun, it seems as though she doesn't... have any family."

"No family? You said that she was put in foster care when her parents died. But surely she is close to them. And perhaps there are other family members?"

Sisithorn shook her head sadly. "Her foster parents died when she was in college. An auto accident, I believe."

"Aunts and uncles? Foster brothers and sisters?"

Again Sisithorn shook her head. "She said that she was... alone in the foster family. So her parents were the only family she had. And now..."

"Her husband's family is her family. Ah, that is difficult. So she has no one to support her. And no one to take her side if she disagrees with her husband's... family."

She almost said "her husband's father" since that was where

the trouble was likely to be. But that wouldn't do. There was nothing to be gained by assigning blame. The members of that American family were all grieving in their own ways.

And yet, the father had a very strong personality. Perhaps in some ways a replacement father for her. As the boy's mother was certainly filling that role. That would make things more difficult. But there was something even more important.

"Then she will need your support more than ever," Ladarat pointed out.

Sisithorn nodded. "I had the same thought. I will try to visit her every day, just to give her someone to talk with."

Ladarat nodded. They were both breathing more or less normally now. And she opened the door to the hallway that would take them to the ICU waiting room, ushering Sisithorn ahead of her.

That was done, then. And her assistant ethicist had done excellent work. But there was just one more question.

"Your hair, Khun...it looks nice. What made you decide to change it? Not that change is bad, of course—change is good. Or it can be good..." Oh dear. In that moment, Ladarat vowed that she would steer clear of discussions about fashion in the future.

"I always used to wear it like this," Sisithorn said. "Don't you remember?"

Ladarat didn't.

"But not since I've known you?"

"That's true, Khun," Sisithorn admitted. "I wanted...to be like you."

Imagine that. Her assistant had redone her hair when she took this position because she wanted to emulate her. Ladarat supposed she should feel offended that her assistant had now embraced a new style, but she was too overwhelmed by pleasant surprise to harbor any negative feelings. She never would have imagined that anyone would emulate her, and now this bright, energetic nurse ethicist had been doing so all along.

CHAPTER 26

A VERY SAD SITUATION

Still deep in thought about the implications of her assistant's new hairstyle, Ladarat didn't notice the strange man until they'd almost reached the sliding doors to the ICU. He was crouched against his familiar wall, again with a view of Doi Suthep mountain. He smiled at them a little uncertainly and gave a deep *wai*, which they both returned. Ladarat pointed at the doors.

"Perhaps you can go ahead," she said softly to Sisithorn. "You could bring the wife out here and we could talk in more quiet circumstances?" Sisithorn nodded, and then she disappeared into the ICU and the doors hissed closed behind her.

The man was looking at her strangely, with a mix of fear and respect that mystified her. Surely he recognized her? But then she realized that she'd put on her white coat for the meeting they'd just come from. Seeing her now in her professional outfit, the man was probably surprised. Perhaps he was intimidated, too. If he truly came from the hills, his experience with medical people would be very limited.

She greeted him warmly and sat on a chair nearby. Not too near, though. She sensed that getting close might spook him in the same way that getting too close to a wild animal might cause it to flee.

After greeting her, though, the man was silent and watchful. Not unfriendly, but cautious. And just like a wild animal would be, he seemed as though he'd be ready to turn and run at the slightest provocation. Ladarat guessed that a question—any question—might send him flying away. So she decided to talk instead. No questions or interrogation. She would just talk, and he could listen or not.

"I am here to see a man and his family," she said. "It is a sad situation. A very sad situation. He was injured, you see, and was taken here. But he and his family are *farang*. They are not from here," she clarified, unsure whether this man's rural vocabulary extended to tourist words like *farang*.

Perhaps it didn't. He was looking at her with a steady concentration that you might devote to thunderclouds boiling in the sky. A mix of fear and concern tinged with fascination.

"Have you heard of this man?" she asked.

In an instant he became flustered, looking down at the ground and then at the ICU doors, which remained shut. He rose to a crouch, and then stood up. But that put his head above hers, which was disrespectful, so he crouched down, bent almost double in a hurried *wai*. Ladarat stood, perplexed, and returned the *wai*.

Then he scurried quickly toward the long hallway, his bare feet slapping on the tile floor. She followed for a few steps, well behind him. Still perplexed by the departure, nevertheless she smiled as she saw that the long hallway was empty, just as she knew it would be.

But she didn't have much time to ponder that brief

conversation and its outcome. No sooner had the man disappeared than Sisithorn emerged pushing the young Mrs. Fuller. The American was looking up, and Sisithorn was leaning over and they were talking conspiratorially.

She needed to focus her attention. This would be a difficult conversation.

THE IMPATIENCE OF STEPPING-STONES

And indeed it was a difficult conversation. But not nearly as difficult as it could have been. The young American woman Kate had a view of her husband's chances that was realistic. Surprisingly so.

Perhaps her clear view of the future came from a lack of fear? You cannot plan well for a future that you're afraid of, Professor Dalrymple tells us. And many people facing the loss of a loved one are crippled by fear. So much so, in fact, that they can't imagine what life would be like without the person. So they hold on and they cling to the person's life. They won't let go, no matter how much that person—the patient—may be suffering.

But not Kate. No, she would miss her husband terribly, of course. Yet it seemed as though she was not afraid of what life would be like without him.

This young woman had been through so much in her short life that the prospect of losing a husband—although certainly tragic—didn't fill her with dread. She knew in her heart that life would go on. So although they didn't come to any decisions at their meeting, they had laid the groundwork, so to speak. And Kate would be able to let go when she needed to.

It had been time well spent. And work well done.

And yet as she sat in her small basement office, facing the

remaining piles of policies that were waiting patiently for her eyes, it did not feel like work well done. Or it did, she supposed, but just not enough. The meeting had gone well, she knew. And it had gone well at least in part thanks to her efforts. She had done some good, and she had helped the Fuller family.

Then why did she feel as though she was failing? Or not failing, exactly. But she felt as if she had stopped midway through a project.

It was the same sensation she had when she bought a row of twelve stepping-stones for her garden. It was around the time of the last Royal Inspection three years ago, was it not? She'd placed seven of them exactly so, but then she'd been caught up in work. And those remaining five stones nagged at her whenever she saw them. She knew in her mind that they were not urgent, those stones. They could wait. Stones may not have much to recommend them, but they do tend to be patient. And yet their unfinishedness nagged at her. Every time she was in her garden, sitting at her little wrought iron table, they chastised her for ignoring them.

"We're still waiting," they said. Sometimes loud enough that she was certain the neighbors would hear. *Maewfaw-baahn* certainly heard them. He would give those unfinished stones a wide berth in his perambulations and midnight prowlings.

But why should she be having this feeling now? As Ladarat asked herself that logical question, though, she knew the answer. She knew it with as much certainty as she knew what those stones were telling her.

She could say that she was an ethicist, and she was. But she was also a nurse, and nurses help people. That's what we do, she told herself. That's *why* we do what we do.

So she knew, just as she did when she left those stepping-stones in a neat pile on the patio, that the Peaflower case was going to nag her with the same insistence that those stones had.

Even more so, to be sure. There were men who were dying. And a woman who was getting away with murder. That was wrong, wasn't it? As wrong as anything in the world of medical ethics?

And didn't she have a responsibility to fix those wrongs if she could?

It was at this point that Ladarat realized three things.

First, she was almost certain that she was talking out loud. To the pile of policies closest to her on the desk. That was not good.

Second, she realized that she needed to solve the Peaflower case. That need had nothing to do with being a detective. She was not a detective. But she was an ethicist. And she did have skills of reasoning and deduction. And above all, she was good at watching and listening. She had an obligation to use those skills, just as she had an obligation to finish placing those stones.

Third, she knew there might be consequences. Khun Tippawan would not be pleased if she learned that Ladarat was ignoring her duties. And it was entirely possible that the director might make such a discovery tonight, if Ladarat did what she needed to do.

Ladarat looked at her watch and realized that she had been lost in this conversation with the stack of policies in front of her for almost twenty minutes. It was almost three o'clock, and she had made no progress on the policies in front of her, or the Peaflower case. Or even in figuring out what she should do.

Easiest, she knew, would be to reach out and take a policy

from the pile. On top, right there in front of her, was the nursing policy about proper visiting hours and family comportment in the obstetrics unit. That was all she needed to do. So simple. She would open that policy and make sure that its approval dates were current.

Much more difficult would be to stand up, gather her things, and make the trip that her conscience was telling her she needed to take. More difficult by far.

Although she had made up her mind to reach for that visiting hours policy, a quote from Professor Dalrymple's good book came into her mind. Unbidden, as usual. The quote simply appeared in much the same way that a text message appears on a mobile phone. Although much more welcome, and useful.

"When a nurse is faced with an ethical choice," the professor counseled, "the option that is most difficult to make is generally the right one to choose."

So. There could be little doubt, in this case, of which choice was the most difficult. There could be little doubt, therefore, about which choice was the correct one.

CHAPTER 28

THE HOUSE OF ROOSTER HAPPINESS

Despite the fact that she was certain what she needed to do, and despite the incontrovertible fact that she enjoyed the support of Professor Dalrymple herself, Ladarat was uneasy as she left the hospital. So uneasy, in fact, that she made her escape via the loading dock, where the Director of Excellence was unlikely to have spies.

Ladarat felt like a young girl sneaking out of her father's Ban Huai Duea School in the middle of the day. Winding her way through the garden that led to the cricket field in back, then taking a left turn before she got there, disappearing behind the high wooden fence. She hadn't done that often, and it had never been her idea. It was true, Siriwan had been a bad influence.

Now here she was, without her cousin to blame. Just her. It was just past three o'clock, and she was sneaking out of the hospital. And with a Royal Inspection on Monday.

But this was an errand Ladarat didn't want to run at night. She suspected that this place of business wasn't somewhere she wanted to be after dark. So it was worth risking the censure of Khun Tippawan. She would do what she needed to do, then go home.

Home...already Ladarat was thinking about dinner. Perhaps

she would get something light. *Nam tok moo*, maybe. Grilled pork and lemon juice and toasted rice. Simple but hearty. And maybe Duanphen's *kanom maprao*—coconut cake—for dessert as a special treat if this errand was as productive as she hoped it might be.

She was still thinking about *kanom maprao*, or maybe *glooai tawt*, weighing their relative merits, as she nosed the Beetle through the seedy back streets of Chiang Mai's river neighborhood. She'd never been to this part of Chiang Mai before. As far removed as it could be from the touristy spots, or the university that she knew so well, it was just up against the river, near enough to the night market to walk to. Yet this was new territory.

She parked in front of a dusty antiques store that looked as though it hadn't seen a customer since Rama VII was king, back in the 1920s. The fact that she'd never been here before didn't bother her, nor did the neighborhood's reputation. The fact that she had no trouble finding a parking spot, though... well, that was a little worrisome.

There were few people on the sidewalks, which was also a little worrisome. And those pedestrians she saw were almost all men. Americans and Europeans, of course. One rowdy group of young men with tight shorts that showed off muscular thighs. Australians.

And Chinese. Lots of Chinese. They made up perhaps half of the people she saw on her side of the street. They were dressed as businessmen mostly. Middle-aged, with a bit of a paunch. And she passed more than a few heavy gold watches on beefy wrists. She hoped they weren't real, because in this neighborhood, you shouldn't flaunt anything that you expected to still be wearing the next morning.

She'd heard the stories of these places. She'd heard about the videos of clients that were sold online, of course. And those who were blackmailed, and robbed, or worse.

All these men around here would risk that—and worse—just for...what exactly? She couldn't understand it. What was the attraction?

These Chinese men in particular were probably all smart, successful businessmen. No doubt they had large brains. Yet tonight, at least, they were not using those large brains to think. Instead, they seemed to have delegated their thinking to another part of their anatomy.

Ladarat finally found a parking space that was perhaps half a dozen blocks from where she was going. She locked the Beetle—a precaution that she didn't remember ever taking. It wasn't until she started walking that she remembered the Beetle had two doors.

Was the passenger door locked? She honestly couldn't remember. When had she ever used the passenger door? That question brought her to an uneasy halt and the men on the sidewalk flowed around her.

She really had been living a solitary existence, hadn't she? I mean, really. Not knowing when you'd last had a passenger in your car? That was truly the classic symptom of a sad, solitary life.

Thoughtfully, she began to walk again, but with more purpose. She would need to work on that, wouldn't she? It just wouldn't do to keep on like this. Somboon had died twelve years ago. And didn't Thais reckon life in twelve-year increments? Perhaps that meant something.

But she would ponder that later. Now, she had to search for a murderer.

Ladarat walked on down the block as the buildings around her became smaller and darker. Back where she'd left the Beetle, at least there had been storefronts, a few of which were still open, with lights on inside. Now, though, only a hundred meters away, the narrow street was lined only with blank brick walls and tough-looking steel doors. There were names and signs above most of those doors, but at least half were in Chinese. The few that also offered English translations followed a predictable theme. "Pleasure Garden" and "Happy Palace" and the inscrutable "Lucky Go-Go," whatever that meant. But she could imagine.

As she hesitated in front of one door, it swung open and caught the back of her right shoulder and spun her around. She turned, annoyed, to see a group of five or six Chinese men emerge. They flowed out through the door and meandered in a drunken serpentine back the way she'd come. Apparently they were cruising from bar to bar. The mamasan—an older woman with her hair pulled back severely in a bun—stood in the doorway watching them go. She was also Chinese, and looked at Ladarat appraisingly. Then she shook her head sadly and disappeared, closing the door firmly behind her.

Rubbing her sore shoulder thoughtfully, Ladarat looked up.

"Fun Time." Its faded neon sign blinked in a regular, slow rhythm as if someone were trying to communicate with a particularly dim-witted tourist.

She kept walking and had almost reached the end of the block when she saw what she was looking for. It was an unassuming building that was in poor shape, even for this block. It had litter on the sidewalk in front of it, and the pavement looked as though it hadn't been hosed down in weeks. There were no windows at all, but it looked as though there might have been once, but they'd been bricked up.

There was a diminutive sign over the door: "The House of Rooster Happiness." The red letters were so smudged and dirty, she wouldn't have noticed the name if she hadn't been searching for the number she'd been given. There it was—just to the right of the door: 9283. This was it.

LOVE IS THE EXPRESSION OF
SIMPLICITY IN EMOTION

Thoroughly unwelcoming, the House of Rooster Happiness offered only an imposing steel door placed dead center. Nor was there any indication of what might be inside. Could this really be the right place?

But she knew it was. Things were starting to make sense. A blind front, with no advertising at all, is exactly what she should have been looking for all along. If this was mostly a matchmaking agency, it wouldn't need to rely on advertising and neon and touts, would it? It would not.

Still, she was a little surprised when she pulled on the door handle and it opened to reveal a low, dark room. The space seemed to stretch back ten meters or more to a bar at the far end that spanned the width of the building. There was a narrow wooden staircase to her left, and to her right there was a collection of small, low tables with velvet-upholstered armchairs that seemed well used and frayed. That was what she noticed first.

It took her another moment to realize that the large room was empty. There was a bartender sullenly mopping the counter, but no one else in sight. No mamasan, and no girls. Where was everyone?

She made her way quickly and purposefully across the empty room toward the bar. Was she being watched? Ladarat snuck a furtive look around her. It felt as though someone had eyes on her, but how was that possible? She and the bartender were alone.

She focused on him. Just concentrate. A small, thin, pinched man, little more than a teenager. Too young to be a bartender unless...this was a family business? Perhaps he was the mama-san's son? Or grandson?

He was halfheartedly wiping the bar counter with a gray rag as Ladarat approached. She made a polite *wai*, which he returned perfunctorily and almost uncertainly. It was as if it was a custom he was unfamiliar with.

"Good evening, Khun," she said as politely as she could. "I'm wondering if you could help me?"

The man shrugged. This, Ladarat thought, is not going well.

"I'm looking for Khun Wipaporn. Is she here?"

At the sound of the mamasan's name, the man's eyebrows rose a fraction of a centimeter and one new wrinkle line appeared above each eye. But that was the only sign he offered that he understood what she was saying. Or for that matter, that he was listening at all.

Without a word, he put the rag on a shelf behind the bar, which was good. Then he turned and disappeared through a heavy swinging wooden door behind him, which wasn't. Oh dear.

Ladarat shrugged and took a seat at the bar. This was truly strange. But then again, if you go venturing into dens of iniquity looking for a murderer, you shouldn't be surprised when things get a little strange. That has to be one of the first rules of being a detective.

She was sitting there, curiously content, and pondering that wisdom, when her attention skated over the mirror that was set into the wall above the liquor racks behind the bar. It was too high for even an elephant to see her reflection. So it seemed to be a silly place to put a mirror, unless...

Ladarat waved in the general direction of the mirror. She smiled. Then she waited.

That should work. But it wasn't working. Ladarat thought very hard about that.

Should she follow the taciturn bartender through the door? That seemed like a generally poor strategy, though. Who knew what was behind that door? Best to stay here. She would await developments.

Another minute went by. Then another. It had been five minutes. And no developments. And no sign of anyone resembling a customer.

That was worth thinking about. What sort of place was this, which could survive without customers?

She was pondering that, and having second thoughts about what she should doing here. In truth, she had just about given up on this whole endeavor. *Maewfawbaahn* would be waiting for her.

And it was...only four o'clock. She could go home early for once. Khun Duanphen would be overjoyed.

Then the door swung open to reveal not the bartender but a heavyset Chinese woman with small eyes and a broad, friendly smile. She was wearing a dark gray business suit that looked to Ladarat's untrained fashion eye as though it had been tailored to fit her improbably sturdy frame. She looked like a prosperous businesswoman. Which, given the empty room and total absence of customers, was more than a little puzzling.

She returned Ladarat's *wai* with a perfect formality and respect. Her son—if that's who he was—could learn some manners from his mother. Before Ladarat could speak, the mamasan greeted her warmly in thinly accented Thai, and offered her tea. No sooner had she nodded—tea would be most welcome—than a beautiful young Chinese woman emerged through the swinging door. She carried a tray that held an elaborate porcelain teapot with a deep blue scroll design and matching cups. The girl poured, setting the cups in front of them, then withdrew silently.

"So," the woman began. "My colleague Khun Siriwan tells me you are looking for . . . a woman?"

Ladarat noticed that subtle hesitation. How much had her cousin told the mamasan? Hopefully enough so that Ladarat wouldn't need to go through the story again. But how much? She temporized.

"Yes, Khun. This woman, Peaflower, is a bad woman. We think that she may have murdered a man. And maybe several."

Wipaporn nodded slowly, as if she were processing new information. But if this were truly new information, wouldn't she show more surprise? She certainly would. So she knew something. Probably Siriwan had told her.

But—and here a very interesting thought appeared in her head—maybe Wipaporn actually knew Peaflower. And maybe she had her own suspicions? That would be very, very helpful. Because if the mamasan was suspicious, she would be more willing to help, wouldn't she? Or perhaps she'd try to cover up? In a split second, Ladarat decided to be blunt.

"You know this woman, don't you, Khun?"

Wipaporn hesitated, but only briefly. She nodded. But she didn't speak.

"And perhaps you've had suspicions of your own?"

"How did you know?"

And Ladarat knew that she had won. "Because, Khun," she said simply. "You are a businesswoman. A successful businesswoman," she added. "And as such, you know better than anyone how a single person can be a threat to a well-run business. The right person, doing wrong things..."

Ladarat didn't need to make her point any clearer. She knew that Wipaporn had been watching Peaflower. She'd probably been thinking about what to do about her. And now... And now here Ladarat was, asking the same questions that Wipaporn should have been asking.

What would Ladarat do if she were in the mamasan's place?

She would help. Of course. She would help to catch this woman. Get rid of her. And be helpful enough during the process that no difficult questions would be asked about her complicity, or what she knew when. Ladarat decided to gamble on that possibility.

"So as a businesswoman, you would want to help us catch this woman, wouldn't you, Khun?"

Wipaporn nodded, smiling. It seemed as though they had an agreement. But what?

The two women sat facing each other in a silence that was curiously comfortable. Ladarat was thinking of a plan. Or rather, she was trying to think of a plan. But what was the mamasan thinking?

"So, Khun," Ladarat began. "What should we do?" She paused. "It's one thing to say that we should catch this woman, but another thing entirely to figure out how to do it." She looked at Wipaporn, whose attention seemed to be focused on a point somewhere over Ladarat's left shoulder. As she was turning to look, her eye caught a movement in the mirror behind the bar. The mirror was about three meters off the floor, so from her angle it revealed only the upper stratosphere of the room. But when she turned, she saw a man. A familiar man.

Wiriya offered a respectful *wai* to both women, first to the mamasan, which was only proper as she was older. Then he introduced himself politely.

For a second Ladarat wondered what he was doing here. Was he the sort of person who...frequented this sort of place? But no, of course he had followed her. Or—more likely, Siriwan had told him Ladarat would be here and he was keeping an eye on her. That was it, wasn't it?

"Of course I know of you, Khun Wiriya," Wipaporn said. "You were injured in the line of duty not long ago, weren't you?"

Wiriya nodded modestly and shrugged. "It was just a day's work."

As he turned away from them to look around the room, Wipaporn raised an eyebrow at Ladarat in way that implied a question. But what? Then Wiriya turned back to the two women.

"Khun Siriwan said you would be here, and I was curious to learn how your detecting was progressing."

Wiriya looked at Ladarat. Ladarat looked at Wipaporn. They both looked at Wiriya.

"It is...progressing," Ladarat said finally. "We have decided that it would be best to try to catch this woman."

"Ah, really? You astonish me. Such a bold plan." He paused, looking from one to the other. "And how exactly will you catch her?" He smiled.

"We thought perhaps we would find a policeman to help us," Wipaporn said, smiling. "Do you have any suggestions for where we could find one?"

"That depends," he said thoughtfully. "Perhaps you could explain how this"—he waved at the room—"works?"

Wipaporn looked puzzled for a moment, then she gestured to an empty chair at the bar. Wiriya sat.

"Of course. Well, you see, this is not a bar most of the time. On weekends, yes, it is a regular bar. But on weeknights, no. If it were, we wouldn't be doing very well." She smiled. "But in fact, we are doing well. Very well. All legal," she hastened to add. "Perfectly legal."

They looked at her expectantly. Perhaps Wiriya knew something of this business? But Ladarat didn't. And she found that she was very curious. How did it work? How could a smart woman like Wipaporn become rich by running an empty bar?

"We are," the mamasan said dramatically, "primarily a matchmaking agency. For Chinese men and Thai girls." Wiriya nodded, but Ladarat was perplexed. The mamasan must have seen the expression on Ladarat's face because she paused to explain.

"After China's one-child policy went into effect in 1979, the Chinese started having more boy children." Ladarat didn't have to ask why that was, or how that happened. She'd heard the rumors. But thankfully nothing like that happened in Thailand. Women didn't have the same status as men, but daughters were as highly valued as sons. It was the daughters of Thailand who took care of you when you were old. And less favorably, it was the daughters who went to work as prostitutes in Bangkok, sending money home. If anything, she guessed, if Thais could select the children they had, they would choose to have girls.

"So," Wipaporn continued, "there is a shortage of marriageable women. And the women who are single have become more choosy. Some do not even marry at all. So you see, Chinese men find themselves in a quandary. Especially middle-aged men, of about our age. They've worked very hard, and have become doctors or lawyers or businessmen. They have the means to support a wife, but they can't find one. And besides, they don't want a woman their own age. They want a young woman, one who will bear children. Those who are very rich or very handsome may make a good match. As for the others..."

Ladarat could imagine. As for the others, they would look elsewhere. To Thailand, of course. But also to Vietnam, Laos, and Cambodia. And increasingly, to Myanmar. All countries with a relatively low standard of living and no shortage of beautiful women.

"So we try to arrange matches to meet that demand," Wipaporn said simply.

"But how?" Ladarat asked.

"Ah, that is our business," the mamasan said proudly. "That is the business I created. Look—you have to find men and women and you have to match them, right?"

Ladarat and Wiriya nodded. That logic seemed unassailable. Sure that was exactly what you needed to do. But how?

"Well, first we get a request from an eligible man in China. Anywhere, in theory. But mostly nearby. Just across the border in Honghe or Wenshan. But mostly in Kunming. He sends a picture and some information about himself." She smiles. "He also sends us an electronic payment."

"How much?" Wiriya asked. "Approximately."

"Four hundred thousand baht," she said. "Approximately."

Ladarat couldn't prevent a sharp intake of breath. And Wiriya didn't try to conceal his surprise, which he revealed with a long, low whistle. Four hundred thousand baht was about thirteen thousand dollars. Almost half of her annual salary.

"And that's for . . . ?" she asked.

"Ah, for that amount, we promise to find a suitable match. Sometimes the first girl we find is acceptable, but sometimes there is more work to do." She shrugged. For 400,000 baht, one could do a lot of "work" and still make a profit.

"But the girls," Ladarat said. "Where do you find them? You must have a very large list of eligible girls?"

"That is the most important part of our business," Wipaporn said proudly. "And the hardest to arrange. These girls who are looking for husbands often find them, you see. Sometimes they find husbands with us, but often they find them elsewhere. So instead of a list, we use a message board. An electronic message board," she clarified.

"How does it work?" Ladarat was still confused, but she was beginning to see. And how it might be very, very profitable.

"Like a real message board, but on the Internet. It's a series of postings that girls can view with a mobile phone. Look, I'll show you."

And she took her phone from her suit pocket. A few clicks later, she handed it to Ladarat, and Wiriya looked over her shoulder. She looked down and saw a man's face. That face sported a broad grin, indicating copious amounts of happiness. Presumably his happiness was caused by the large yellow speedboat the size of a city bus in the background. It was included, of course, to show how rich and powerful he was. That, she supposed, was a good reason to be smiling. Of course, if that boat wasn't really his, some girl was going to be very disappointed.

She took the phone and scrolled down to show them the man's name: Cheng Chi Weng, age forty-four, and occupation "entrepreneur."

"So you see, it's a buyer's market. The girls can pick and choose."

"Do you have a record of the...matches you've arranged?" Wiriya asked.

Wipaporn shook her head. "No, Somsak, my nephew, deletes them as soon as a meeting takes place. No point in taking up storage space, he tells me."

Wiriya looked as though he was going to ask another question, and in fact, he began to open his mouth. Instead he just nodded.

"So what does a girl do if she sees a man she's interested in?" Ladarat asked.

"She would send a text to Somsak, mentioning the man's name. He handles all the technical aspects of the business. He is a very smart young man. Not like my son." Wipaporn gestured at the man who had been behind the bar but who was now sweeping the stairs. "Hopeless." She shook her head.

"Somsak was the one who created the message board. Then he'll send her some more information about the man. His income, where he lives, whether he's ever been married. And then if she still likes what she sees, she'll upload her information to the man's profile on the message board. So he can log in to see who has responded. If there is interest, we arrange a meeting here."

"And these meetings," Wiriya asked, "are they always for marriage?"

"Well, one can never predict the course that romance will take. Didn't Confucius say that love is the expression of simplicity in emotion?"

Perhaps he did. Ladarat wasn't sure. But wasn't 400,000 baht rather expensive for finding simplicity? Especially if a man could fly to Chiang Mai and wander down this street himself?

"And if marriage does not ensue?" Wiriya asked.

"Then we sometimes will give a partial refund."

"How often does that happen?"

"Rarely," she said. And she smiled a very thin smile that was not really a smile at all. "Even if there is not a successful marriage, most of our clients don't ask for their money back."

Ladarat thought that was odd, although there was no accounting for how men behaved. But Wiriya seemed to be suspicious as well—he was watching Wipaporn closely.

Ladarat thought of the boat in the background as she handed the phone back. "But what if a man were to be less than honest about his...characteristics?"

The mamasan gave her a stern look. "These men should be very careful about lying. That would not be good for them to attempt."

"So, Khun." Now Wiriya had adopted an exaggerated politeness. Which meant that he was suspicious. "I'm curious. You say that these men pay...three hundred thousand baht?"

"Four hundred thousand."

"Ah, my mistake. So you said. Four hundred thousand baht. That's a lot of money, even for a very wealthy man, isn't it?"

"It is a bargain, though, to find your soul mate. Don't you think?"

Wiriya shrugged but continued to watch her carefully.

"Are you married, Khun?" the mamasan asked.

Wiriya shook his head warily, perhaps wondering how this clever woman had turned the tables on him so effortlessly.

"Ah, well, for many men, marriage is easily worth that much or more. Perhaps not for you, but men place a different price on that which they desire, no?"

"But to pay that much and not to find your soul mate," he said. "Well, that would be a source of dissatisfaction, would it not?"

"Perhaps that is true," Wipaporn admitted. "But there are certain...compensations."

"Compensations?"

"Well, when the man arrives, we typically arrange a meeting with the girl."

"And where would that meeting take place?"

"Why, here, of course."

"Here, as in *here*?"

"Here, and...upstairs."

"Upstairs?"

"Well, these men travel some distance to get here. They need a place to...freshen up. And sometimes they may meet the girl upstairs as well."

Now this was interesting. Wipaporn was looking very uncomfortable as she was telling them this. Strange. This was a successful businesswoman who was describing a successful business. Yet she seemed nervous. Granted she was also talking about what seemed to amount to prostitution. And Wiriya was a detective. But prostitution was hardly unusual in Thailand, as they all knew perfectly well. Typically it was off-site, not upstairs. But Ladarat's cousin had run precisely such an upstairs arrangement for years. So why was Wipaporn so distinctly uncomfortable?

"But what about the girl?" Wiriya asked, changing direction. "She comes in, looking for a marriage proposal. And when the man decides he's not interested...Or he decides he's interested, but not *that* interested, what happens then?"

"Well, we do have ways of compensating girls when romance does not go well. Heartbreak can be very painful,"

230

she said virtuously. "We do what we can to help the girls get back on their feet after rejection."

Fair enough. And this was interesting, but it wasn't helping them catch a murderer, was it? No, it was not.

"So," Ladarat said. And she suddenly realized that this was the first time she had spoken in a while. "So how would we catch this woman? How would we get the evidence that we needed?"

Wipaporn and Wiriya exchanged a look that Ladarat couldn't for the life of her figure out. It was almost as if they had a secret that they weren't sharing. But that was silly. Wasn't it?

"We would lay a trap," Wiriya said simply.

"That's right," Wipaporn said. "We find a potential husband that this woman would find attractive, and then we arrange a meeting."

"But how do we find her?" Ladarat asked. "How do we create a profile that will be sure to find this..." Wiriya was looking at her and smiling. "Ah. We include his name."

"And," Wiriya said, "we make him as unappealing as possible."

"Why unattractive?"

"To make sure that no other girls would be interested. We want only one girl to respond, and we want to be sure that girl is the right one."

"So you make him boring," Wipaporn said.

"And an undesirable partner." Wiriya grinned.

"And make him ugly," Ladarat suggested.

Wiriya and Wipaporn laughed, a bit too heartily. It really wasn't that funny. Ladarat smiled. Then her two conspirators exchanged glances.

"Khun Ladarat..." Wipaporn said carefully. "This trap?"

"Yes?"

"It needs bait."

"It does?"

"It does. It needs a person. A real person."

Why was she looking at Ladarat like that?

"Do we have such a person?" Ladarat asked.

"We do," Wiriya announced with a smile. "And perhaps he is ugly, but he would prefer not to be described as such."

Oh dear.

"But how would we know if we'd found the right woman? We don't know what this woman looks like. And she might not be using her real name."

"She would use her real name if she were interested in marriage," Wiriya pointed out. "And we're pretty sure that she is. In fact, that's exactly what she's looking for."

"But how would that trap her?" Ladarat asked. "If we find her, that's one thing. But just finding her won't help us to prove that she killed these men, would it?"

Wipaporn looked from one to the other. "I think I can help with that," she said. Ladarat sat quietly, waiting for details. But the mamasan didn't seem to want to say more.

Eventually it was settled. They would post Wiriya's picture, giving him the not-very-original name "Zhang Wei." And they made up an unappealing profile for him. He was forty-two—too old to be considered a good catch even by the lax standards of this place. And they captured the most unflattering mobile phone picture they could. They had to go outside and halfway down the block to find a nondescript brick wall to take the photo in front of. It wouldn't do to have Peaflower recognize the bar in the picture's background.

Then they all came back inside, and Wipaporn took out a laptop and began typing out a profile. And it was in the description that they did their real work. He was widowed. Three times, they decided. That would be enough to ward off all but the most determined pursuit.

But it was Ladarat who created the crowning touch. Make him a writer, she suggested. A successful businessman who now spends his time writing self-help books for aspiring entrepreneurs. Mention how much he loves to work at home. Both Ladarat and Wipaporn made faces. The last thing any self-respecting girl would want, they knew, was to have a husband who was at home all the time.

"But..." Ladarat saw what seemed to be a big hole in their careful plan.

Wiriya and Wipaporn looked at her expectantly.

"When they meet..." She paused. "If they meet. Well... Peaflower will be expecting a Chinese businessman, will she not?"

Her two accomplices nodded. "Of course," Wipaporn said.

"And I'll dress the part," Wiriya added. "Perhaps with a big fake Rolex." He smiled.

That was well and good, but there was one thing Wiriya couldn't fake. "You don't speak Mandarin, do you?" she asked. "Surely with this...history of interactions with Chinese men, Peaflower will speak Mandarin. Perhaps Cantonese as well. And almost certainly she'll speak in Chinese to put her new potential husband at ease. And when she does..."

She didn't need to finish that thought. The baffled expressions of her accomplices made it very apparent that they hadn't thought of this detail.

They looked at Ladarat with a combination of puzzlement and appreciation.

"It was lucky of you to have thought of that," Wipaporn said.

"But not luck at all," Wiriya added. "You have this ability to put yourself in other people's shoes. To think about what they would do, and what they would want." He smiled. "No, it is more of a skill."

Ladarat was flattered that these two people—who certainly had many talents when it came to people—thought that she, too, had such abilities. But that pride faded rapidly as she realized they didn't have a solution. As soon as Peaflower and Wiriya met, the game would be over.

None of them could think of a solution as Wipaporn uploaded the profile to the message board. "Well," she said. "That's all we can do for now."

"And the problem of our Chinese businessman who only speaks Thai?" Wiriya looked glum.

Wipaporn shrugged. "Let's hope we think of a solution before she arrives. If she arrives."

"How long will we have to wait?" Ladarat asked.

"It depends," Wipaporn admitted. "A day? A week? Maybe Peaflower is lying low for a while. Or maybe she became so rich she isn't looking at all? But if she is, we'll know soon."

CHAPTER 30

THE POISONER'S ART

Wiriya had been strangely solicitous as he walked her back to her car. Quite unnecessarily so. After all, it was only eight o'clock and the streets were crowded. But they talked about the note that had been left on her Beetle's window and he'd told her she should be careful. Very careful. She didn't tell him about the durian. That just would have upset him, and he had enough on his mind, especially now that he was about to be hunted by a murderer.

Then Khun Wiriya said something that surprised her. She looked out of place, he'd said. And that could lead people to take advantage.

Now, sitting on her back porch in the moonlight, with *Maewfawbaahn* curled up against her feet, she wished she'd asked him what he meant. "Out of place?"

Of course she looked out of place. Did he think she routinely frequented such streets? She smiled and took a last bite of the *kao niew moo yang* she'd been fantasizing about earlier—grilled pork skewers and sticky rice. It would keep well. The simplest dishes—like the simplest people—always withstood time the best. She'd save the rest for lunch tomorrow.

But what did he mean? Did she really look more out of place than he did? She didn't think so. Although his suit jacket was obviously made of good cloth, it was also obviously old. Well cared for, but aged. Not the kind of garment a man would put on if he was going out for a night on the town. So he didn't fit in any more than she did. Which was a good thing.

Maybe he meant that she looked too trusting? He didn't say that, but she'd heard it before. And it was a useful attribute to have, was it not, if you wanted to get people talking to you? People would tell you things they wouldn't ordinarily say, if they thought that you would believe them without a second thought.

Did that attribute prepare her to be a detective? She could imagine that it might. If people were to tell you things they wouldn't ordinarily say. If they were to let secrets slip . . . Well, maybe detecting would simply be a matter of listening.

She smiled and reached down to scratch behind *Maewfawbaahn*'s left ear—his favorite spot. She should just look trusting. She should just be herself. What could be easier?

A moment later, *Maewfawbaahn*'s head wasn't where it had been, and her fingers closed on air. He bounded in quick hops over to the gordonia bushes that lined the back wall and disappeared behind the oversize leaves that parted like a curtain and closed behind his tail. A mouse, maybe. Or a snake. He was always hunting. But fortunately he was a very bad hunter. If he ever caught anything, he never brought it home, which was one thing to be very thankful for.

Maewfawbaahn, she decided, was not a trusting soul. And that led her to think back to these poor Chinese men. They would not be trusting souls either, would they? She didn't think so. Making such long-distance marriage arrangements was risky—surely they knew that?

And then when they met this woman, well, they wouldn't let down their guard, would they? No, they would be careful.

She thought about that for a moment or two, as a subtle

movement of the gordonia leaves against the far wall marked *Maewfawbaahn*'s relentless pursuit of an evil mouse.

If they were not trusting—if they were still skeptical—what would they do? How would they act?

Well, for one thing, they would probably not believe their good fortune. They would conclude that this was a little too good to be true. So they would be suspicious. They would be fearing a trap.

Would they go back to Peaflower's home? They would not. They would surely have heard stories of unsuspecting men who were lured into an unfamiliar place and beaten up and robbed. So they would prefer to stay in public places—hotels and restaurants.

Then how had she managed to poison them? If indeed Khun Wiriya was right, that is, and they were poisoned. Her mind wandered and she imagined scenarios that might fit.

She somehow puts something in his food in a restaurant? But that would be difficult to disguise. Perhaps with enough spices? Perhaps with a very spicy dish like *tom yam* soup?

That was possible, but unlikely. What if it didn't work? What if the man had a fine sense of taste? Some men do. That wasn't something she could be sure of in advance. And, too, there was the problem of how Peaflower could order a dish for him that she herself wouldn't touch. And she'd need to ensure that he ate all of it.

No, there were too many problems and potential failures. And if there was one thing Ladarat knew about Peaflower, it was that she didn't take chances. She would be certain of the outcome before she ever walked into the House of Rooster Happiness to meet her next victim.

So what's the best way to disguise a poison? That would be the poisoner's art. The science—finding a substance that would kill—seems like it would be relatively easy. But how to induce your victim to take the poison that you've prepared?

Ladarat thought about that for a good long while. Long enough for *Maewfawbaahn* to return—empty-mouthed, fortunately—from his hunt. Again he curled up at her feet, proud that he'd kept the tiny yard safe from vermin.

Safe...that was it. What was safer than medicine? Medicine from a trusted doctor?

What if...Peaflower managed to get drugs from a doctor? A doctor that the victim would trust? And what if she somehow substituted the poison for the drugs?

But that would be difficult. How to disguise poison as a drug? As a pill or a liquid? Ladarat didn't know much about poisons, but that seemed like it wouldn't work.

So...what if she used a drug to poison him? Then it would be simply a matter of substituting one dangerous drug for another.

She would just need to get him a medication that he was expecting. A medication that he wanted to take. Then she'd substitute something like an opioid or a sedative, or maybe both. In a high enough dose that he would fall asleep. Then he'd stop breathing. Very soon he would be dead.

The trick, though, would be getting him to want to take any medication in the first place. In hopes of stumbling on an answer, she let her mind run along, while she tried to keep up.

He arrives, and they meet. They spend the evening at the House of Rooster Happiness, perhaps. Or perhaps they go to a hotel. Perhaps they don't spend the night together. She would want him interested, but she wouldn't want him to turn around and leave. She'd have to *keep* him interested.

So she leaves him in his hotel. She promises they will meet the following day.

But...the following day he doesn't feel well. She's done

something to him. A sprinkle of laxative in one of his drinks, perhaps. Or aspirin, which would cause stomach discomfort. A little gastrointestinal upset was easy to arrange. That, Peaflower could be sure of.

So when they meet the next day, he is feeling out of sorts. He'll stay in his hotel, he says. He'll spend the day resting.

She's helpful. She is the perfect future wife. She can't let her future husband suffer, can she? He wouldn't expect that. So she offers to get him a prescription for something that will calm his stomach.

But the man refuses. He's in a foreign country. He doesn't know the doctors here. He doesn't trust them. If he were at home, he would call one of the best doctors in Kunming, who would make a house call for him. But here? Were these Thai doctors any good?

No, no, he'd say. It will be all right. I'll be better. It's nothing.

Then Peaflower would play her trump card. There's a Chinese doctor not two blocks from the hotel. Very well respected. He treats many Thais who are in influential positions in government. And many ethnic Chinese. Very wealthy...

Eventually the man relents. He wouldn't trust just anyone, but if it was a Chinese doctor, and an important one... well, that was almost as good as his own doctor back in Kunming.

But how would Peaflower arrange to get a prescription? Would a doctor write a prescription for a patient he's never seen? Even for a stomach tonic, probably not. And still there was the problem of how she'd get an opioid and a sedative. How would that work?

Maybe Peaflower really did use some form of poison, but Ladarat had a feeling that this was a case of switched medications. It was more... clever. Anyone could use rat poison, but Ladarat had a feeling that this woman was proud of her cleverness.

So she'd need to get her new man to a doctor. And she'd need to get a drug that could be lethal, like morphine, from somewhere. And she'd have to switch them somehow.

Ladarat was stumped. Somehow, the woman would need to get those prescriptions without the "patient" being present. How could that be possible?

She thought about that problem for almost an hour. Even *Maewfawbaahn* decided that enough was enough and he slunk inside through the patio door she'd left open. She just couldn't see how a doctor would be willing to write those prescriptions. And if the man were actually in the clinic with the doctor, who handed him the prescription, wouldn't he get it filled immediately?

Ah, so that was it. The man would be feeling poorly, so he would go straight back to the hotel, while Peaflower filled the prescription. Then she would replace the stomach medicine for something far more dangerous.

Ladarat basked in the feeling of success for a whole minute but then realized her mistake. What if the doctor didn't write a prescription? Or what if he provided the man with medicine that was in the office? There were too many possibilities and ways that her plan could go wrong.

And, too, there was the problem that this woman was a serial killer. She did this again and again. So any plan would need to work not just once but perhaps a dozen times. Not necessarily with the same doctor, but probably so.

But how? Think.

Think about what you do know. And go back to the beginning.

They meet. He has made arrangements to stay in a hotel.

Where? Well, the Shangri-La, obviously. It was where businessmen, and especially Chinese businessmen, stayed.

But if she did this repeatedly, she wouldn't be able to use the same hotel, would she? She would not. So it could be anywhere.

A few moments ago, she'd thought that Peaflower would have mentioned a Chinese doctor near the hotel. That had just been a guess, but it made sense, didn't it? And it would have to be near the hotel. She'd want to get out and back before the man started feeling better.

That meant she was looking for a doctor—a Chinese doctor—near many high-end hotels that cater to foreign travelers. That would be outside the southeast corner of the old city, between Chang Klan Road and the Ping River.

So they were looking for a Chinese doctor near the Shangri-La who provided a prescription about a week ago to a man named Zhang Wei. He should be easy to find, shouldn't he?

She looked at her watch. Almost ten o'clock. Too late. Or was it? Her hospital's medical records department would still be open. There was always someone there.

This close to the inspection, it might be her friend Panit Booniliang. But if it wasn't, then it was probably his nephew.

She stood and stretched, then carried her plate and the leftover *kao niew moo yang* inside. She picked up the phone and dialed the medical records number. She was unaccountably pleased when the nephew answered, just as she'd predicted.

He didn't seem surprised to hear from her. It was almost as if he'd been waiting for her call. Of course, he must be bored. Any interruption would be welcome. So she told him what she wanted. He sounded skeptical at first, but all she had to say was that she needed the information for the hospital inspection. That was enough.

After she hung up the phone and began to get ready for bed, there was one question that was still nagging her. If her theory was right, then these men died in a hotel. So Peaflower would need some way to remove their bodies, undetected, which would be difficult. She'd also need to transport those bodies to an emergency room unnoticed, which would be almost impossible. So how did she do it?

And there was still the problem of the drugs that actually killed the man. If she was correct, it would be drugs like morphine. A doctor would never provide those without seeing the patient. That was the second problem with her theory.

Those two problems should have been enough to make her doubt herself. And perhaps, a week ago, they would have. But much to Ladarat's surprise, now they weren't. She was convinced that she was right. Everything else made sense. Everything else fit together. Even if this one piece didn't...well... she would figure it out in time.

Wan sao

SATURDAY

NOT SOMEONE YOU WOULD EVER
EXPECT TO COMMIT A CRIME

M*aewfawbaahn* was still sound asleep when a harsh, mechanical chirping sound filled her small bedroom. After a moment spent contemplating the likelihood of an invasion of robot birds, Ladarat reached over blindly in the dark, and succeeded only in swatting her little phone onto the floor. Undaunted by this rough treatment, her phone kept chirping relentlessly until she leaned over and found it under the bed.

As she picked up the phone, part of her mind registered the time in the upper-right-hand corner.

Five thirty-four.

Five thirty-four in the morning? On a Saturday? Who on earth would be calling her that early?

But she knew who it was. That is to say, she used her powers of deduction to determine who the caller *had* to be. Suddenly wide awake and giddy with excitement, she pressed "Answer."

"Khun Ladarat? We found your woman," the mamasan said without preamble.

"Ah," Ladarat said. She felt that in this moment something more emphatic was called for. But she was surprised to find that she had no idea what she should say now. They'd progressed beyond the bounds of detection. What should they do?

"Should we... tell Khun Wiriya?"

"I already have. And I told Peaflower that her man just happens to be in Chiang Mai on business today and tomorrow. She'll meet him at the House of Rooster Happiness at five o'clock this afternoon."

Clearing her head, Ladarat grasped the tail of a thought she'd had as she was drifting off to sleep last night.

"Could you text me her picture that she posted on her profile?"

"Of course, Khun. But why?"

And Ladarat explained what she had in mind.

"That is very careful thinking," Wipaporn said admiringly. "You are a real detective, for certain."

Ladarat knew enough about this businesswoman and her "business" to suspect that such flattery came easily to her. But she also realized that didn't really bother her. Perhaps it was even true? Perhaps she was really a detective?

A week ago that immodest ambition would have embarrassed her. But now it seemed silly not to consider it. Wasn't she helping to track down a killer? And wasn't that what detectives did? Her phone bleeped a message and the picture of a young woman appeared.

So this was Peaflower.

It was strange indeed to be looking at this woman's face after such a hunt. Especially since she seemed so... plain. She was pretty, of course. She wouldn't be successful in her... activities if she were not. With a rounded, heart-shaped face and a slightly pointed chin, she had the soft, gentle features of a girl from Isaan.

She also had bright green eyes and what seemed to be long hair pinned up in a bun. And although the resolution on Ladarat's phone was limited, it seemed as though Peaflower had left a few wisps of hair free that tickled the back of her neck. She wore simple diamond stud earrings—just two—and a thin silver necklace.

She seemed...demure. The perfect picture of a young woman looking for a stable, solid husband to take care of, and who would take care of her in return. Not someone you would point to and say, "This woman, she is a murderess!" Not someone you would ever expect to commit a crime.

"That is amazing." Ladarat recognized that wasn't the most professional response, but it really was amazing. And Wipaporn didn't seem to mind.

"I know—I'm surprised, too. It was so easy."

But maybe too easy. "You're sure that she's the right woman?"

"I've met her before," was all Wipaporn said. Of course, she would have seen the woman's pictures as she arranged other meetings with other men.

"Besides," Wipaporn said, "Who else would be so interested in Khun Wiriya?"

Ladarat thought about that question for what felt like a full minute after she'd ended the call. Who indeed?

And she was still thinking about that question twenty minutes later as she tried to go back to sleep. For a short time, she thought that a return to sleep might be possible. But now *Maewfawbaahn* was awake. And once he was up, there was no point in thinking about sleep.

He was half sitting like a sphinx on the pillow next to her head, staring at her with a strange and almost unworldly attention. She felt a little like how a mouse might feel, finding herself eye-to-eye with such a determined predator. The cat wouldn't blink, and his attention didn't waver.

It was just as well she was awake. She yawned and stretched. So much to do today. There was the coming inspection, of course. And the American. And the man in the ICU waiting room—she needed to find some plan for him before the inspectors arrived on Monday.

It was that problem more than anything else—even more than *Maewfawbaahn*'s unflinching stare—that convinced her she might as well get up. This was not unusual, after all. She often worked much of the weekend. Too much perhaps?

But she enjoyed her quiet time, too. Sitting in her garden, reading. Or perhaps strolling the markets by the river to hunt down the freshest mangoes and papayas and strawberries. In fact, Ladarat had thought that this might be one such weekend. Certainly she'd earned it.

And perhaps it still could be. She would go to the hospital early and do what she could. Perhaps no one would notice that she was there? Perhaps she would be able to work just half a day? Then there might be a trip to the market, and perhaps the booksellers. And perhaps a cup of tea by the Ping River.

CHAPTER 32

THE POWER OF GOOD NEWS

Ladarat held that hope in her mind all the way to the hospital. And even as she walked down the still, dark basement hallway, she was imagining the market stalls piled with fresh strawberries and dragonfruit and the tiny bite-size apple bananas that were so sweet.

But that hope didn't last long. She'd just arrived in her office and had barely put her bag in her desk drawer when the phone rang. Involuntarily she looked at her watch. Seven o'clock? Who thought she would be in her office at this hour on a Saturday?

The answer, apparently, was the ICU nurses. There'd been a "development" in the American's case. That was all the nurse would tell her. There'd been a development and could she please come as soon as possible?

She could. Why not?

And, too, she was worried. Very worried. Any development in the American's case was unlikely to be a good one. She ran through a list of possibilities as she made her way down the still-deserted basement hallway and pressed the elevator button. Too distracted even to wrestle over whether she should take the elevator or the stairs. So the elevator won by default. It was a relief, frankly, not to think about something for a change.

Unfortunately, choosing the quick way up six floors gave her less time to think about what might be waiting for her. Still, she knew it wasn't that the American had died. The nurse would simply have said so. Perhaps his family was creating a disturbance? But again, she would have said that. What would be so strange—or so uncomfortable—that she wouldn't have wanted to try to explain over the phone?

There really was only one explanation, and Ladarat had just reached that conclusion by the time she walked quickly through the waiting room. On the way, she noticed with some relief that the strange man was not there, but that was the only mental detour she had time for. A minute later, at the nurses' station, she found the head nurse and three other nurses, clustered together with Suphit Jainukul.

They all looked up expectantly as she crossed the floor. It seemed as though they were waiting...for her. Why?

But she was pretty certain that she knew.

"The American is...awake?"

Their expressions convinced her that she was not wrong. Only the director nodded, though. The others seemed too confused to say anything. In their confusion they deferred to the director, who just smiled.

"Ah," he said simply. "You heard."

She didn't have the heart to tell him that it was simple deduction. As Professor Dalrymple said, if you remove every explanation that is impossible, what remains—however unlikely—has to be the true explanation. Or words to that effect.

Then Khun Suphit beckoned to her and the two of them crossed the room to stand outside the glass door of the American's room. His face was still very puffy, and his head was swathed in bandages, but...

"He woke up so suddenly early this morning that he pulled

the breathing tube out of his trachea before anyone could react. We thought of replacing it, but he seemed to be awake and breathing on his own. We sedated him just a little so he wouldn't struggle, but he's starting to wake up now." Indeed, they could see his eyes were open.

What was even more surprising was the presence of the hospital's assistant nurse ethicist by his bedside. As they watched, Sisithorn laid a compress on his forehead and seemed to be talking to him. One could only imagine what she was saying. Whatever it was, though, seemed to calm the young American. His eyes closed and he fell asleep as they stood there. Sisithorn beckoned to another nurse who had materialized next to her and they traded places. Then she squirted some hand sanitizer from a dispenser by the door and offered a *wai* to both of them before rubbing the alcohol mixture into her skin.

"Ah, Khun, you have heard?"

Ladarat nodded, wondering with a small part of her brain how Sisithorn had learned about this before she did. It was not appropriate for her assistant to be called in first. Not appropriate at all.

She turned to the director, but before she could frame a question, he said that Sisithorn had been there already. She had been there, he said, just as the American began to show signs of waking up.

"So diligent," he said, smiling. "You are fortunate indeed to have such an assistant."

"Indeed," was all she said.

The director smiled and nodded. "Your assistant has taken a very strong interest in this case, it seems."

Well, there would be time to sort this out later. For now, there was only one question that needed to be asked.

"Have you told the family?"

Now the director looked sheepish. "Not yet...it's still early. But of course we need to. It's just that..."

"They will be surprised?"

"That, and they will think that we were stupid to be so... pessimistic just yesterday." The director grinned in embarrassment. "Just yesterday, I said that he wouldn't survive. And now here he is—awake." He shook his head. "It makes us look foolish."

What he didn't say was potentially even worse—that he would look foolish in front of any inspectors who reviewed this case. The inspector would see what they told the family. And he would see that the doomed patient was alive now... That would be bad. That would be very bad.

But there was nothing to be done. And besides, what was important was that the American seemed like he might recover. So that was what she told the director.

"His family will be very pleased," she suggested. "So pleased, that they will forget everything they'd been told."

The good physician didn't look convinced. Nor did Sisithorn. So Ladarat turned to her assistant. "Do you remember when you got this job?"

Sisithorn nodded respectfully, her eyes fixed on the linoleum tile beneath their feet. "Of course, Khun."

"You said everyone had told you that you would never be hired. That there were hundreds of very strong applicants. That you wouldn't stand a chance. Am I right?"

Sisithorn nodded. "You are right, Khun."

"So when you found out you got the job, were you angry at the people who told you those things?"

Sisithorn shook her head.

"No, of course you weren't. You were simply happy to have the job. That is the power of good news—it allows us to forget everything that came before." She turned back to the director. "And that is what this family will feel. They will be so happy—and so grateful—that they will not dwell on what you've said in the past."

The director smiled a genuine smile. "Well," he said, "you know Americans. And how they think."

The inspectors, of course, were another matter entirely. But they would cross that bridge when they came to it. In the meantime, they would need to tell the family. Ladarat was just thinking about how to do that when Sisithorn volunteered. She would go with Dr. Wattana, she said. They were here when the American woke up, so it was only right.

Dr. Wattana? It took Ladarat a moment. Ah, the ICU fellow who looked like a bespectacled stork.

Then one of the nurses was waving frantically at the director and pointing to the phone in her hand. He shrugged and thanked Sisithorn.

When they were alone, Ladarat asked Sisithorn what she would say to the Americans. "What are you going to tell them? You must make certain not to cast aspersions on his doctors, you understand? You must be very careful..."

She trailed off. She sounded, she knew, like an overprotective parent. Sisithorn was smart and capable. And she had a relationship with the American's wife and his parents. That would count for a great deal. And...well...she shouldn't worry so much.

Before Sisithorn could answer, Ladarat simply told her assistant to ignore what she'd just said. "Do you have any questions for me?" was all she asked.

Sisithorn shook her head. "No, Khun, I don't think so. Dr. Wattana will be with me. And as you said, we are bringing good news. And...Khun?"

"Yes?"

"I don't think this will be a surprise to them. I think...they expected good news. Kate in particular. She was ready for bad news, but she still had very strong hopes, I think. It's been as though she thought some miracle would happen."

Ladarat nodded. "Exactly so. They won't be distressed by this change because they never really believed what we told them before, any more than you believed the people who said you wouldn't be able to get this job."

Then Ladarat left Sisithorn in the ICU to go find Dr. Wattana. She hoped that they would go soon. It wouldn't do for the family to come up to the ICU and discover on their own that the patient had woken up.

But there was no danger of that. Sisithorn knew that time was of the essence. More important, she knew what time meant, which was one of the main reasons Ladarat had hired her. She hadn't been the best qualified applicant, it's true. But she was the only one who had arrived early for her interview. That was why she got the job.

CHAPTER 33

AN ANTICIPATED DEATH
THAT IS NEVERTHELESS UNEXPECTED

The waiting room had begun to fill up with families, but the mysterious man hadn't yet appeared, so Ladarat headed down to medical records. She took the stairs, now that she wasn't preoccupied. And she was pleasantly surprised to find that when she reached the basement, she felt virtuous. She would do this more often. At least four flights of stairs every day, she decided. Four was an auspicious number. And more important, it was a rather small auspicious number.

In the medical records room, she was surprised to find Chaow Willapenna behind the counter. He offered her a tired *wai*, looking up at her under sagging eyelids.

"Have you been here all night?" She'd heard that his uncle Khun Panit worked long hours, but she'd had no idea that they would work overnight like this.

"Yes, you see, we still have much to get ready for ahead of the inspection." He waved at the stacks of charts behind him. "My cousin at Rajavithi Hospital in Bangkok told me yesterday that when his hospital was inspected last month, the inspectors asked to see charts of current patients in the hospital dating back two years. Two years! Can you believe it? So yesterday we began to get those old charts from storage."

"But that must be charts for almost a thousand patients..."
She knew the hospital was full. That would be a huge number
of old charts to find in storage.

Chaow smiled wearily. "Fortunately, it's too important to
trust to me, so my uncle has gone to do it himself. Unfortunately, he's taken most of our workers." Then he perked up.
"But here, Khun, I have what you asked for. I had a few free
minutes this morning—it didn't take long." And he handed
her a small slip of paper, neatly folded in half.

Ladarat thanked him. It was amazing to see such dedica-
tion in a Thai of his age. Most kids would simply grab any
convenient excuse, like the need for old charts. They would be
"off the hook," as the Americans say. But this young man did
what she'd asked anyway.

Letting him get back to work, she took the result of his
searches back down the hall to her office. It wasn't until she shut
the door behind her and sat down at her plain wooden desk that
she realized how tired she was. And it was only...8:05.

She'd accomplished a great deal. But she was already
exhausted. It was truly going to be a long day. And this day
would most likely not include a trip to the market or a browse
in the booksellers, or a cup of tea by the Ping River.

Ladarat unfolded the slip of paper to find only one name:
Arhit Tantasatityanon. She couldn't be certain, but the long
name was a good indication that this doctor was a relatively
recent immigrant to Thailand. By law, surnames had to be
unique to a family. So once the short names were taken, immigrants had to stretch for surnames that were increasingly
long. And since most immigrants were Chinese...

And his address was in the tourist district, just where she
thought it should be. Not more than three blocks from the

Shangri-La. So only one physician in that area had seen a man named Zhang Wei in the past week.

How Chaow had managed to get that information was still a puzzle. But last night he'd promised that it would be easy. They asked for this kind of information all the time, he'd said, to complete a patient's chart when information was missing.

So now she had a name and a phone number. It was still early, too. If she was quick, she might be able to talk to the doctor if she caught him before he began to see patients. Or should she go in person?

What would Khun Wiriya do?

As Ladarat sat down at her little desk, though, she realized that was the wrong question. She wasn't a detective. Maybe technically she was, at this time, a detective. But she didn't have the sort of personality that would convince people to give her information. She couldn't be convincing and she certainly couldn't be threatening. One look at her oversize glasses and diminutive figure, and anyone would say: "This is not a person I need to take seriously."

Perhaps this insight should have distressed her. But it did not. It truly did not.

One must work within the limitations that one is given. One should not attempt to swing through the trees like a monkey if one is an elephant. And vice versa.

That was not wisdom gleaned from the good Professor Dalrymple. But it was, Ladarat thought, wisdom nonetheless.

Besides, she could sound much more authoritative on the phone, she knew. And on the phone, her mild manners wouldn't be a liability. And there was always the chance that this doctor wouldn't be seeing patients on a Saturday. Unlikely, but it would be silly to waste a trip. So, before she could start to have second thoughts, she picked up her phone and dialed the doctor's number.

It was still early, but perhaps the office staff were already answering the phone. If not...

She was surprised by a man's gruff voice. He answered in heavily Chinese-accented Thai, and she had trouble understanding him at first. He said hello again and seemed about to hang up when she launched into the speech that she had been practicing the night before.

She introduced herself as a nurse at Sriphat Hospital and then—a guess: "Are you Dr. Tantasatityanon?"

"Ah, yes. My office manager called in sick—I am all alone here today. How can I help you, Khun?"

"I am trying to understand the events that brought a man to our emergency room last week. He was one of your patients, I believe, a Khun Zhang? Zhang Wei?"

The doctor thought for a moment, but not long. "Of course. I've been caring for him for...at least four or five years. A very sad case. Is he well?"

Ladarat would need to tell the good doctor that his patient was not, in fact, particularly well.

"No, I'm afraid he isn't."

"Oh?"

"He is not well at all."

"That is too bad."

"In fact, he is dead."

There was silence on the line for a few moments as the doctor processed this information.

"He went to your hospital?"

"Well, he didn't actually *go* to our hospital." Then she explained that his wife had appeared with him and that he was dead when he reached the emergency room.

258

The doctor seemed to be surprised. So Ladarat took a risk.

"And how was he the last time you saw him?"

"Well, you see, he doesn't usually come to clinic."

This was interesting.

"And when was the last time do you think he came to clinic?"

"I would have to check my records to be sure, but I think it was perhaps several years ago."

This was very interesting.

"Perhaps about the time that you first started seeing him as a patient?"

"Perhaps," the doctor admitted. "You see, he is—was—very frail. His cancer has spread to his organs, causing him pain when he moves. It has been a surprisingly slow-growing cancer, though, and one that he has been able to live with for some time. But coming to clinic has been... a challenge."

"And yet you provide him with medications for his pain?"

"Oh yes. His wife is a delightful woman. She takes excellent care of him, and gets his medications for him. Every three months she comes in. But there has never been any concern about abuse of his pain medications, you see. Always the same dose..." He paused for a moment. "That is really too bad. But if I may ask, how did he die?"

"As you said, Khun, he did have cancer at an advanced stage."

"Of course he had advanced cancer, it is true. But he also seemed to be stable, if one could describe a seriously ill patient with that word. It was as if he could continue on like this forever. His death was anticipated but nevertheless unexpected, if you understand me. On her last regular visit, about three months ago, I refilled all the usual prescriptions. Morphine, of course. And also lorazepam, to help him sleep. You know the drugs? You said you are a nurse?"

Ladarat said she knew the drugs. Though perhaps not as well as Peaflower seemed to know them.

"And then just last week, his wife asked again for an antibiotic for a gastrointestinal infection. He suffered from such infections frequently—a result no doubt of his weakened immune system. Every few months she would come for another prescription."

Ladarat considered for a moment, not liking the implications of this new development.

"But was there a cause of death determined?" he asked. "Could it have been this infection? You see, often in cases such as this, there is an event that causes an abrupt decline. Either an infection, or a blood clot in his lung perhaps. Or bleeding?"

"Khun..."

"Yes?" He seemed distracted, but at least she had his cooperation.

"Is it possible—just possible, you understand—that your patient Zhang Wei has been dead for some time?"

"But...you said he died just last week."

"Yes, it's true that a woman brought a man by this name to the emergency room last week. And it's most undeniably true that he was quite dead when he arrived. But is it possible that this man—who seems to have had the same name as the man you're thinking of—is actually a different person?"

"But...why would that be? Are you saying that there are two men with the same name and with the same diagnosis? That perhaps this man in the emergency room is not my patient?"

"No, actually what I'm suggesting is that there may be several men with the same name." And she told him what she thought might be happening.

She gave this information a moment to sink in. In that time, she noticed that the doctor seemed genuinely surprised. She also noticed something else. He didn't seem to resent the implication that perhaps he had been aiding in these murders, even unwittingly. He didn't point to the law, and what he was allowed to prescribe. Nor did he say that he was just doing what any caring doctor would do. That was what she would have expected him to say if he had a guilty conscience. And that was a relief, because she wasn't at all sure how she should proceed if she had reason to believe that the doctor was some-how involved. That would be very difficult.

Instead, he only asked her what he could do to help. And that, fortunately, was easy.

"You would be able to recognize this woman—the man's wife?"

"Of course. And my office staff would be able to recognize her as well. As I said, she came to see me quite often."

Yes, Ladarat knew exactly how this doctor could help.

A HUNCH

She barely had time to savor what could only be called a victory of detection, when she heard a soft, almost apologetic knock on her door. She rose to open the door, a maneuver she'd often noticed could be accomplished—almost—without leaving her chair. Such were the modest dimensions of her little closet of an office.

When the door opened, though, she could only stare at Dr. Jainukul standing there. He offered her an overly polite *wai* and waited impatiently to be invited in. In that moment, he seemed like a lost child. One hand was fidgeting nervously with the stethoscope in the right pocket of his white coat, and the other was clicking nervously on a pen in his left pocket. Click. Click. Click. Click.

"Ah," was all she could think of to say as she stepped aside to let him in. She gestured to the chair in front of her desk and sat quickly, facing him. This, she thought, would be very interesting. What could be important enough that the director couldn't have mentioned it when they were together an hour ago? And what on earth could be so important that he couldn't simply have called her? This would be interesting indeed.

"Khun," he began. "You know I've tried to be very patient in the matter of the man in the waiting room."

Ladarat nodded. Yes, she supposed he had been patient. And she supposed that she had not made much progress. She waited.

"But you see, the inspectors will be here soon, and..."

"Yes?"

"This man—he has just...*defecated* in the garden outside the hospital reception area! I heard the security guards talking." He shook his head. "Can you imagine what the inspectors will think if they see this? The health implications alone are enough to get a serious citation. And if we get a citation..."

He didn't need to explain what would happen if their hospital received a citation. It would be a tremendous loss of face for everyone. Everyone in a hospital would feel that, from the director down to the janitors. Everyone would be embarrassed. And of course, the other hospitals in Chiang Mai would know...It would be very bad. Very, very bad.

"Ah, I see," she said. "Yes, that would be very bad. But I believe there has been...a development."

"A development?"

She couldn't say more. It was still only a hypothesis. But Ladarat was fairly certain that she was correct. It was a strong hunch. Or maybe instinct. Regardless, she was almost certain that she would be able to resolve the case of the strange wandering man today.

The director nodded and stood, offering her a deep *wai* as he did. "I know you can resolve this problem, Khun. I have no doubt. Thank you." And he *wai'd* again as he turned to leave.

That, Ladarat thought, was mysterious. The way that he seemed to trust her. Strange, indeed.

Of course, he was desperate. And when we're desperate, we trust anyone who offers an answer.

As Professor Dalrymple said, even the most incompetent nurse looks like a hero to a patient who is truly in need.

And yet...he really seemed to think that she could solve this problem for him. He trusted her. And she had inspired confidence. Imagine that.

But could she solve this problem? Yes, she could. At least, she hoped so.

CHAPTER 35

THE ELEPHANT'S MIND IS THE MAHOUT'S MIND

Ladarat had already pushed the "up" button for the elevator when she had a crucial second thought. She turned and walked quickly back to her office, taking off her white coat and hanging it on the hook on the back of the door.

There. She should have thought of that earlier. That would have been a significant mistake.

She wondered what other mistakes she might be making, but there was no time for second-guessing now. She would go up to the ICU and let intuition be her guide. Intuition, and luck. And fortunately, luck seemed to be on her side.

The waiting room was almost full. It was Saturday, after all, and many friends and family from the Northeast and all over Isaan had come for the weekend. A five-hour bus ride had brought them to Chiang Mai.

Ladarat scanned the faces scattered across the room, noticing that they didn't seem to be paying any attention to her. Of course, without the white coat, she was just another family member looking for someone she knew. It occurred to her in that moment that perhaps she should wander the hospital this way more often. Incognito, as they say. She would learn a great deal about the way the hospital ran.

Well. As soon as this inspection was over, that was exactly what she was going to do. Who knew what sorts of ethical problems were lurking, unseen and unnoticed? She would wander about, and she would eavesdrop. She would be...a detective. She almost smiled.

But then she remembered why she was here. She didn't see the man, but she knew that she wouldn't from where she was standing. If he was here, he would be seated on the floor, right over...there. And there he was.

She took a step back and pulled her mobile phone from her purse. Just one quick call.

A moment later, her call completed, Ladarat made her way awkwardly across the room, stepping over children's toys and knapsacks and food baskets and the occasional wayward child. Smiling and nodding so as not to give offense, she was blocked in her progress down a narrow passage between two rows of seats by two small children—not much more than infants, playing with a bright blue inflatable ball that reached to their shoulders. She would have been content to stop and watch, but their mothers leaned in and whisked them up onto laps, smiling as they did.

Finally, she was through. She walked purposefully to the section of the wall where the man had planted himself. As always, he'd positioned himself to gain a heartening view of the mountain outside the window.

He looked up and greeted her with a deep *wai*, which she returned. Odd, he didn't seem particularly surprised to see her. Nor did he seem to remember his previous abrupt disappearance. It was almost as if he took her irregular materializations for granted as manifestations of the natural world, just as he assumed his were to her. These meetings were like a sunset or...more prosaically, a tree falling. There was no point in being surprised, his demeanor seemed to suggest. These things just happened.

"Khun..." She wasn't sure how to begin this conversation. She wasn't sure at all. But she hoped that the formal address might lend some gravity to a situation, which was rather peculiar. Here she was, leaning over this man, who was eyeing her with an open honesty tinged with wariness.

"I thought we might perhaps talk...outside?"

The man nodded hesitantly. Of course, that was it. This man from the country would be more comfortable outside. And, of course, that would be the perfect place to have a conversation.

A small part of her brain—the rational, logical part—noted that this man should ask her what she wanted to talk about. This man should naturally resist ambiguous invitations of this sort. But the man didn't even ask her what she wanted to talk about. The invitation to go outside was enough.

She led and he followed, as she'd hoped. So with barely a glance behind her, she turned left and led him through the door and over to the stairs she had recently discovered.

They trooped down the steps without speaking. And as he had in the hallway, the man let her lead. Down the stairs they went, the man's bare feet making a soft slapping sound on the linoleum tile. Slap. Slap. Slap.

As they reached the first floor, the slapping sounds behind her slowed, and she realized the man was hanging back. But Ladarat pretended not to notice, and she forged ahead through the door to the ground-floor hallway that connected the main hospital building with the new wing that housed the ICU. It was a short walk down the hall to the right, and then out the door to the little garden nestled between the old and the new buildings.

As she expected, the garden was not crowded. It was still early, so most people at the hospital were either visiting or working. There was a small family at a table near the fountain, having a breakfast picnic of sticky rice and chili paste and roasted fish. And several hospital employees were sitting alone, talking on their mobile phones.

There was also a couple—an intern and a nurse—sharing a quiet moment in the corner. She thought for a moment of how she used to meet Somboon, in a garden much like this one at Aek Udon Hospital in Isaan. But now was not the time to think of such things.

Just behind them in the doorway were two monks, who passed them and went to sit by the fountain. They were engaged in an animated conversation, and seemed not to notice the people around them. A matter of great theological import, no doubt. One was old and the other was just a novice. Both wore the saffron robes of the order and had shaved heads that exposed them to the merciless sun. They popped open orange umbrellas to shade themselves and continued their conversation quietly.

She didn't have an umbrella, so she led the man to a ledge on the far end of the garden, thinking that he'd be more comfortable there than sitting on a chair. She found a corner in the shade of the hospital behind them, and she sat facing the building, so the man would face the mountains over her left shoulder. She thought that would give him comfort. He followed suit, but more slowly. He seemed warier now.

But he also seemed more relaxed, if that was possible. Before it was as though he was on edge in an irrational way. But now . . . it seemed as though he was more himself. Wary, yet comfortable.

He watched her with the same patient regard that he might give a wild animal who was not unfriendly but was nevertheless unpredictable.

She would start gently.

"It is sad about the American, is it not?"

The man looked at her quietly, with a resigned expression. He nodded slowly but said nothing.

"This person you're visiting...it is the American, is it not?"

Again, the man looked at her quietly and nodded. Still he didn't speak, but she had a feeling it wasn't that he didn't have anything to say. It was more that he was waiting. He knew that she had more to say, and so he would bide his time. That degree of patience, she thought, was unusual. And it convinced her that she was right. If she'd had any uncertainty when she invited him out to the garden, that uncertainty was gone now. She could be more direct.

"You know, I suppose, that the American is getting better."

A puzzled look.

"The man, I mean. Of course the woman is getting better. But you knew that, because you've been watching her. Haven't you?"

A slight nod.

"But now that man is starting to wake up. It's thought he may make a good recovery."

There. She'd said enough. Now it was his turn. But he surprised her by standing formally and giving her a high *wai*— his fingers at the level of his wrinkled forehead, and bent so low that he was almost doubled over.

"No, no, Khun, you mustn't thank me. I...I did nothing. It's his doctors and nurses. I only bring news that I thought you would want to know, given your...concern with the case."

"That is very good, Khun," the man said finally. "I am relieved." A pause as he looked up at the mountains over her left shoulder. "I am so relieved."

269

Then the man became suddenly serious and his smile disappeared in an instant. "This is a great relief, you see. Because of course it was my fault, Khun."

That surprised her more than it should have perhaps. "But...it was an accident involving an elephant, was it not? Why would that be your responsibility?"

As the silence between them stretched out, she decided to guess.

"The elephant is yours, is it not, Khun?"

The man nodded miserably.

"But how are you responsible, Khun? Is it not the elephant's doing that caused these injuries?"

"Of course I am responsible, Khun." The man seemed genuinely surprised. "If not me, then who?"

"Surely accidents happen? And...elephants have minds of their own?"

"Ah, but the elephant's mind is the mahout's mind. They are one, do you understand? For an elephant to commit such a crime, it is the same as if the mahout commits the crime. Do you see?"

She didn't. The morality of elephants was something far beyond any ethics textbook she had ever read. Although Ladarat was intensely curious about what thoughts the good Professor Dalrymple would have on the issue of elephant morality, her otherwise excellent textbook was alas silent on this. Perhaps someday she would write to the professor to ask her to consider the morality of elephants. But now, she needed to come to an arrangement that would separate the man from the ICU waiting room.

"I'm not sure I understand, Khun. Perhaps in time you will be able to explain it to me. For now, though, I need to ask you to help me."

"Of course, Khun. But what can I do?"

What indeed?

"Well, the American woman is in a delicate state. When she saw you in the hallway several days ago, she became...distressed. Do you understand?"

The man nodded. "Of course I understand. It is natural. But I do not mean to cause her distress. I only meant to... watch. To find out how she is progressing. That is why I'm here."

There was a question in the back of Ladarat's mind. Something that she was missing. But what? No time to figure it out, though. Not now.

"No, you do not mean to cause distress. I understand. But your presence here seems to do that. It is an accident, but true nonetheless."

Now the man was nodding, but uncertainly. "So what should I do?"

"First," Ladarat said, sounding more authoritative than she felt, "you should avoid the waiting room upstairs." She paused. "You should not be there. The American woman will be going in and out to see her husband even more often now, and she will see you. And she will be upset."

The man nodded. "I understand. But...how will I know how the American is doing? How will I know if he makes a recovery?"

How indeed? But the words were out of her mouth before she realized what she'd said. "You will apologize to the Americans."

"But...they will be angry with me. They will be very angry."

"They may be upset, it's true. But they will not be angry. You must tell them what you told me about the elephant and the mahout. And the mahout being responsible. You must tell them that's what you believe. You must tell them that this is what's in your heart. Once they hear that, they will decide that you have a very big heart to feel such things. And they will forgive you."

"They will?"

Who knew? Perhaps not. Still, Ladarat thought that was a good possibility. So she nodded.

"Yes, I believe they will. But you must avoid the waiting room in the meantime, do you understand?"

The man nodded.

"Good. I will try to arrange this for tomorrow morning. In the meantime, we will need to find someplace for you to stay."

"But I can stay here, Khun." And he waved a gnarled hand at the garden around them.

Oh no. No, he most certainly could not stay here. The only thing that would be more interesting to the Royal Inspector than a man in the waiting room would be a man bivouacking in the garden. That would not do. That would not do at all.

But fortunately this was one problem she had anticipated. She stood, and the man stood, too. The monks talking by the fountain stood and the eldest approached them.

They all made high, formal *wais*, the man's highest of all. Overwhelmed to be talking with a nurse and two monks, he seemed unsure what to say. So he kept both hands pressed together just beneath his eyebrows, smiling nervously.

"These monks will give you a place to stay for as long as you need it, Khun. There is no need for you to sleep on a floor, or in the stairway. It is not right. The monks belong to a monastery that is just across the street."

The man nodded and smiled, relieved. He made another deep *wai* to the monks, and then to her.

She thanked the monks and they both smiled. "We are happy to be of service," the older one said. "You were lucky Prasert here answered my phone for me. I often ignore it. You see, there was the India-versus-Pakistan test match that just ended."

Ladarat looked at him blankly.

"Cricket?"

Ladarat shook her head.

The monk shrugged, then smiled. "We must go."

Then the two monks disappeared inside, still in animated conversation, the man trailing behind them. He would make himself useful in the monastery, she had no doubt. He probably had skills as a gardener and a carpenter. It was too bad that there were no elephants to care for.

She stood there for a moment, thinking about that. Elephants. Elephants need regular care, do they not? That's what was bothering her a few moments ago. Who was caring for the man's elephant? The one who hurt the Americans? Surely someone was caring for it? She would need to remember to ask when she saw the man tomorrow.

For now, though, there was work to be done. She'd solved one issue ahead of the impending inspection. But there were many, many more that needed to be dealt with. And if she could solve this one, she thought proudly, then she could solve anything.

CHAPTER 36

ONE MUST ALWAYS NEGOTIATE FROM A POSITION OF POWER

As she pushed open the heavy wooden door to the House of Rooster Happiness, Ladarat was preoccupied with thoughts of her Beetle. There'd been no room to park anywhere nearby, so she'd found a smaller alley about three blocks away. That alley held a jumble of small storefronts that were all closing for the night, so it was probably deserted by now. And she'd left the Beetle there all alone.

She hoped it would be okay. But of course it would. It had survived this long, hadn't it? In truth, it was older than she was. So it could take care of itself. She smiled at the thought of a car fending for itself as she laid down her bananas on the *Hing Phra* shrine and made a deep *wai*. She said a quick prayer, asking Buddha for help in what she was about to attempt.

A bunch of bananas was hardly adequate payment for such a request. If the Buddha were inclined to favor her request, surely he would do so without a pile of ripe fruit in the bargain? But that was Buddhism for you—it was all about covering your bases.

A moment later the mamasan herself emerged through the swinging doors behind the bar, carrying a small tea tray. Moving silently, she appeared like a ghost. After they greeted each other, she apologized that she would need to leave Ladarat alone.

"There is much to be done," she said by way of explanation. "My nephew Somsak is having technical difficulties. But Khun Wiriya will be here soon." And she was gone, as silently as she'd arrived, leaving Ladarat alone again with her thoughts.

And she devoted those thoughts to the mahout and his elephant. It didn't seem right that he would leave his elephant and come here. It was understandable, of course, that he would want to know what happened to the American. It was even understandable—though perhaps not to a hospital inspector—that he would want to stay close all the time.

And yet... wasn't the elephant his source of livelihood? And didn't they work together as a team? It seemed strange indeed that the mahout would simply leave and come to Chiang Mai. Even if he put his elephant in the care of someone he trusted, it was difficult to imagine doing that for any reason that wasn't a matter of life and death. To do that voluntarily, on a... mission? That just didn't make sense.

But what was the alternative? That the man wasn't really a mahout? No, the American Kate recognized him. And besides, if he weren't the mahout, why on earth would he be here?

Ladarat continued to try to puzzle this out, but she was no closer to an answer that made sense when Wiriya came through the front door. Just as Ladarat had, he made a high *wai* to the Buddha inside the door and deposited a bunch of overripe bananas in front of the shrine. She thought she saw him smile as he did so. One could only hope that the Buddha was very fond of bananas.

As they greeted each other, she noticed that Wiriya had dressed with particular care for his assignment. In place of the worn gray sport coat she'd become strangely accustomed to, now he wore a deep blue suit with chalk pinstripes. The suit made him look slimmer, and about ten years younger.

As Ladarat poured him a cup of tea from the pot that Wipaporn had left behind, Wiriya noticed her interest in his suit. He smiled.

"One must always negotiate from a position of power."

"Indeed?" That was all she could think of to say.

"Indeed. And I think this is a woman who respects power, so we are playing by her rules."

Ladarat found that surprising. This is a woman, remember, who is making a living by stealing from men with power. Killing them, and then stealing.

"But why do you think she respects power? She has not demonstrated much respect for anything, or anyone, has she?"

"Ah, but she has. You see," he explained, "the men she is preying on are the men she respects. Or perhaps I should say they're the men she fears. She doesn't like them, it's true. And...at the risk of sounding like a forensic psychiatrist, I would venture to guess that she hates powerful men."

"And how do you know that, Khun?"

"Well, I don't know it. Not for certain," he admitted. "But there are many ways to make a living, and many ways to steal. Yet our woman has found a way to make a living that would seem to involve murder. That suggests to me that this is personal. That she is targeting these men, not just because they're rich, but because she has a powerful hatred for these men, as a group."

"Ah, I see. But why would that be?" Actually, Ladarat could think of many reasons why that might be. The Chinese who had come to Thailand in the early twentieth century had become quite successful in business. And many—though certainly not all—were ruthless as well. It was not difficult to imagine that members of this successful group had made some enemies. And one enemy in particular.

The detective was of the same opinion. He shrugged. "Perhaps her family was bankrupted by a Chinese lender. Or perhaps a Chinese business put her father out of work. Who knows? It's just that this seems too personal, and too . . . vengeful, for it to be simply a strategic crime."

They both thought about that possibility for a moment, as Wiriya sipped his tea.

"So you think this may be . . . revenge?" Ladarat asked.

"Perhaps. But it is too much, don't you think? I mean to say, one murder of the person responsible . . . well, that could be counted as revenge. But two? Or a dozen? At some point this stops being revenge and is more like . . ."

"A habit?"

"Yes, I suppose. A habit. Now this is the way that she thinks of the world. You know, I heard a story once about tigers in India. That normally they don't prey on people. People are just . . . part of the environment. But once a tiger kills a man, then it begins to think of people as food. That first kill changes the way that they look at us." He paused, and they both thought about that for a moment.

"So it seems to me that this woman—and here I'm speculating—has fallen into just such a pattern. Now she sees these men as prey. They may seem powerful to others, just as they once seemed powerful to her, as they took her father's business, or whatever it was one man did to enrage her. Maybe once she was afraid of them. But now? Now they are just her prey."

"It seems as though you have thought about this a great deal."

Wiriya smiled, embarrassed. "Yes, I suppose I have. You see, it would mean a great deal to me personally to be able to solve this case. With much help, of course." He smiled.

"I have a reputation in the police, of course. But reputations don't last forever. Already there are young men on the force who don't know me. They're young and ambitious and… well, unless I prove myself, soon I'll be assigned to investigating unpaid parking tickets."

Ladarat wanted to ask him if that were really true. Somehow she doubted it. This was a man who had been injured in the line of duty. He had a commendation from the king himself. Surely that was enough to ensure his status and his reputation?

But then again, she could easily imagine how that might not be true. It took very little, in fact, to damage one's reputation. And, of course, time did the rest. Just as she was about to ask him whether he wanted to stay a policeman forever, the door behind the bar opened.

Ladarat gave a start of recognition. There, in front of her, was the man from the ICU waiting room. And the stairwell.

Now he was dressed more comfortably in track pants and a Ramones T-shirt. But if there had been any doubt in her mind that this was the same young man, a glance at the enormous wristwatch on his left arm was enough to convince her.

He offered a deep *wai* and an apologetic smile. Behind him was the mamasan, looking distinctly uncomfortable.

Before Ladarat could formulate a question, the mamasan intervened.

"I'm sorry I didn't mention Somsak earlier. You see, when I first learned that you were investigating this Peaflower woman, I became worried. I thought perhaps we needed to watch you.

And then, when you began to make progress, I thought we should try to...dissuade you."

"But at our meeting..."

The mamasan nodded. "Yes, by then I'd realized that the best thing to do—the right thing to do—was to trust both of you. So..." she said. "No more durians. But Somsak has been keeping an eye on you."

"Because..."

"Because Peaflower is dangerous. Very dangerous. She has much to lose. And Somsak had an advantage, you see. He knows what Peaflower looks like. But she wouldn't recognize him. So by keeping him close to you, as a..."

"As a bodyguard?"

"Exactly so. As a bodyguard. He could warn you if he saw Peaflower anywhere near you."

Ladarat wasn't certain whether this revelation made her feel better or worse. Better, perhaps, because the mamasan had been watching out for her, at least in the end. But worse, somehow, because people had been worrying about her, and protecting her.

There would be time later, she knew, to sort those feelings out.

"Now I must get ready," the mamasan said. And she disappeared through the door behind the bar.

Somsak had been staring fixedly at the ground the entire time, but now he looked up at Ladarat and offered another high *wai*, bending at the waist.

"I'm very sorry, Khun Ladarat, for frightening you. And for the durian." He stood upright, his hands at his sides. "It's just that your car, the Beetle, it is such a beautiful car. And a classic. I couldn't think of a way to get your attention without damaging it in some way. So I thought..."

"A ripe smell would be a harmless threat." Ladarat smiled. "Yes, I suppose it was. And the smell is decreasing gradually. By the time the smell is gone entirely, the car will be an antique."

"But, Khun, it is an antique," Somsak protested. "And very valuable. Especially to Americans."

So the fruit seller had said. But Ladarat had assumed he was just exaggerating. And speaking of the fruit seller...

"The fruit seller, is he all right?"

Somsak looked confused for a moment, then he smiled. "Of course. I didn't want any witnesses, so I gave the police a tip that he was selling durians out of season. The police carted him off with his durians. After I'd bought one, of course. But I promised him I'd watch his cart for him until he'd paid his fine. It didn't take more than an hour. When he came back, he found the baht you'd left him. And I left him five hundred baht for his trouble. I think it was a very profitable day for him."

Somsak looked at his large watch. "But now we must hurry." He beckoned Wiriya to follow him as he scurried toward the stairs by the front door.

Wiriya rose but then stopped. "I will go and...await developments."

He turned back to Ladarat. "That doctor. The Chinese doctor you thought you'd be able to find, did you—"

"Yes, I think so. At least, there's a Chinese doctor in the hotel district near the mall who said he's given many prescriptions for a Mr. Zhang Wei, but all by way of the man's wife. He hasn't seen the man in years."

"And the last prescription was..."

"Just last week."

"Could he identify a photograph of her?"

"I sent it to him after I spoke with him this morning and..."

She opened her phone quickly, checking her e-mail. Nothing. She shrugged. The doctor's office manager was out sick, so he had warned her that he might not be able to reply to her until late afternoon.

"Maybe he will reply soon?" she said hopefully.

"Maybe." Wiriya smiled at her. "No matter. But if he does, give me . . . a sign." Then they were both gone.

A sign? What sort of sign would that be?

A very pretty Chinese girl, not the one she'd met on her first visit, appeared a moment later to gather up the tea things, and then motioned for Ladarat to follow her through the door behind the bar. At first she thought she was being ushered out of the way, and that she'd be stashed in a back room somewhere. But the girl led her through the door and then into the mamasan's office just to the right. The office was plain and businesslike, with an oversize desk plunked down right in the middle, and piled with neat stacks of paper that looked like bills and invoices.

What caught Ladarat's attention wasn't the desk but the wall of video monitors against the far wall. There had to be . . . she counted them. Sixteen in total, in two horizontal rows. And Wipaporn was seated in front of them. She turned just long enough to offer a polite *wai* and to gesture to the chair next to her. Ladarat took a seat and looked at the monitors more closely.

There were two that seemed to cover the front entrance, and several more that showed the main room from various angles. So the whole time she'd been out there, someone had been watching her?

Well, probably not. Her eye caught a flicker of movement in one monitor far to her right. She leaned behind the mamasan to get a better look, and realized that anyone looking at these monitors most definitely would not have been watching her drink her tea. There were far more interesting options on offer.

"Oh my. Is that..." She tried to sound composed. As if videos of naked couples were something that she experienced every day. (But for the record, they most certainly were not.)

"Don't trouble yourself about that," the mamasan said. "Besides, the man is well known in the tourism ministry. Very well known. It wouldn't do to have people mention they saw him here."

Ladarat wasn't sure how to tell her host that from this angle, it was difficult indeed to see any part of this man that would lead her to recognize him later, if they were to meet on the street. He was safe from her, at least. But if privacy was such a concern, then...

"You seem to have many video screens, Khun." As always, Ladarat was a master at stating the incredibly obvious.

Wipaporn smiled for the first time. "Tell me something, Khun Ladarat. In your work, you are responsible for the ethics of an entire hospital, are you not?"

Ladarat nodded, not sure where this was leading.

"So in order to ensure ethical behavior—that is, behavior by the rules—you need a series of safeguards, do you not?"

Again Ladarat nodded. It was true, they had their chart reviews and consent forms, and ethics consultations...

"So when men come here, we expect that they will play by the rules. That they will follow the rules agreed upon. And if they don't, well, this is our system of safeguards."

"So...you will know if a man...breaks the rules?"

"We will know, but it's more than that. We will be able to explain to the man exactly what it was that he did wrong. In terms of safety and compliance with the rules, it is essential to be specific, don't you agree?"

Ladarat did agree, and indeed she couldn't have put it better herself. It was certainly essential to be specific about what the rules were, and what a transgression involved. Especially in a country like Thailand, where rules could be bent and changed and shaped to fit the moment. She had to respect someone who was so committed to the letter of the law.

But what law was that, exactly? And what "rules"? And how does a video camera help enforce those rules?

Wipaporn leaned over and put her finger on a blinking orange light beneath the video screen that displayed the couple. Ladarat tried not to look at the screen as she attempted to make sense of the blinking light.

It took her a moment, but finally she understood. "It's a . . . recording?"

"Indeed it is. Many of them. For every client." She smiled in a way that was a little eerie. "So you see, Khun, there is no danger of our clients breaking the rules. We are very clear about our expectations. And if there is any dispute . . . well, this is our safeguard."

Ladarat was tempted to ask what sorts of disputes might arise, but she was reasonably certain that she really didn't want to know. Nor, truly, did she want any more information—visual or otherwise—about the important man from the tourism ministry.

Instead she pulled her mobile phone out of her bag and checked her e-mail quickly. Still nothing. No, there it was. A very brief message from the very tired Dr. Arhit Tantasatityanon.

"That is her."

Ladarat smiled to herself at a bit of detective work well

done. Wait until she told Wiriya. He would be impressed. Speaking of whom, where was he?

She scanned the monitors again. There, one of the monitors right in the middle of the line. She hadn't seen him at first. The monitor was only black and white, and his blue suit blended in with the dark background of the bed he was sitting on. He was sitting so still, in fact, he could have been a piece of furniture. Ladarat smiled as she thought about the detective as a piece of furniture in her own house. An armchair, perhaps. *Maewfawbaahn* would be pleased.

Then the mamasan pointed to the front door monitors as a woman approached. She seemed sure of herself and didn't hesitate as she turned toward the front door and entered. Together, they watched her progress across the large downstairs room and up to the bar, where Somsak was waiting. He offered her an informal *wai*, which she returned perfunctorily. Then he emerged from behind the bar and followed her to the stairs.

As Peaflower reached the first step, though, Somsak seemed to have a last-minute thought. He said something that caused Peaflower to whirl around. From the second step, she towered over Somsak and he took a couple of steps backward.

What was this? Ladarat glanced at Wipaporn, who was drumming her bright red manicured nails on the desk. She had a steady but fast rhythm. Click-click-click-click-click. She didn't take her eyes off the monitor and simply shrugged in response to Ladarat's unspoken question.

He was warning Peaflower away. He had to be. What else could he be saying?

The camera's position only revealed Peaflower from behind, but her gesticulating arms offered a clue to a careful observer that she was not pleased with the news that there was a police-man upstairs whose goal it was to arrest her. This news did not seem to be brightening her day. Somsak opened his mouth to speak twice, but each time was left with his jaw hanging, useless.

Finally, though, he seemed to regain the power of speech, and it was his turn to harangue their visitor. He pointed up the stairs, and then at the door, talking the whole time.

Peaflower heard a little of whatever he had to say, but apparently that was enough. She came down those two steps in a hurry, giving Somsak a quick choice to move or be pushed out of the way. He chose to move.

Peaflower headed for the door much faster than she'd come in and had almost reached the *Hing Phra* shrine at the edge of the camera's field of view when she pulled up abruptly. Peaflower stood there, perhaps thinking. Or perhaps listening to Somsak—both their backs were turned so it was impossible to tell who was speaking.

Eeehhh. This was anxiety-provoking. What was he saying?

Ladarat thought for a moment, glancing at Wipaporn, whose drumming had increased speed. Still, she wouldn't meet Ladarat's eyes. And still she said nothing.

Was he giving up their plans? No, that couldn't be it. If that were the case, Peaflower would be gone. She wouldn't be standing in place, not twenty meters from where a detective wanted to arrest her for murder. And yet Somsak most cer-tainly had said something... concerning.

And Wipaporn seemed almost as worried as Peaflower was. So whatever was going on downstairs, she wasn't aware of it.

Whatever it was, though, seemed to have been resolved to Peaflower's satisfaction. She turned, finally, and walked sedately—almost regally—across the main floor and up the stairs. Somsak stepped aside to let her pass and then followed meekly, like a royal retainer.

Just as Ladarat hoped she might get a good look at the woman, the two of them were lost from view. But then they reappeared at one end of a long hallway that was lined with doors on either side.

So all was well. Or was it? Wipaporn's manicured nails had ceased their drumming, which was good. And she was even smiling slightly.

"What..."

But Wipaporn just shook her head. "I'll explain in a minute."

She leaned over and spoke softly into an old-fashioned microphone that was resting on the table between them. "Your friend is here. In the hallway."

Wiriya didn't seem surprised to hear a voice issuing from the ceiling. If Ladarat was surprised by his nonchalance in response to this disembodied voice, she was stunned when he turned toward the camera, targeting it exactly, and gave a cheerful wave.

In that moment, all of Ladarat's pride in having tracked Peaflower to the Chinese doctor evaporated as she realized that her part in this whole endeavor was actually pitifully small. Wiriya had known about the rooms all along. And about the video cameras. Presumably he'd worked this out with the mamasan in advance? And the dance between Somsak and Peaflower, Ladarat was sure that was part of the plan, too. But what?

No matter. She *had* played a part, hadn't she? Of course she had. She could say that proudly.

And this was no time to dwell on matters of credit, or pride. Wipaporn was focused intently on the video screen as

Peaflower pushed the door open. The corner of the door was just visible in the lower-left part of the screen and it obscured the woman for a moment. Then the door closed with a soft click that was easily audible through the speakers on the desk.

Finally, Ladarat found herself with a close-up view of the woman who had caused all this trouble. Unmistakably the same woman in the photo, although that photo had been taken earlier. Much earlier, perhaps. It was five years old at least, and maybe more. Even from this perspective, the resolution of the video camera was quite good. The better to ensure adherence to the rules. In any case, there would be no doubt about who this woman was. The doctor would have no trouble identifying her. Nor probably would any one of several dozen hospital staff who met Peaflower, however briefly, during one of her late-night deposits of the latest dead ex-husband.

WHEN DEATH DOES NOT BRING PEACE

Wiriya stood to greet her, offering her a respectful *wai*, which—to her credit—she returned. The camera revealed the two of them in profile, the detective on the left and Peaflower on the right. Each seemed to be waiting for the other to speak first. Ladarat had assumed that Wiriya would take the lead. He'd tell the woman everything that he knew. He'd overwhelm her and force her to confess. But he didn't seem to subscribe to that strategy.

In fact, it was looking as if he didn't really subscribe to any strategy whatsoever. He was just...standing there. His hands were clasped at his waist in a pose of quiet confidence. And he was looking at Peaflower with an amused smile. It was if he was waiting for something. Not waiting for her to speak. Just waiting for...something.

If Peaflower was confused or disturbed by this behavior, she didn't show it. Instead, she seated herself on the one chair in the room, facing the camera. She smiled, crossed her legs primly, and folded her hands in her lap. In that moment, she looked like the perfectly demure future wife. Gentle and submissive. She gestured to the bed, the only logical place for Wiriya to sit.

Then Peaflower said something in Chinese that Ladarat couldn't follow. Ahh...this is bad. This is exactly what they'd been afraid of. She will know that Wiriya is no Chinese businessman from Kunming. She will be certain in the next few seconds. And she will run.

Ladarat turned to Wipaporn, who said nothing. Indeed, there was nothing to say. They had tried but failed.

Watching Peaflower's face closely, Ladarat saw a hint of... what, exactly? Not fear. Or even concern. It was a subtle twitch of the mouth that suggested annoyance.

A woman is in a closed room with a strange man who is behaving strangely. Other women might be concerned or afraid. But this woman is simply annoyed. She must have considerable confidence. She must be a strong woman. And perhaps also a dangerous one.

Still Wiriya said nothing. He just stood there, leaning lightly against the wall at his back, with his hands folded loosely at his waist. His expression didn't change. No—there. He smiled. Just a little.

Ladarat recognized that smile immediately. It was the winner's smile. *Yim cheua cheuan*. It was the magnanimous smile that the winner bestows on the loser.

And Peaflower recognized it, too. Although it took her a moment to determine what that smile meant for her. Her expressions flowed from one of polite interest to concern to aggression. But never fear. At no time in that five-second shift in the weather did she ever look afraid. And even now, as she must have been realizing that she'd been caught, her fixed smile denoted hostility.

"I know you're not a Chinese businessman from Kunming," she said in Thai.

So there it was. Their plan was over. So simple and elegant, but they had failed.

But then Peaflower said something that surprised Ladarat.

And judging from the proud smile on Wipaporn's face, it pleasantly surprised her as well.

"I know that you're here as part of an immigration investigation, are you not?"

Wiriya said nothing, but a faint smile and flick of his chin suggested that this information was not the surprise to him that it was to Ladarat. Wipaporn was smiling broadly.

"Somsak came up with that on his own," she said. "Such a clever boy."

Ah, so that was it. That's what Somsak had been saying in the front entryway.

"He told her that there was an inspector who was doing routine passport checks at the request of the Thai immigration service," Wipaporn suggested. "That would keep her from running away as soon as she realized your friend doesn't speak Mandarin."

They turned their attention back to the screen in time to see Peaflower reach into a handbag that she'd placed on the floor next to her. With a flourish, she produced her passport and handed it to the detective.

Wiriya accepted it with a nod but still without speaking. He glanced at the page with Peaflower's picture, looking from the picture to her, as if he were checking her identity.

Apparently satisfied that this murderer was a Thai citizen, he handed the passport back to her, and it disappeared into her bag. It was only as she was thanking him for his time in a sweetly deceptive voice that Wiriya finally spoke.

"I'm not here about your passport."

Even if Peaflower had managed to maintain her equanimity up until this point, this was more than she could tolerate. Her facial expression cycled through confusion, fear, anger, and back to confusion in the space of a second.

"But...Somsak...the man downstairs..."

Wiriya shrugged. And smiled.

Peaflower seemed to have realized that she'd walked into a trap. What kind of trap, she wasn't sure. But she must know that the man in front of her dressed as a Chinese businessman who was supposed to be an immigration inspector wasn't either of those things.

Yet there also seemed to be a cool calculation unfolding in her head. Sure, she seemed to be thinking. This wasn't what she had expected. But she had gotten out of tough situations before. Much tougher than this. She would see where this led.

And indeed these thoughts seemed to have played out to their logical conclusion, and Peaflower shrugged and smiled. And focused her attention on the detective, who continued to lean against the wall.

Then she looked up contemptuously toward the camera, noting that it was there, as she expected it to be. Interesting. She waved in much the same way that Wiriya had only a few minutes earlier. But then she seemed to dismiss the camera altogether.

Despite Peaflower's display of bravado, Wiriya was still smiling the winner's smile in a way that was starting to be a little eerie. No doubt precisely what he intended.

Wiriya didn't say anything, but now he seemed more relaxed. Almost friendly. But why?

Finally it was Peaflower who broke the silence.

"Okay, so I know you're not...a client. Or an immigration inspector. But you must be very clever, to have gotten past my sister."

At this, Wiriya arched an eyebrow. It was barely perceptible, but Peaflower saw it.

"Ah, you didn't know the mamasan is my sister? We grew

up together as children. We are family. And you are...nothing. She is on my side in this."

Ladarat snuck a look at the mamasan. She didn't turn away from the monitor, but only gave an almost imperceptible shrug.

Was nothing as it seemed? And now whose side was the mamasan on? Surely not on theirs. Ladarat glanced around, but they were still alone in the office.

She felt acutely out of her depth, but what was she to do? Besides, Wiriya didn't seem to be worried. So she, Ladarat, would not be worried either. She would...await developments.

"Then who are you? Let's start with that. Who are you to be so clever and sneak past my good sister? Then you can explain why you brought me here."

Wiriya seemed to be thinking carefully about whether now was the time to speak. He waited five seconds. Then ten, as if he were considering the merits of an enormous decision. Finally, he spoke. But when he did, it was in a voice that Ladarat had never heard from the detective. Warm and soothing, he spoke as a radio announcer would, very late at night. He spoke as if he were trying to reassure the woman in front of him.

"Ah, Khun Anchan. Forgive me for my silence. I was simply waiting for the right moment. But let me explain." That tone induced another flicker of annoyance to flash across Peaflower's face. But it disappeared almost as quickly, leaving a demure expression that was as calm as it was unreadable.

Peaflower seemed to relax a little. Now, at least, they were in territory that she could understand. This man in front of her—she didn't know why he was here, but presumably he wanted something. And if he wanted something, then they could negotiate. Peaflower glanced down, and let her shoulders slump. In an instant, she became a poor, simple country girl. Simple and trusting.

"As you wish," she said, looking up briefly.

But in that quick glance up at Wiriya, Ladarat saw that she was scheming. Calculating. Reviewing her options. Oh, she was clever.

Wipaporn saw it, too. "She is playing the simple Isaan country girl. She will use all of her wiles on your friend."

Just as you have, Ladarat thought. You and your nephew. At the same time, she found herself wondering what that list of wiles included.

"First," Wiriya said softly, "I didn't bring you here. You brought yourself, did you not? Everything you've done over the past—how long has it been? A year? Two years? Five years?" The detective waved a hand dismissively.

"No matter, we'll get to that. However long it's been, everything in your past has led you here. You see"—he smiled—"you and I have to be here now. It is fate."

Now Peaflower looked confused. As if she was starting to sense that things were not going well. As if perhaps this was a situation she wasn't going to be able to evade so easily.

"I don't believe in fate," was all she said. Then she sat there quietly, waiting for the detective to make the next move. Which he did.

"We know all about you," he said. "We know everything." Then he was silent as Peaflower thought very carefully about what "everything" might consist of.

Apparently she didn't think it would include much of importance. "Then you have the advantage on me, Khun." She smiled in a way that might be construed as charming, but Ladarat wasn't worried. She was reasonably certain that the detective would be immune to these particular charms.

Particularly since he knew perfectly well where those charms had gotten other men before him. That knowledge, she thought, would be a pretty effective anti-aphrodisiac.

"But I am impolite. I forgot to introduce myself. I am Detective Wiriya Mookjai, of the Chiang Mai Police." And he reached into his left breast pocket and produced his identification, flipping it open with a practiced flick of his wrist.

Peaflower froze in place, her face becoming an ugly and bitter mask. In an instant, she'd aged ten years or more, her features becoming sharp and her mouth pinched like a witch's. She looked mean, and evil. But not defeated. Not yet.

Almost as soon as her face had changed, it melted back again, and her features softened into those of a young girl. A young, innocent girl. And her profile shifted, too. Where her gaze a second ago had been direct, chin up and glaring, now she was demure and almost scared.

It was an act. Ladarat knew that perfectly well. As did the detective. But it was a brilliant performance, she had to admit. Even Wipaporn was impressed.

"She's always been able to do that," she said a little sadly, as if this ability were an illness. "She can be a little girl, or a comforting wife or—if need be—a ruthless adversary. All in the space of a second." She shook her head.

"It's remarkable, but it's what led to all of her troubles." She paused. "It's what led her to this moment, I suppose."

And Wiriya seemed impressed, too. He was silent for a moment, as if searching for the right words. But he didn't soften. In fact, it was almost as if these quick changes galvanized him into being more direct than he would otherwise have been.

"We know, for instance, that you've used this establishment's services to find 'husbands,' haven't you? And, no"—anticipating her retort—"that isn't a crime. Fortunately for many lonely men, it's perfectly legal. What is not legal, though, is killing them."

"Of course not, Khun Wiriya. Of course murder is not legal," she said in a plaintive little girl voice. "Who could possibly think it was?"

"Some people"—he paused—"might become confused about just what is legal and what isn't."

"Well, let me assure you that I am not one of those people."

"That would be good, if it were true. But you see, we know perfectly well that it isn't." He didn't wait for her to interrupt, but instead plowed ahead.

"We know, for instance, that you looked for 'husbands' with a very specific name. Such consistency is perhaps laudable, but when your previous husbands have died, one has to wonder at the importance to you of that particular name. So I am curious. Does that name have sentimental value? Is it perhaps a lucky name?"

Peaflower was quiet but watchful. It was as if the tables were turning against her slowly. She recognized that change in the game but wasn't ready yet to turn and run. So the detective continued.

"We also know, as I've said, that these 'husbands' of yours seem to have a very high mortality rate." He allowed himself a small smile. "One would be tempted to conclude that life with you must be a risk factor much like smoking is. One might almost be tempted to say that you were dangerous. At least"—he paused—"to men with an unfortunate name."

"Yes, it's true that I have suffered much loss in my life. I am truly a poor woman who has been unlucky in love. But is that a crime, Khun Wiriya? Can I be arrested for being unlucky?"

"No," the detective admitted. "Being unlucky is not yet

illegal. But sometimes luck needs a little bit of help to turn one way or the other. Haven't you found this to be true, Khun Anchan?"

Peaflower didn't answer. She was still trying to figure out what this detective was certain of, and what he was guessing about. And that was worrisome, because Ladarat knew that he was mostly guessing. They had what was probably called circumstantial evidence. A series of connections and coincidences. But would that be enough to convict her? Probably not. If it were, Wiriya would simply have arrested her.

And it seemed that Peaflower was having the same thoughts, and reaching much the same conclusion. So she was ready to try to be tough. She would deny everything. And she might get away with it.

Perhaps that was why Wiriya decided to change his tactics. He seemed to pull himself up a little straighter, and he folded his arms across his chest. The net effect was that he appeared ten centimeters taller. His voice changed, too, dropping an octave and becoming rougher. He began talking in a faster rhythm, making points quickly, as if to head off any interruption.

"We know you have a marriage certificate from a man named Zhang Wei, dated about five years ago. Whether you killed that man is, unfortunately, not known to me. But I wouldn't be surprised if he met an untimely end. Since then, though, we know that you've been using this marriage certificate to collect the life insurance of unsuspecting Chinese men with the same name. You lure them here from nearby regions of southern China—Kunming, especially. You draw them here and you establish that they do indeed have a life insurance policy and that they have no dependents. Then you kill them, confident that Chinese law will award you at least some of the life insurance money as the recognized spouse. Even if the family contests the claim, you are sure to get something. And we suspect that you've done this not just once, but many times, dropping these men at emergency rooms around our city in order to obtain an immediate death certificate."

Peaflower looked stunned for a second, but only a second. Recovering almost instantly, she managed a laugh that, although not entirely convincing, was still quite impressive from someone in her difficult predicament.

"Of all the things you believe that I've done, Khun Wir-iya, there is one aspect of these...accusations...that is most surprising. Exactly how do you believe that I've killed all of these men? I'm just a single woman, small in stature. And weak, too. How do you propose that I've managed to murder these men?"

Ladarat snuck a glance at Wipaporn, whose previous fin-ger tapping had resumed with renewed energy. Her gaze was still fixed on the monitor, but in the few seconds that Ladarat watched her, the mamasan took a moment to look around the room, and at the door to her left. In short, she looked like a very nervous woman.

Ladarat thought for a second, then turned back to the mon-itor. She decided it was time to be helpful.

She knew how to be helpful. That was easy. But what about Wipaporn? Whose side was she on exactly? She'd brought them all here, to be sure. But they were sisters, were they not?

Well, she would find out.

She leaned over to the microphone on the table and pushed the button just as she'd seen Wipaporn do a moment ago.

"Dr. Tantasatityanon sends his regards and asks that you not come to him anymore for prescriptions."

Wipaporn looked at her and nodded. Her finger tapping

ceased, and she looked resigned and sad at the same time. Wiriya smiled up at the camera. He looked pleased.

Peaflower, however, did not.

"So this doctor...Tantasatityanon? This Dr. Tantasatit-yanon believes that I got prescriptions for my husband?"

"For several husbands, in fact," Wiriya said smoothly. "In the time you've been getting prescriptions for Mr. Zhang, there have been several deaths of Mr. Zhang. And yet those deaths seem not to have diminished his need for pain med-ications. So sad, really. One always hopes that death brings peace, but it seems that even repeated deaths did not bring relief of suffering. Even after cremation, these men are still suffering and in need of the good doctor's services."

Wiriya paused to let that observation sink in. Then he reminded Peaflower that what she'd done to procure prescrip-tions of opioids was illegal. "And that's punishable by twenty years in prison. Longer, in fact, than a sentence for murder often is. And may I remind you that there is no doubt about your guilt in this matter at least. We have a doctor who is will-ing to testify that you obtained these prescriptions under false pretenses. And he has already identified a photo of you. So there is no doubt that you are the culprit."

"So my crime is..."

"Your crimes are murder. There is no doubt in my mind about that."

Now the detective's voice had turned rough. He'd left the calm, benevolent interviewer far behind. Now he sounded like a detective. And Ladarat remembered for a moment what he'd told her about wanting—needing—to solve this case. She hoped that ambition didn't bring out a side of him that she'd rather not see.

"I know that you've killed several men. And I know how.

Perhaps I can't convict you of those crimes. But that doesn't really matter to me. I'm not trying to solve a big case or make a name for myself. I'm happy to live out the rest of my time in the police without solving another case. But I do want to make sure you go to jail. It doesn't matter to me what crime you're convicted of, as long as it's one that will put you in jail for a long, long, time."

Now Peaflower looked truly concerned. Almost scared. It was as if she'd finally realized that this was not a man to be bargained with or bought off or... bribed in other ways.

"So this is your choice. You can either confess to this latest murder, or we'll prosecute you for illegally obtaining narcotics. And if, in the process of that investigation—and conversations with doctors and experts—we determine that there is enough evidence to prosecute you for all of those murders, well, then we'd do that, too."

Wipaporn's finger tapping resumed, but more slowly than before. Almost thoughtfully.

"Your friend the detective," she said, "is very clever." She said that as if it weren't entirely welcome news.

Back on the screen, Peaflower seemed about to say something, but then lapsed into watchful silence. So Wiriya went on.

"During the investigation of the narcotics charge, for instance, we'd look very carefully through the prescribing records of the Chinese doctors in the city. Particularly the ones near the center of town. And particularly the good Dr. Tantasatityanon, who I believe will want to be very helpful." He snuck a quick look at Peaflower's face.

"Yes, I think that would be an excellent place to start. We'd look at all of those records very carefully. And of course we'd check hospital records to see if there were other prescriptions being filled by a woman who matched your description. We'd look very long and very hard. And maybe, just maybe, we'd turn up additional evidence of wrongdoing." He paused.

"Do *you* think we might turn up additional evidence? That often happens, you know," he said conversationally. "Often we look for one crime and we find another. Sometimes several others. So you never know what we might find. Or...perhaps you do?"

Did she? What exactly had she done, and what kind of a trail had she left behind her? How careful had she been and—more to the point—how careful did she *think* she'd been? Because that was going to be what mattered right now.

There was a silence that seemed to stretch out forever as Peaflower weighed her options. Every few seconds her eyes would dart to the camera and Ladarat had to check an impulse to lean back.

But finally, after a last sweeping glance around the room, as if looking for a chance of escape, Peaflower seemed to collapse. She slumped forward as if someone had taken her backbone out entirely. Ladarat never would have believed it could happen, but it certainly seemed as though Peaflower was giving in.

Then she was gone. In the space of a blink, Peaflower had simply vanished. Ladarat looked around the office in confusion, but Wipaporn turned her attention to the other screens and pointed to one on the far left. Ladarat turned just in time to see the blurred image of Peaflower's face flit by the camera, only to appear on another screen. And then another. In no more than a few seconds, she was racing down the stairs.

She was going to get away. Ladarat couldn't believe that they had come this far, only to watch this murderer run out the front door. And they'd never find her again—Ladarat was certain of that. With all the resources at Wiriya's disposal, they hadn't been able to locate her. And now that she knew she was being hunted, she would disappear.

Too late, Ladarat resolved that she would chase this woman. She would at least try to catch her. Because they had to do something, did they not?

But as she turned toward the door, the mamasan caught her arm and pointed at one of the screens that showed the *Hing Phra* shrine next to the front door. As they both watched, Peaflower flew off the last step and across the floor. Just as she reached to push the door open, a massive shadow detached itself from the wall next to the shrine and enveloped her as implacably as a hand might capture a moth.

Peaflower struggled and screamed loud enough for Ladarat to hear her through the closed office door. But she made no progress whatsoever. And as the shadow and its quarry moved back toward the stairs and into the light, Ladarat knew that struggling would be futile.

Jonah was by far the biggest person Peaflower had ever encountered. Easily twice her weight, and struggling against those arms was a lost cause. One might as well struggle against a mountain.

He seemed to be trying to talk with Peaflower for a moment, but then she pulled a hand free and slapped his face. Ladarat could hear the sound of the impact, and Wipaporn winced. But Jonah simply shrugged. Then he bent over and hoisted Peaflower over one shoulder much as one might carry a bag of rice.

A few moments later, Jonah and his burden reappeared in the room in which Wiriya was sitting comfortably on the bed. As soon as Peaflower felt her feet back on the floor, she took a step toward the door, but something in Jonah's expression

301

must have convinced her that another attempt at escape would not be wise. And so, seemingly resigned, she resumed her seat. Jonah took a step back out of the camera's range, but presumably he was still close at hand.

"You already know enough to convict me on charges of falsifying a prescription," she said. She looked perfectly composed, but she sounded out of breath. Or perhaps now she was truly nervous. Or perhaps this, too, was an act. "So why should I tell you anything?"

"To teach me," Wiriya said gently. "I want to learn how you did what you did."

"But why? Why would you want to learn...from me?" Now Peaflower sounded genuinely curious.

"To help me understand the murderer's mind. How you think. And why you did what you did."

At this, the mamasan's fingers seemed to take on a life of their own. Their drumming increased in pitch, but with a scattered rhythm that sounded like raindrops on a tin roof—haphazard and chaotic.

"Just...to teach?"

"Just to teach," Wiriya confirmed.

"And not..." Peaflower glanced at the camera. "Not recorded?"

Wiriya's smile was a combination of amused befuddlement, as if he'd never heard of such a thing. "Are there cameras in a place like this? Video recorders?"

Peaflower shrugged. "My sister wouldn't do that to me."

Would she? Ladarat wondered. She snuck a glance at Wipaporn, whose face was inscrutable. Her fingers, though, continued their rhythmless clacking.

"Very well," Wiriya conceded. "We won't record."

"You'd best not," Peaflower warned. She seemed to be

getting her spirit back very quickly. "She's as guilty as I am." And Peaflower glanced up at the camera.

"So if I describe what I've done...?" Peaflower asked finally.

"We'll stop there. No need for dredging up old secrets."

"Just...to teach?"

"Exactly so. Think of this as a chance to educate an old policeman."

Wipaporn touched Ladarat's arm lightly, as if she didn't really want to attract Ladarat's attention. They looked at each other for a long moment, as if Wipaporn was coming to a decision. Then, finally, Wipaporn pointed to a blinking light under the screen that held Wiriya and Peaflower.

"There is enough tape there for a long conversation. Longer, probably, than your friend will need. But if the tape runs out, here is another." She placed a well-manicured hand on an old videocassette next to the microphone.

Ladarat was certain something was happening that she should be paying close attention to. Something important. But most of her attention was still focused on Peaflower, who seemed to be thinking very carefully about what to teach Wiriya.

So compelling was Peaflower's consternation that Ladarat found herself staring at her expression, the mamasan next to her temporarily forgotten. Only a few seconds passed, but during those seconds, Peaflower's smile was transformed to one of sadness, something like resignation.

When Ladarat turned back to Wipaporn, she realized she was alone in the room. The mamasan had vanished. A quick glance at the rows of monitors showed her hustling out the door.

CHAPTER 38

GIVE MEN EXACTLY WHAT THEY EXPECT

Peaflower sighed. No doubt she was shrewd. And tough. But she also realized when she was not holding a winning hand.

"What do you want to know?"

If Wiriya was surprised by this sudden turnaround, he didn't show it. Presumably that was a skill that real detectives learned. Along with negotiating from a position of power, presumably one also had to expect the unexpected.

She herself was proof that that was good advice. For instance who would have guessed a week ago that she'd be sitting in a place like this on a Saturday night listening to a murder confession? You never could tell, could you?

"Just tell me how it worked. With the last man. Tell me what you did."

Peaflower sighed. "All right. It really wasn't very complicated, and there's not much to tell at all. But if you really want to know…"

The expression on Wiriya's face indicated that he did very much want to know.

"My late husband—he died six years ago—was named Zhang Wei. A common Chinese name, as you probably know. They say there are hundreds of thousands men in China with the same name. So I thought, maybe one of them is looking for love? Maybe one of them would find me attractive?"

She paused, perhaps waiting for Wiriya to say something gallant. He didn't. Instead, he took a small spiral notebook out of his other breast pocket, opened it, and began to take notes.

Peaflower shrugged and continued. "So it was easy enough to meet another man with his same name."

"But how did you find a man with the same birthday so the marriage certificate matched the death certificate? Surely that would have been impossible?"

Peaflower looked confused for a moment, then she laughed. "So you'd think that would be necessary, wouldn't you? In order to convince an emergency room doctor that the man I've brought is who I say he is, you'd think I'd need some form of identification. But in fact, they don't look too closely. When you arrive at an emergency room in the middle of the night with a man you say is your husband, and when you have a marriage certificate and his birth certificate... well, let's just say they are very willing to be convinced that everything is as it should be."

For a moment, it seemed as though Peaflower was going to stray, and that she'd begin talking about the men she'd murdered. Perhaps that was exactly what Wiriya was hoping for. But if he was, he was going to be disappointed. Instead, she sat there in silence.

"So you met this man Zhang Wei—the most recent one—through this establishment," Wiriya prompted. "And then what?"

"We corresponded by e-mail and then by phone. He was much slower than you were. More... selective."

"Ah, well... I've been told by a close friend that I'm quite ugly." He smiled and snuck a quick look at the camera. "So I could not afford to be too selective."

Oh dear.

"And then what happened?"

"Then he wanted me to meet me at Kunming, where he lived, but I said he should come here.

"He was reluctant at first, but eventually I convinced him. It took more than a month but finally he arranged a visit to Chiang Mai. He said he was coming here on business anyway, but I think he came here just for me. So we met here and then we went to his hotel, the Shangri-La. Do you know it? Very nice."

Wiriya nodded.

"Anyway, we went to his hotel and we spent the night there. But the next morning he wasn't feeling well. Upset stomach. It was the spicy *panang gai* we had for room service that night before. He said Thai food didn't agree with him."

Ladarat could imagine that. *Panang gai* was one of her favorites—crispy fried chicken in red curry and coconut milk. Wonderful, but very spicy, and very rich.

"And what was in the Thai food that didn't agree with him?"

Peaflower looked at him blankly for a moment. Then she began to smile.

"It was ipecac. A syrup that loosens your bowels and makes you throw up. You or I would taste it in food—or at least we'd know something was strange. But a Chinese man not used to our food...well...to him it's just one more example of why he should have stayed in China."

"Very clever. Yes, I know it, but it doesn't last long. Maybe a couple of hours at most. Wasn't he better the next morning?"

Now Peaflower was grinning happily. It was as if she'd forgotten for a moment that she was confessing to murder.

"Ah, but he was still feeling weak, so I went to the drugstore

306

to get him a tonic that would improve his strength. But before I got back, I opened the tonic bottle and put in—"

"More ipecac." Wiriya nodded. "Very smart. So by later that morning, he was probably feeling very ill. He was probably convinced that he had some infection that needed medical treatment, am I right?"

Peaflower nodded. "But not just any medical treatment. His experience with Thai food had convinced him he needed a real Chinese doctor. Well trained, with the best credentials. So I said I knew just the doctor, and he had an office right near the hotel. I could describe his symptoms and get a prescription for antibiotics. It would be better for him to stay in the hotel room and rest."

"And he agreed."

"Of course he agreed. He should have been suspicious, but Chinese men always expect that women will do their bidding. A woman offers to do something for them, they accept. It's the way they're programmed."

She was still smiling, but it was a smile of revenge. Her own version of the winner's smile. *Yim cheua cheuan.* But she wasn't the winner now, was she?

"So then you went to the doctor—the same one who had treated your husband?"

"My real husband, yes. He had pancreatic cancer and other ailments. He was weak and tired most of the time." She seemed to think about that assessment for a moment. "So I would say that he had an infection and he would give me a prescription for an antibiotic, of course."

"Of course? Why wouldn't he ask to see your husband—his patient? Why would he simply trust you?"

Peaflower shrugged. "I'm not sure, but he probably thinks

I'm the dutiful wife. So kind and loyal and caring. That's the secret to a trick like this. You need to give people exactly what they expect. If they expect you to be rude or nice or confused or angry—be what they expect. Do what they expect. The more you act in a way that fits with their view of the world, the less suspicious they are. I fit so well with the stereotype the doctor carries around in his head of the way wives should be, that he never thought twice about a part of the story that doesn't fit, like the fact that this man with pancreatic cancer is still alive so many years later."

Ladarat made a note to herself to think about Peaflower's advice about anticipating other people's expectations. There seemed to be a lot of wisdom in that. When someone does what we think they should do—when they behave as we expect—we stop paying attention to them. Like all of the people in the waiting room outside the ICU. She'd walked past them a couple of times a day all week, but she couldn't remember any faces. It was only the one man who was acting in unexpected ways who was memorable. And Peaflower had learned that. She made herself and her actions invisible, because at least superficially she was doing exactly what a wife was supposed to be doing.

Wiriya was nodding. "You'd make a good detective, Khun Anchan. A very good detective. But once you got the drugs from the pharmacy, how did you get Khun Wei to take them? All of those pills at once?"

"Well, all of the medications were liquid. Highly concentrated. So I emptied out the bottle containing the antibiotic and filled it with the pain drugs I'd gathered from my last visit to the doctor. I told the gullible Mr. Zhang that the doctor said he should take them both at the same time. All at once."

Then she giggled. A strange, girlish sound coming from such a person.

"No, that's not quite true. Actually what I said was that the doctor told me that he should *try* to take them both at once, but that most people couldn't because they tasted so bad. Most people had to dilute them and take them over twenty-four hours." She giggled again. "And of course, once I said that, he had to prove himself. He had to prove that he could drink the whole bottle at once. Like a man. Stupid, but that's the way that men are."

"Indeed," Wiriya said slowly. "Indeed. And you are truly a remarkable psychologist, Khun Anchan."

Perhaps some of Wiriya's response was merely flattery to get her talking. But Ladarat suspected that he really was impressed. Ladarat certainly was.

"So he drank the bottle all at once..."

"That was about a thousand milligrams of morphine and a hundred milligrams of lorazepam."

If Wiriya could have heard Ladarat's sharp intake of breath, he would have looked at Peaflower with very different eyes. Ladarat knew that a normal dose of morphine for someone who isn't used to it is about ten milligrams. And lorazepam is half a milligram.

"And then what happened?"

Peaflower looked at him strangely. "Then, he went to sleep and never woke up."

"That's all? That was enough to cause him to die?"

"Well, he was lying in bed, and I don't know, but I think he may have gotten smothered in the pillows. He wouldn't have been able to move, you see. So in the wrong position, and weak and unconscious...well...the pillows might have smothered him."

Odd that she was being so careful, even at this stage, not to incriminate herself more than she absolutely had to. But that wouldn't matter. She'd admitted everything. Everything except the ending.

"So then what happened?"

"So I bribed one of the bellhops in the hotel to help me drag him to my car. He was dead—or almost dead, but you couldn't tell unless you checked for a pulse, and the bellboy wouldn't do that. Then I drove him to the emergency room and gave them the story that you know—that my poor husband was suffering from multiple medical conditions, including heart failure, and died suddenly. Such patients often die suddenly, you know. Here was his birth certificate, and here was our marriage certificate, that he'd put in an envelope in his study for just such an eventuality."

"So then you got the death certificate, but what about the life insurance money? How did you know what his policy number was, and what company?"

"Ah, I appealed to his vanity, of course." Ladarat sensed another lesson in male psychology was on its way, and she wasn't mistaken.

"As we corresponded, he tried to convince me that he was wealthy. I said I'd heard that before. He asked me what would convince me, and I told him…"

"You wanted to see his life insurance policy. Very clever. You weren't asking for his bank account, so there was nothing for him to be concerned about sharing. If you weren't married, there's no way that information could harm him."

"Exactly so."

"But why didn't you ask about my life insurance policy?"

"Ah, well, you see things were moving too quickly. There was no time. And besides, it was a small investment of time only. I knew I could meet you here within a day. And if things did not work out, there was no point in asking about life insurance."

Alas, Wiriya did not ask Peaflower whether, in fact, things had worked out. Instead, he asked about the way that life insurance policies were handled in China. A dull subject perhaps, but he was being careful.

"And in China?" he asked.

"A wife generally gets the insurance policy by rights," Peaflower explained. "Even if the husband doesn't name her. As long as there is a valid death certificate."

"Which you had from your... first husband."

"Exactly so. Although not always. And not all of it. Sometimes there are legal challenges, which..."

"Which you avoid."

"Exactly so."

"So these arrangements are not always... fruitful?"

"Perhaps not. But nothing in life is certain."

Wiriya took a deep breath, as if he was preparing for a difficult question. Ladarat leaned forward, paying close attention. What question could possibly be more challenging than the ones she'd already heard?

"I must ask, Khun—your focus on Chinese men, is it motivated by... personal reasons?"

For the first time in their conversation, Peaflower looked at the detective in confusion. Then she smiled the *yim thak thaan* smile: the smile of disagreement. It said in essence, "I know what you're trying to tell me, but you're wrong, so I'm not going to listen."

"Was there a reason you chose to devote your attention to Chinese men? Rather than Thai men, or Americans, or..."

Wiriya trailed off, looking unsure of himself for the first time in their interview. Perhaps he had not considered this line of questioning in advance? And perhaps he did not anticipate that their interview would proceed this far. At a loss for words, the detective lapsed into a silence that seemed to stretch on for minutes.

"Chinese men," Peaflower said finally, "are all the same."

"How so?" Wiriya leaned forward, nodding respectfully. This wasn't a matter of interviewing tactics, was it? No, the detective seemed genuinely curious.

There was another pause. Not as long as the last, but long enough for Ladarat to wonder whether Peaflower was going to answer. At last, though, she did.

"Chinese men," she said, "they don't want wives. They want... servants. Women to do their bidding. That's all we are to them. So why not make a living from these men?"

Wiriya paused for a moment as he seemed to search for an appropriate response.

"But many men have this characteristic, do they not?" he asked. "Many men want servants rather than partners. Thai men, in fact, often have this reputation. Yet you focused on Chinese men. May I ask why?"

Peaflower shrugged. "Certainly many men share this characteristic, it is true. But perhaps you do not?"

Now Wiriya shrugged. But he didn't speak. He waited.

"What is a characteristic in many men is perfected to a high degree in the Chinese," she said quietly. "I learned this at a very young age. After my father died when I was two years old, my mother remarried a Chinese businessman. He treated her poorly for the rest of her short life. He wouldn't even pay for special medical care when she developed cancer. He took her instead to the state-run hospital, where she got no treatment."

Wiriya nodded encouragingly. He was a good listener.

"When my mother was dying, this man—her husband—began to turn his attentions toward me."

"When you say his attentions, Khun Anchan, you mean..."

"His sexual attentions. Yes. That's what I mean. I was only fourteen, although old enough, apparently. But what he didn't know was that I was also old enough to run away from home and find work in Bangkok, then here in Chiang Mai."

"I see," was all Wiriya said. Indeed, what else was there to say? Ladarat watched the detective closely now. Would he show empathy? Should he?

That was the better question. The more ethical question. Should this story—if it were true—excuse the actions of this woman? At least partially?

Perhaps. But this was a woman who had just admitted to killing several men. For revenge, yes. But also for financial gain.

The detective, though, seemed more positively disposed. He was still leaning forward and listening carefully to Peaflower's tale. Was he harboring doubts?

But then he asked another question.

"And this man—your stepfather. What was his name?"

"Zhang Wei."

Then Peaflower smiled the smile of a woman who was immensely proud. She smiled the smile of a woman who had won a national competition of skill and wits. She did not, however, smile the smile of someone who had confessed to murder. It was strange indeed how her pride overwhelmed her sense of what was right. And her own spirit of self-preservation. People could be evil, but they could also be silly.

Ladarat looked closely at the console and clicked the "stop" button. Then she removed the tape and put it in her handbag. There would be time enough later to puzzle through the ethics of what she'd just heard. For now, though, it was enough to know that they had captured the confession of a murderer.

CHAPTER 39

THE PROTECTION OF *JAI DEE*

An hour later, after the police had come to take Peaflower away, cataloging the videotape as evidence, Wiriya tried to explain their suspect's bizarre confession as he walked Ladarat to her car.

"We see this. It's not uncommon, really. Imagine that you've done something very, very clever. Something that not one person in a thousand would be able to dream up. But then imagine that you couldn't tell anyone what you did. No one would know. And no one would appreciate how smart you are. Think how awful that must be."

But as she walked beside him, she could see from his profile that the detective was smiling.

"That doesn't seem so awful," she said.

The detective laughed. A deep, hearty chuckle. "No, I don't suppose it would be for me either. But if you really thought you were more clever than anyone else, and if you felt that no one appreciated you...well...I could see how the urge to brag would get the best of you."

"But not for someone who is *jai dee*."

Wiriya laughed again. "Yes, it's true. Not for someone who is *jai dee*. In *jai dee* there is protection from many dangers, is there not?"

Ladarat agreed that this was true. One could avoid many misfortunes simply by being virtuous.

"But honestly," he continued, "we don't see many murders committed by people who have a good heart."

There was one other aspect of the case that was bothering her. And that aspect had to do with someone else who wasn't *jai dee*.

"So...the mamasan?"

"Yes?"

"She will..." What was the phrase? "Get off free?"

Wiriya smiled a sad smile that didn't have any Thai name.

"She will." He shrugged. "There is not much we can do—she is gone. Far away by now, and probably back across the border in China, if she's smart."

Ladarat thought about that for a few moments as they walked in silence. That ending seemed...wrong somehow. But perhaps not everyone pays for all crimes.

They stopped at Loi Kroh Road, a busy street that ran right through the heart of the tourist district. Old taxis and battered private cars barreled ahead, and schools of mopeds swirled around them like small, predatory fish. All seemed oblivious to two polite pedestrians waiting patiently to cross.

When she'd come this way just a few hours ago, she'd forded this street from within the relative safety of a crosswalk a block away. But Wiriya took her elbow gently and led her out into the swirling traffic. The stream of traffic parted for them as if by magic, and cars and mopeds flowed around them.

"You must be firm," Wiriya explained as they reached the safety of the opposite sidewalk. "You must signal your intention, and drivers will react accordingly."

Ladarat thought about that as they turned the corner to the *soi* where she'd left the Beetle. Certainly one must be clear about one's intentions. That stood to reason. But she had great difficulty imagining how the presence in a street of someone of her diminutive dimensions might cause any driver to react.

She stopped on the sidewalk and Wiriya stopped beside her, looking around for her Beetle.

"Your car is not on this street?"

"Apparently not."

There was a pause as Wiriya thought about this information. "But you left it on this street?" he asked finally.

"I did."

"Ah. I see."

But Ladarat, who was not a detective, did not see. Who on earth would want to steal a forty-year-old Volkswagen? Of course, she thought loyally, there was nothing wrong with it, per se. But as a target of theft, well, wouldn't a thief be better off stealing a horse and cart?

"I suppose I'll need to file a police report," she said. And, she thought, now I'll get a new car after all. She was sad to see the Beetle go, of course. It had sentimental value. But really, it wasn't a sensible car.

"I can give you a ride," Wiriya offered. "Besides, you'll never get a taxi in this neighborhood. You'd need to walk over to the night market, and in that time I could take you home. I can fill out the report, too. Do you have insurance information and a car title at home?"

Ladarat nodded, still a little too shell-shocked to think clearly.

CHAPTER 48

LET SLEEPING DOGS LIE

The police formalities hadn't taken long. Wiriya called a uniformed policeman who had met them at her townhouse to take a statement and filled out the paperwork that would go to the insurance company. Odd that she was saving one insurance company from paying a murderer, but she was asking another to pay her for her car. That was the way that karma worked.

While Wiriya and the policeman sifted through her title and car registration, filling out forms, she explored her kitchen, looking for something that she might be able to make them for dinner.

Nothing.

She looked again. Refrigerator? Cupboards? She turned up a grand total of a bag of raisins, a package of Digestive Biscuits, a jar of peanut butter, and a bottle of *tom yam* spicy sour soup mix. Oh, and five cans of cat food. She pondered for a moment the sort of meal she might be able to make from that motley collection of foodstuffs.

"I'll be right back," she called out to the men in the living room.

Duanphen's cart was just closing. But she still had *gang massaman*—a new dish for her. From the south, it was halal

318

chicken curry with potatoes and a brown mild gravy. Just the sort of thing you'd serve to a substantial man, she thought. And for something lighter, *tom um gung*—spicy prawn soup—and *kai jiew moo ssap*—a Thai omelet with fish sauce and pork, deep fried. And *glooai tawt*, of course. Finally she picked up two mangoes from the fruit cart just down the street. Crisis averted. As an afterthought, she picked up a six-pack of Singha from the corner 7-Eleven. Wiriya looked like a man who would appreciate a beer at the end of a long day. Come to think of it, so would she. Her day, arguably, had been even longer than his.

When she got back, the policeman was gone and Wiriya was out on the patio, with *Maewfawbaahn* on his lap. They appeared to be getting along splendidly.

Ladarat didn't make any pretense of serving and presentation. No need for Wiriya to get the wrong impression about her. Instead, she brought the Styrofoam containers to the patio table, where she'd spent so many nights, taking plates and utensils and serving spoons from the kitchen on the way.

Wiriya smiled. "You didn't need to go through all the trouble of cooking for me."

"Yes, well, I'm such an excellent cook, I love to be able to show off my skills. And I'm very good at making Styrofoam food containers. They're my specialty."

As she opened the boxes and set them down in the middle of the small table between them, she asked Wiriya a question that had been on her mind ever since the beginning of the case. Now, she figured, was as good a time as any to ask.

"Why...did you come to me about this case? You could have come to anyone in the hospital. Or even someone in the Ministry of Health. They would have access to all of the records that I found, wouldn't they?"

The detective thought about that as he took a bite of the omelet. Then he smiled and nodded.

"You are an excellent cook, Khun Ladarat. And so quick." He was quiet for a moment.

Then he swallowed and shrugged. "To tell the truth, I wasn't sure what the result would be. If it were murder, well, that's one thing. I know how to deal with murder. But what if it were less straightforward? What if there were..."

"Nuances?"

"Exactly so. Nuances." He seemed to be rolling that word over in his mind appreciatively.

"Like what?"

"Well, what if this woman was a victim of abuse by her husband, for instance?"

"That wouldn't make her immune to the law, would it?"

"No," Wiriya admitted. "It wouldn't. Not really. But it might affect whether the law should be involved."

"How so?" Ladarat helped herself to some of the curry. Just a bit.

"Marriage has its own set of rules," he said thoughtfully. "Its own set of laws."

"So if someone breaks those...laws?"

"I'm not sure," he admitted. "But it seems to me that if there were conditions of abuse, or even infidelity, then those...laws were broken. In that case, one might be excused—at least partially—for circumventing other laws."

"And the story that Peaflower told you—were those the sorts of nuances that you thought might exist?"

"Yes, unfortunately. In my experience, whenever a woman harms a man, the man always bears some of the blame."

"But not exactly in this case, no? The male culprit, if there was one, was Peaflower's stepfather."

Wiriya agreed that this was so. "However," he said, "these more recent men were hardly blameless. They thought they could buy a wife off the shelf. Perhaps they did not mistreat Peaflower, but they showed a disregard for her as a person that suggests that they would have. I could never imagine finding a wife in such a way. In the best marriages, it has always seemed to me, mutual respect must develop first." He paused, toying with a piece of chicken. "Respect and...cooperation."

"Ah." Ladarat took a sip of Singha, hoping it would clear her head. It did not.

"Anyway. Ah...so you thought that if I looked into this first, I could determine whether there were any of these... nuances?"

"Exactly so." The detective seemed to be relieved to be back on firmer ground. "And if there were, and if perhaps this woman were acting in self-defense, well...then I hadn't really begun an official investigation."

"You would let sleeping dogs lie."

"I would what?" Wiriya looked genuinely surprised, his bottle of Singha hovering midway between table and mouth. "Why...dogs?"

"It's an American expression," Ladarat explained. "It's how they say that one should leave well enough alone."

Wiriya thought about that for a moment as he split the remaining omelet between the two of them.

"It's wise to let a sleeping dog lie," he said finally. "I had no idea that Americans were known for their wisdom."

"They have their moments," Ladarat admitted.

Wan aatit

SUNDAY

AN ELEPHANT APOLOGIZES

It was still very early—not even seven thirty—and the hospital garden was quiet. Only the low voices of a small group of medical students in a far corner broke the silence. They had their books open, and their steady murmur was a counterpoint to the fountain's mumbling.

But was this the right place for the meeting she had planned? She wasn't so sure. What if the Americans wanted more privacy? What if there were outbursts? But at least the mahout would be more comfortable out here. And if he was comfortable... well... maybe that would help.

She arranged two of the light aluminum tables next to each other, then gathered eight matching chairs around them. The scraping of the chair feet on the concrete sounded harsh in the silence, and two of the medical students looked up. But a second later they were back to their studies. It only took a moment, and she had the tables and chairs together. She thought for a second, then made space to accommodate two wheelchairs.

There. She'd done what she could. That would have to be enough.

Uncertain what to do, she looked around at the garden. There were Siam tulips, and silver-leaf ginger, just like in her own garden. Funny how she'd never noticed them before. Of course, she hadn't really been out here much. Just for a brief respite on busy days, for a cup of tea, or to take a call on her mobile. But she'd never really been out here alone, with nothing pressing to do. With no one to talk to or listen to.

So it was for the first time that she noticed how the splash of the fountain echoed against the hospital wall behind her. And how the breeze swirled a few leaves around and around in lazy circles. This was a moment of peace that she would never have experienced if she were with a group, or engrossed in a phone call.

Then she heard voices behind her and she turned to see a small army making its way through the door. There was the father, Mr. Fuller, in the lead, chivalrously holding the door open for his daughter-in-law, who was being pushed in a wheelchair by Sisithorn. Then the son, pushed by his mother.

They all emerged and Mr. Fuller turned abruptly, letting the door close with finality behind him as he stalked across the patio, trying to retake the lead. It seemed important for him to reach Ladarat first. She couldn't imagine why that would be but realized that she really didn't want to find out.

He looked angry. More than angry—it looked like he had something he needed to prove. His face was set in a hard mask, and Ladarat noticed he didn't even look to his left as he strode past his family.

It was a race, of sorts. But at first it looked like he wouldn't get in front of them. Sisithorn was walking at a brisk clip, wearing a fixed distant smile—*yim thak thaai*. She'd easily outdistanced Mrs. Fuller and her son. But Mr. Fuller was gaining, and as they passed the fountain, he overtook them, striding out ahead with a sense of purpose that was bewildering to behold.

Once he was out in front, though, he seemed to slow down

and take on a more dignified pace as befits the head of a family. And it was with a calm expression that he reached Ladarat first and, much to her surprise, offered a *wai* that was very polite. His hands rose to the level of his nose. It was the sort of *wai* that siblings might offer to each other, and Ladarat was touched. But she was also confused. She'd expected the man to be angry. And perhaps he was. But he wasn't showing it.

Instead, he simply stood in front of her.

"Thank you. I just wanted to say thank you for everything you've done for our son and our daughter-in-law."

That was hardly what Ladarat had expected. But if there was one thing she'd learned from her year in America, it was that Americans always surprised you. You never could tell.

"It is nothing," she said, trying to hide her surprise. "Nothing. It is what we do."

"Yes, but, I mean, I know you did extra. I know you and your colleagues did more than what you would normally do. Because... because of who we are. And... and I just wanted you to know that we appreciate it."

He looked as though he wanted to say more. But the rest of the entourage had arrived at the finish line, and Ladarat introduced herself to the husband, thinking that he didn't look like he'd been declared dead. Even all of that gauze didn't hide the bruises that mottled his cheekbones and forehead. But he was clearly handsome in a blond, American sort of way, with green eyes that darted back and forth between Ladarat and his father.

She offered him a *wai*, which he returned, clumsily but with a smile.

"I'm glad to see you well." It was all she could think of to say, but it hardly seemed appropriate to the moment.

"Thank you, Khun Ladarat. My parents have told me how

much of a help you've been. I'm very grateful." It took her a moment to realize that Andrew was speaking in Thai. Heavily accented Thai, with tones that were a little off-kilter, but easy enough to understand.

"Your Thai is very good, Khun Andrew. You have learned well."

"Thank you, Khun. I was a teacher of English previously. But I found it helped to know Thai, if I was expecting my students to speak English."

And that, Ladarat decided, was a good rule. If you want to teach someone your way of thinking, you need to be fluent in theirs.

"I'm sorry that you're still in a wheelchair, but Khun Sisithorn tells me the strength in your legs is coming back?"

Andrew smiled. "Yes, thanks to the excellent care I got. The injury to my spine didn't damage any nerves, and they tell me I'm healing very fast." He wiggled the toes of both feet, looking down proudly. "I should be able to start walking in another week."

The Fuller family gathered around the table, moving Kate's and Andrew's wheelchairs side by side. The two newlyweds held hands as they sat next to each other, and Ladarat thought she'd never seen two people look happier than those two did in that moment.

"Khun Ladarat..." Sisithorn spoke up for the first time. "Where is the man? Shouldn't he be here by now?"

Ladarat had had the same thought, but she'd decided that he would appear at the right time, and in the right way. Hadn't he spent the better part of the last week watching and waiting? If anyone knew when to appear, it was him.

And so they sat in silence for what seemed like a full minute. Kate and Andrew in unison turned their faces to the blue sky overhead, marveling in the daylight and fresh air and sunshine. And Andrew's parents looked on with relief and pure enjoyment, as if the pleasure these two young people were experiencing was all of the pleasure they could ever want for themselves. They held this pose for what seemed like hours but which probably wasn't more than a minute or two.

Then, out of the corner of her eye, Ladarat saw the mahout materialize out of the bushes behind the family. He crossed the stone patio noiselessly, his bare feet making just a whisper of sound as he padded over to Ladarat's side and offered a deep *wai*. He didn't look at the family, only at Ladarat.

"You will translate for me, Khun Ladarat?"

She nodded. She noticed that he'd taken considerable effort with his appearance. He'd bathed, and his clothes seemed, if not new, then lightly worn. Now he wore loose cotton trousers and a lightly frayed yellow cotton button-down shirt. He looked for all the world like a farm laborer cleaned up and going to town.

He offered the others a deep *wai*, bent at the waist. Then he gave Ladarat a quick glance and looked down fixedly at his feet as he began to speak.

"I wish to say how sorry I am for all of the trouble I caused," he said slowly. He glanced at Ladarat, who translated. She thought it was odd to offer this direct translation, without a preamble or explanation, but it seemed to be what the man wanted, and the two young people and the parents were staring fixedly at him, waiting.

"And it is my fault. I want you to know that. You must know that," he said. "For a mahout, the elephant is an extension of himself. What the elephant does, the man does."

He stopped and for the first time looked at Ladarat. He waited a long moment, as if to be certain that Ladarat was translating correctly. She knew that he didn't speak any English at all, and yet his fixed gaze made her more careful than she might otherwise have been.

"And so your sadness is my sadness, too. And for that, I am deeply sorry."

And he knelt on the stone patio and placed his hands level with his shoulders. He brought his forehead down to meet the stone once, twice, three times. And then he sat back on his haunches.

It seemed for a moment as though he was waiting, but Ladarat realized he was just too weak, and too tired, to get up. The poor man had been waiting here for a week, with little food other than what he got at the monastery last night. Sleeping in a stairwell when he could. And gnawed by anxiety that the American might die.

She wasn't at all sure how the Americans would respond, but she decided in an instant that she wouldn't wait to find out. She rose and bent over the man, taking him firmly by an elbow and helping him to his feet. She pulled a chair over from behind her and sat him down. It was obvious from his expression that he was uncomfortable, and she knew he'd probably rather be on the ground. But she wanted him to be seated among them as an equal so that the Americans could respond to him as an equal. This wasn't the time or the place to mete out charitable platitudes, as Americans are wont to do.

Oh, it's not your fault.

Oh, these things happen.

That wouldn't do. No, they would need to acknowledge that this was indeed the mahout's fault. And they would need to forgive him.

They seemed stunned by his admission, and they sat there in silence. Then, to her surprise, it was Kate who spoke first.

"The elephant. I think you told us her name was Pha mai?" The mahout nodded uncertainly.

"What happened to her?"

"She had to be killed," the mahout said simply. "It's the law. When an elephant attacks a person, it has to be killed."

Ah, so that was why the mahout could make a journey to Chiang Mai. There was no elephant at home to care for. That elephant was his life and his livelihood. And now it was gone.

But it was Andrew's response that surprised her the most.

"So you have no way to make a living now?" he asked in Thai. Ladarat scanned the confused faces and translated for the Americans. The boy nodded his thanks, but his attention was focused on the mahout.

"That is true," the mahout said quietly. "I can't afford to buy another elephant. They cost hundreds of thousands of baht." And he swallowed as he said that, as if that amount of money was beyond his understanding. "But it is the way it should be."

Ladarat translated.

"You worked with this elephant for a long time, didn't you?" Andrew asked in Thai.

The mahout only nodded.

"That is very sad," Andrew said in English. "He has been hurt worse than we have," he said to no one in particular. He was looking at his wife, but Ladarat got the feeling that he was speaking to his parents. "We are recovering, but his livelihood is gone." He paused. "Personally, I don't think there is a need for an apology. He has suffered more than we have. Too much maybe." Then he looked at his parents, who nodded hesitantly. Then to his wife, who smiled and squeezed his hand.

"Then, Khun," Andrew said in Thai. He turned toward the mahout. "We forgive you. And we thank you for doing so much to help us after we were hurt. If it weren't for your quick thinking, we would not be alive." And he offered the mahout a deep *wai*. His wife followed suit almost immediately, as did his parents, after a moment of self-consciousness.

There didn't seem to be anything else to say, and so the mahout rose and made a *wai* to everyone gathered around their little table. Then he walked past the Americans as silently as he'd come, floating over the stones and disappearing into the bushes as an elephant melts into the jungle.

Wan jan

MONDAY

CHAPTER 42

HOW TO CARE FOR AN AGED CAR

Ladarat's office was a picture of neatness that didn't do justice to the morning of chaos that the inspectors had wreaked. She'd no sooner arrived at 7 A.M. than a group of three of them found her. Whatever store of *sabai sabai* she'd stored up yesterday afternoon and evening was gone in an instant.

Apparently the inspectors had wanted to interview the night shift nurses, and so they'd come at 5 A.M., striding around the wards as if they owned the hospital. They'd poked into corners and checked the expiration dates on medications. Even the fire extinguishers—they'd wanted to know when they'd been inspected last. And then they'd wanted to talk with her, the nurse ethicist. Endless questions about cases she could hardly remember. But she'd gotten through it eventually, and now they were over in the outpatient clinics, doing whatever damage they could.

When the phone rang, she assumed it was someone from the clinic asking for help. But it was Wiriya.

"Ah, Khun Ladarat. I didn't expect to find you in your office. I thought you had a Royal Inspection this week."

Ladarat sighed. "We do. Oh . . . we do. I'm hiding."

Wiriya chuckled, and Ladarat decided she very much liked that sound. It was very comforting, but just a little bit cynical at the same time. As if daring her not to take things too seriously. Which she vowed she wouldn't do. Just as soon as these inspectors left.

"I have some good news, Khun," was all he said.

"Good news?" Ladarat realized she shouldn't sound so surprised. However, in fairness, good news had been in short supply in her life lately.

"About your car. You see, the police have found it."

She sighed with relief. She hadn't realized how much she missed it. When she had to take a *sengteo*—a pickup truck taxi—to work this morning, that was an inconvenience. But she really did love that car.

"Is it all right? I mean, it's not damaged?"

Again, that chuckle. "No, but the thief apparently did a few things to it."

Ladarat waited, fearing the worst. Engine removed? Wheels stolen?

"Well, to begin with, your brakes were very old, so he replaced them. And new tires, of course. Those tires were fifteen years old at least."

Ladarat was having trouble processing this information. Did you have to change tires? Didn't you just wait for them to go flat?

"And he fixed the locks, so they actually work. Oh, and he put a new stereo in. It sounds very nice."

"Ah," was all Ladarat could think of to say.

"So I thought I would drive it over to the hospital for you. Unless..."

"Unless?"

"Well, I drove it to a reputable garage to have it checked out, and the man there wants to buy it. He says it's a classic. He'd restore it perfectly and then sell it to an American. Lots of Americans want to buy a Beetle that's in perfect condition, without many kilometers on it." He paused. "He's willing to pay six hundred thousand baht."

Ladarat thought about that proposition for a full minute as Wiriya waited on the other end of the phone. The Beetle did have sentimental value. That was true. But wouldn't it be better to see it restored? And honestly, what would she do with it? She didn't know how to take care of an aged car.

"You don't need to make a decision now . . ."

But she'd made her decision. Almost without realizing it. She would sell the car to the dealer. That was the right thing to do. With just one caveat.

A SMALL GIFT TO THE BOON LOTT ELEPHANT SANCTUARY

It wasn't until after dark on Friday evening that Ladarat could prop her feet up on the other chair on her patio—the chair that Wiriya had occupied a week ago. Just a week ago? Really? It felt like it was years ago that they'd sat out here eating *kai jiew moo ssap* and talking.

So much had happened since then. It had been a long, long week. The inspectors had...inspected from Monday through Friday. Each long day, they started at 5 A.M., and continued right through to past 7 P.M. Today, Friday, it was past nine o'clock when she left, and close to ten by the time she swung down off the *sengteo* that she'd flagged outside the hospital. But it was a weekend, so Duanphen was open late, and she'd gotten a plate of *kao ka moo*—pork that had been simmered for hours in a rich broth seasoned with cinnamon and anise. It required so much time to simmer that it was usually only available late in the evening. Some sticky rice and *tom yam* made a meal.

The inspection, at least, had gone well. Very well.

As she'd expected, there were no difficult questions about the American's unexpected recovery. Indeed, the inspectors interviewed both the young people and their parents, all of whom couldn't say enough good things about the care they'd received.

There had been some...consternation when the mahout appeared in a downstairs waiting rom. Shoeless and thread-bare, his materialization caused fits of anxiety among the well-meaning receptionists. One had apparently heard inflated stories about the strange man who was stalking an American patient, and she called security.

But even that ended well. Apparently the man had a cousin—a distant cousin, but a cousin nonetheless—on the sanitary inspection team. So the mahout heaped lavish praise on the cleanliness of the hospital, noting particularly how the cleaning staff waxed even the basement floor of the stairwell. So they passed the inspection with high marks. They received a 98 percent, which was higher than any other hospital in Chiang Mai had received in the past five years. That, she thought, was something to be very proud of.

And in that week, she'd finally sold the Beetle. It was time, she knew. And when she met the mechanic, she knew she'd found someone who would give it a good home. She particularly liked the way he talked excitedly about the car's inner parts, and how they were in very good working order, considering. It was like he was talking about something she herself had personally accomplished—keeping an old car running. When in truth she knew she deserved very little credit. All she'd done, really, was to drive very little. No more than the short trip back and forth to the hospital every day, with a very few side trips.

Perhaps she could have gotten more money for it? But 600,000 baht was plenty. Plenty, at least, for what she had in mind.

In short order, she arranged for the sale. The mechanic

found her a lightly used car, which was previously owned by a professor in the Chiang Mai University History Department. Nothing fancy, but it was all Ladarat need. And he sent the balance, about 300,000 baht, directly to the Boon Lott Elephant Sanctuary, an organization started by an idealistic young British woman named Katherine Connor. The sanctuary saved elephants from brutal work logging teak and trained them for lighter, happier work in tourism. There was even an elephant that the sanctuary was hoping to rescue, so Ladarat was able to arrange that ownership would pass from the current owner via the sanctuary to the mahout. So he would have a living, and a life.

She'd heard that the mahout wanted to name the elephant Ladarat. She wasn't sure how she felt about that. But then it wasn't really her choice. Anyway, she would like to meet her namesake some day.

And the American—he continued to progress quickly. He was even starting to get out of his wheelchair with difficulty. Not surprisingly, his parents wanted him to travel home as soon as he could, but inexplicably he wanted to stay. Ladarat had heard that he and Kate were taking an apartment near the hospital so he could come in for physical therapy once or twice a day. He wanted to practice his Thai, and perhaps even to stay here. There was talk that he might open a travel business.

Peaflower, of course, went to jail. Certainly her case had been complicated by...nuance. But not enough to make a difference.

Still, Ladarat could not quite convince herself that justice had been done. Certainly Peaflower deserved to go to jail. That much was clear.

But was it fair to say that Peaflower was entirely responsible for what she'd done? Ladarat could imagine a different story in which a much younger Peaflower's life might have taken a very different road. What if her mother had married a kind, caring man? Chinese or not.

Would she still have grown to become a murderer? She most certainly would not have. She was, one might say, a murderer by chance.

It was true, of course, that her history didn't determine that she would become a murderer. She could have survived that childhood to emerge as an adult who did not kill Chinese men. She deserves some of the blame, but surely not all of it? So there was perhaps some wisdom in Wiriya's plan to charge her for only the most recent murder.

Whether Peaflower would cooperate, though, was anyone's guess. As they'd learned that evening in the House of Rooster Happiness, this was a woman who was very proud of herself and her cleverness. Once she was in a courtroom, granted the opportunity to show the world just how clever she was, it seemed entirely possible that she would become eloquent. But time would tell.

Time would tell, too, about the future of her fledgling detective agency. Ladarat would take it slowly, that was certain. Didn't she have enough careers already? She was already a nurse and an ethicist. It was difficult indeed to imagine how she could find time to be a detective as well.

Although just this afternoon one of the monks at Wat Sai Moon had asked her quietly whether she might look into a small matter. Apparently a group of nurses at Loi Bahn Nursing Home had been making very lavish donations to the temple and to other causes, such as the Chiang Mai Canine Shelter. The monk admired their charitable inclinations, of course. And making merit in this way was a core tenet of Buddhism.

But he could not understand how these women could afford such largess on their modest salaries. And he worried that they were stealing from their elderly patients to fund their charity. Since it raised difficult ethical questions, he'd pointed out, would she help? She said that she would.

She'd even begun to think about calling herself a detective. At least in between Royal Inspections. If she were to be a detective, Ladarat knew that she would need to be an ethical one. That is, she would solve ethical problems. It was one thing to catch a murderer. Many detectives could do that.

But Khun Wiriya had paid her that compliment of saying that he valued her advice when there was...nuance. Ethical nuance. So that was the sort of detective she would be. How that would turn out was anybody's guess, of course. But she herself was game for another adventure.

Other outcomes were easier to predict. Sisithorn and Dr. Wattana seemed to be spending a lot of time together. Sisithorn said it was related to the inspection, and perhaps it was. Who was Ladarat to judge? But still, she thought there was more...togetherness there than any inspection could possibly explain.

And speaking of togetherness...well, it was too soon to tell about her and Wiriya. They'd had dinner together once this past Tuesday, and it went well. She was even able to relax a little, and he told funny stories about his colleagues who had been caught taking bribes. Including one cop who demanded such generosity from the owner of a go-go club that the owner quit and the place was taken over by a McDonald's.

Yes, it was, truly, too soon to tell. But he was willing to put up with her limited culinary skills, and *Maewfawbaahn* was certainly fond of him, which was a good sign. In any case, it was time for her life to take a different direction. Learning the skills of a detective was all well and good. But that was a hobby. There was real life to be lived, too. And she'd been neglecting that for too long.

ACKNOWLEDGMENTS

In the past ten years, I've been very fortunate to be able to travel often to Thailand. On those trips, I've been welcomed by the Thai people, and I've had a wonderful time exploring Thailand's culture, language, and food. But my most meaningful experiences, and my fondest memories, have been in interactions with my physician and nurse colleagues there. It's struck me many times that Thai culture highlights some of the best aspects of health care and healing, and offers lessons that I've learned a great deal from in my work as a doctor. Ladarat is, alas, not an actual person. However, her skill and wisdom are very real among the colleagues in Thailand I've worked with over the years, and I'm grateful to them for helping me to become a better physician.

MEET THE AUTHOR

David Casarett, M.D.

DAVID CASARETT, M.D., is a physician, researcher, and tenured professor at the University of Pennsylvania Perelman School of Medicine. He is the author of three acclaimed works of non-fiction, *Last Acts: Discovering Possibility and Opportunity at the End of Life* (Simon & Schuster, 2010), *Shocked: Adventures in Bringing Back the Recently Dead* (Current/Penguin, 2014), and *Stoned: A Doctor's Case for Medical Marijuana* (Current/Penguin, 2015). His studies have resulted in more than one hundred articles and book chapters, published in leading medical journals such as *JAMA* and *The New England Journal of Medicine*. His many awards include the prestigious U.S. Presidential Early Career Award for Scientists and Engineers. He lives in Philadelphia.

INTRODUCING

If you enjoyed
MURDER AT THE HOUSE OF
ROOSTER HAPPINESS,
look out for the next
Ethical Chiang Mai Detective Agency novel,

MERCY AT THE PEACEFUL INN OF LAST RESORT

by David Casarett, M.D.

A WOMAN POSSIBLY CRYING

The frail woman sitting alone below in the courtyard was sad. That much, Ladarat Patalung could see. Ladarat could also see that the woman wasn't Thai. She seemed to be European, in her fifties perhaps. A simple pale blue cotton dress with oversize buttons down the front and a plain gray cardigan made her seem doll-like, especially when viewed from Ladarat's office window, two stories above. And like a doll, she was almost perfectly still. But every once in a while, after a surreptitious glance at the doctors and nurses and families around her, she would raise a fingertip to the corner of her eye—sometimes the right but more often the left—as if she was brushing away a tear as casually as she could.

"Khun Ladarat?" A gruff but amused voice gently interrupted Ladarat's musings.

"There is something interesting out there in the courtyard? More interesting perhaps than the case of murder that we were discussing a moment ago?"

Ladarat Patalung shifted slightly in her chair so she would be less tempted to sneak glances at the sad woman. The possibly sad woman. Her visitor was correct, of course. However important a possibly sad woman might be, she could not be as important as the matter at hand. So Ladarat turned her full attention to the heavyset man who was sitting on the little wooden chair facing her desk.

As the nurse ethicist for Chiang Mai University's Sriphat Hospital, Ladarat Patalung received many important visitors on many important errands. Indeed, it had been almost three months ago that this very chair had been occupied by the heavyset man who occupied it now. And just as it had then, today the chair meekly protested the bulk that it found itself supporting.

That bulk belonged to Wiriya Mookjai, a forty-two-year-old detective in the Chiang Mai Royal Police. She knew his age to the day because they had celebrated his birthday together with a meal at Paak Dang, perhaps the nicest restaurant in Chiang Mai, perched on the banks of the Ping River, which ran through the city. Like her late husband, Somboon, Wiriya had an expansive appetite. And at that birthday dinner, he had sampled a dozen delicacies for which Paak Dang was justifiably famous, including their *kao nap het*—succulent roasted duck over rice, drizzled with intensely flavorful duck broth.

And meals like that had perhaps given him a bit too much bulk. Her little chair was right to protest. It was far more accustomed to the weight of the nurses who more typically sought her counsel. But Wiriya was handsome and…solid. That was the thought Ladarat had whenever she saw him. That he was solid. Solid and dependable.

Those three months ago, he had come to ask her help when he had a suspicion—no more—that a murder might have occurred. And not just any murder, but a serial set of murders. Something unheard of in this quiet, sleepy city of Chiang Mai in northern Thailand.

His suspicions had been correct, and they had solved the case—together—with Ladarat acting as a detective of sorts. An ethical detective, which was what the *Chiang Mai Post* called her.

And she and Wiriya had become something of a couple. More a couple than not a couple, if that made any sense. And now he often made social visits to her new office—granted to her because of her sudden fame and perhaps her new unofficial job title as nurse detective. But today, Khun Wiriya was here on business. Possible business.

Ladarat looked down at the pad of yellow lined paper that lay open on the desk in front of her, still blank except for today's date written in a neat hand at the top of the page. It was ready to receive whatever thoughts might be worthy of writing down. But as of yet, she had no such thoughts.

It would be a shame to waste a fresh page, so she wrote "Murder?" in small letters in the upper-right corner of the page, as a way of making some sort of progress in her note taking, yet without giving undue weight to that single word. Then she added a second question mark, and then a third.

Indeed, "murder" was just a possibility. Even less of a possibility than that sad woman sitting alone on a bench in the courtyard. So on the far-left side of the page, she wrote "Woman, crying." Then three question marks, just for the sake of symmetry. So far, the left side of the page seemed to be drawing ahead of the right, as far as plausibility went.

"These are . . . murders, do you think?"

Wiriya shook his head, then shrugged. "I honestly don't know what to think. Murder? Suicide? Kidnapping? All we know with certainty is that over the past three months there have been at least eight people, all foreigners—*farang*—who have received entrance visas through Suvarnabhumi Airport, but who haven't left the Kingdom of Thailand through official entry and exit ports."

They came but didn't leave? It seemed a stretch—a very pessimistic stretch—to think of these as murders simply because—

Phhtttt.

Ladarat looked around, startled. And even Wiriya—normally unflappable—jumped just a little, causing the little chair to register yet another futile protest.

She had forgotten that they weren't alone. A small bundle of wiry white and brown fur lay curled at her feet, with the approximate shape of one of those annoying piles of dust that seem to find refuge under sofas and beds and other large, immovable pieces of furniture. On occasion the ball of fur would assume the shape of what could charitably be described as a dog of an indeterminate breed. A little terrier and beagle and who knew what else.

And every so often, Chi—because that was the ball of fur's name—would emerge from whatever dreams were entertaining him, raise his head, look around, and utter a sound like a wet sneeze. That *phhtttt* seemed to summarize his deep disappointment with his present company, which was clearly inadequate for a dog of his great intellect. Then he would go back to sleep, biding his time until his talents would be appreciated.

Chi was a therapy dog. Not an exceptionally talented therapy dog, truth be told. And he was rather fat, thanks to the doting attention and treats lavished on him by nurses and patients and the food stall vendors lining the sidewalk in front of the hospital. He was also quite lazy. So as therapy dogs go, Chi was not an outstanding specimen. But he was inarguably Chiang Mai University Hospital's *only* therapy dog. And that uniqueness had perhaps led Chi to overestimate his importance and thus to underestimate the amount of work he needed to do to continue to earn his keep.

Ladarat was caring for him, since his owner, Sukanya, a pharmacist, wasn't allowed to take him to the hospital pharmacy where she worked. So Chi was shuttled back and forth between them, with other hospital staff stepping in to take him for walks and on rounds to see hospitalized patients whose days might be brightened by his appearance in their doorways. Although sometimes it was difficult indeed to imagine why or how he could have that effect on anyone.

Phhtttt.

It was easy for dogs to feel they were special. Being a special dog didn't necessarily come with special responsibilities. Chi just needed to wag his long-fringed tail frequently, looking cute. As position descriptions go, that would be very easy. Easier than being a nurse. Or an ethicist. Or a detective. And certainly much easier than trying to be all three.

Speaking of which, Ladarat was supposed to be at least one of those things right now. She looked down at her notes, such as they were.

"So perhaps they are still here?" she asked. "These tourists?"

It wasn't unusual, Ladarat knew, for people to fall in love with her country, and to stay longer than they had planned. Perhaps that was what had happened to these people. They had just found a quiet bungalow in the mountains of the Golden Triangle, or on a beach on Koh Tao, or any one of a number of small, largely untouched towns and villages. They had found a village, and an embarrassingly cheap standard of living, and they had forgotten to leave.

"Ah, perhaps. But if they have made that decision to stay, they don't seem to be telling their families of their plans. Indeed, it's been either families, or"—he corrected himself—"the families of at least eight people so far, who have called various embassies to inquire about their whereabouts."

"So you suspect... foul play?"

Wiriya grinned. "A detective is never so lucky as to stumble across two such enormous cases of foul play, as you put it, in one career. That would be unheard of. And greedy. No, I've had enough fame for a lifetime."

And Wiriya was not being modest. If Ladarat had become a minor celebrity, Wiriya had become the toast of the town, as they say. He was given his own investigative division on the police force, and a promotion. Now he was Captain Mookjai. And—as he was today—Wiriya often wore suits that were neatly pressed. Several steps up from the rumpled trousers and shirts that had been his previous nondescript uniform.

But the best evidence of his fame, and by far the most treasured, was a letter of commendation from King Bhumibol Adulyadej himself. Ladarat knew that Wiriya kept that letter framed in his office for everyone to see. But she also knew that he kept a miniaturized version, folded up in his wallet and with him at all times.

"But," he continued, tapping a pen nervously on his knee, "I'm worried."

"Worried?"

"Yes, these people are all foreigners. They're all wealthy, with homes and families and jobs. These are not the sort of people to disappear. At least, not the sort of people to disappear without a trace. And certainly not the sort of people who would disappear without any contact with their families."

Dutifully, Ladarat wrote "Disappeared. No trace." on the right side of the page. Then she added a question mark.

"No trace? No trace at all?" She thought for a moment, also tapping her pen. "But surely they stayed ... somewhere? Perhaps somewhere in Bangkok?"

"It is difficult to trace the paths of these people. Very difficult. Even finding where they might have stayed in Bangkok is a challenge. But we do know that at least three of them—two Americans and one man from Germany—flew directly to Chiang Mai from Bangkok. We were able to get passenger manifests from Thai Airways so far. But for others who flew other airlines, or those who took a train or a bus..."

"Would a foreigner really take a train or a bus? That is so slow, and uncomfortable. Most tourists want to ... get where they're going." Ladarat herself had thought of taking the bus to the ethics conference in Bangkok she would be attending on Friday, but she had balked at the time required. That was something better left to the young backpackers.

Wiriya smiled. "It's true, that's the case for many visitors. Tourists, as you say. But some tourists want to save money, and a bus from Bangkok to Chiang Mai costs only two hundred baht. And others consider themselves travelers. They take the most difficult routes, by the most inconvenient modes of transportation."

"And you know this because..."

"I know this because they often get lost, or lose their money foolishly, and show up at a police station in Thma Puok or Ang Thong or Kanchanaburi, asking for a ride home to New York City, or wherever they came from."

Ladarat smiled. Yes, people traveled in Thailand with far more adventurousness than they did in many other countries. There were few dangers, and Thai people were generally very friendly and welcoming. So that led many travelers to take risks they wouldn't take in, say, India or Cambodia.

"But you don't think these missing people got lost?"

"No, we would have heard from them. Or their families would have. It's true, one person just arrived in Thailand last week. She might phone her family any day now, perhaps saying that she was sick with a stomach infection and that she's been in a hospital somewhere. But the first person on our list, he vanished three months ago. It is unlikely that he will suddenly reappear."

Ladarat thought about something else. "These are all foreigners? Western foreigners?"

Wiriya nodded.

"Eeey. That is bad."

And it was. Not just bad for tourism, but bad for the image of Thailand as a friendly, welcoming, and above all safe country. And Wiriya admitted as much.

"The director of the Department of Tourism asked me to look into this personally, and to help the families trace these people, if I could."

The way he said that explained much of Ladarat's feelings

for this kind man. He did not say this in a boastful way, as many people might. Not: "The director asked me personally, because I am so important." But rather: "I must do this because I've been asked. And I must do it conscientiously."

Thinking about the implications of the Department of Tourism's involvement, Ladarat wrote "Very bad for tourism" underneath "Disappeared. No trace." Unsure of where this was going, she thought perhaps the result might become one of the strangest haikus ever written.

"And," Wiriya added, "there is one more thing. One more... fact."

Ladarat waited, her pen poised to record this fact, whatever it might be.

"The most recent disappearance? The one a week ago? It was an American woman. From San Francisco."

"And?"

"And she was in this very hospital for several days, before she checked out, apparently against her physician's advice."

"What was she in the hospital for?"

Wiriya shook his head. "I don't know. I don't have access to those records. But you, I suppose, could—"

"I could do nothing of the sort. Looking up the medical records of a patient? What if the hospitalization was not related? That would be a breach of privacy."

Wiriya looked down, suitably chastened. "Of course, of course. I only asked because... well... I thought it might be a simple matter."

And of course he asked because her explorations of medical records were what had helped them to catch the last murderer. But not this time. At least, not yet.

"Do you know where she went?"

Wiriya reached into the chest pocket of his suit and removed a folded piece of paper. He smoothed it on the desk and slid it toward her.

On the paper in uneven letters in smudged blue ink was a name: Sharon McPhiller.

And: Nong Chom Village, San Sai District.

Then: The Peaceful Inn of Last Resort.